I0611251

Secret Service

THE PRESIDENT'S BODYGUARD

ZOE NORMANDIE

ENTWINED PUBLISHING

The President's Bodyguard
ISBN # 978-1-80250-255-8
©Copyright Zoe Normandie 2025
Cover Art by Kelly Martin ©Copyright July 2025
Interior text design by Entwined Publishing
Published by Entice, an Entwined Publishing imprint

Published in 2025 by Entwined Publishing, United Kingdom.

Entwined Publishing is a division of Totally Entwined Group Limited.

THE PRESIDENT'S BODYGUARD

Chapter One

White House, Washington, DC

The East Room felt like a stage where Cassidy Evans was the one person who hadn't memorized her lines. The air buzzed with a polished energy — the clink of glasses, the hum of power, and the subtle sway of people who knew they belonged here. She didn't.

A month into her assignment, Cassidy had thought it would get easier. But it hadn't. In fact, it had only gotten worse. Her colleagues seemed like they were always a step ahead of her, always a step above her. She was the outsider. The one they talked about behind closed doors. The reporter who didn't know how to fit in, how to play the game.

She stumbled through the crowd, the clicking of her heels softened by the chatter around her. She needed to get out of here, to disappear into the shadows where she wouldn't be noticed. She found the doorway and slowly backed out of the room. She could feel the night breeze on her back — almost finding freedom.

But fate, it seemed, had other plans.

As she stepped back, and before she could even register the movement, her heel landed right on someone's foot.

"Watch it, Evans." The words were laced with venom, each syllable like a dagger she could feel in her chest.

Duke.

Of course it was Duke.

She barely had time to react before his hand shot out, grabbing her arm with a force that made her skin flare with heat. His fingers tightening around her wrist were like a vise, cold and unyielding. He spun her with effortless force, pulling her just inside the door, out of sight of the others.

"Don't trip," he said, so smooth it made her skin crawl.

"Get off me."

And there she was, cowering in front of Duke Armstrong — tall, broad-shouldered, dark hair, dark eyes, with a crisp black suit that screamed authority, the kind that could only belong to someone in the Secret Service. She jerked back instinctively, but it was no use — his grip was steel.

"Still pissed at me?" His tone was mockingly light, almost playful, as if he enjoyed seeing her discomfort. He fed off it, the bastard. His breath was warm against her ear, a whisper of danger that made her pulse race in a way she didn't want to acknowledge.

She stiffened, jaw clenched. "Let go of me."

But Duke only grinned, the same arrogant, knowing smile that made her want to lash out.

Her face flushed as she shook him off her, taking an intentional step away from him. "You think you're winning," she said, her voice hollow. "But I'm done here. I'm done with this whole damn circus."

He raised an eyebrow, amused.

Cassidy didn't let him see her break. She turned but barely made it a few steps before she saw the president marching down the hallway. He was flanked by the usual entourage of assistants, but as he passed by the open doors of the East Room, his eyes flicked over to her. It was a brief glance, but it made her stomach twist.

Before she could look away, the president's gaze lingered, and with a subtle motion, he nodded in Duke's direction. Of course, he was the one the president would call to his side. His loyal servant. *His nephew.*

Duke immediately turned to follow. His smile slipped, his gaze hardening—issuing an unsaid warning. It was there in the way his jaw clenched, the way his eyes narrowed.

Cassidy stood there for a moment, feeling her heart slam against her chest. Duke moved to the president's side, falling in line with the others as they continued their path down the hallway.

The sound of her own breathing was the loudest thing in her ears as she turned on her heel, her mind a blur. She didn't want to make a scene. She didn't want anyone to see the unraveling thread that was her composure.

She couldn't stay here. Not like this. Not anymore.

The lies, the games, the endless humiliation. It had been months of Duke toying with her — giving her fake names, twisting the truth, and then watching her crumble as she tried to keep up with him. Duke was always one step ahead, always the one in control. And she? She was just the joke.

As she moved toward the patio doors, she caught the eye of a young staffer standing nearby. The girl's expression was anxious, a slight tremor in her voice as she said, "You're not supposed to go out there alone."

Cassidy didn't stop. Didn't even slow down. She waved the girl off without a word as she slipped through the door and into the evening air.

The cool breeze hit her like a rush of relief, sharp and refreshing after the stifling heat inside. For a moment, she just stood there, inhaling deeply, trying to fill her lungs with something other than the suffocating atmosphere of the East Room. The tension in her chest eased just a little, the air outside tasting almost sweet in comparison to the chaos she'd just escaped.

She didn't look back. She couldn't. She wouldn't.

The gardens lay ahead, a quiet refuge, and beyond that, the side exit where the press buses waited. She had to get there, away from this place, away from Duke and the White House circus.

But as she rounded the corner, her steps faltered.

There, leaning casually against the marble columns, was Congressman Richard West. The faint glow of a cigar dangled from his fingers, the smoke swirling lazily around him. He took a slow drag, exhaling through his nose, eyes half-lidded in a lazy, predatory way. She recognized him immediately — her editor had warned her about him, told her to steer clear at all costs. West was infamous for his reckless behavior, the kind of man who thought he could get away with anything when he had a drink in him. He was a predator in a suit.

She froze, debating whether to turn and go back inside. But it was too late.

"Look who it is," West slurred, his voice dripping with a mix of condescension and amusement. "Little lost lamb wandering out here all alone." He took another drag of the cigar and flicked the ash onto the gravel at his feet. "Shouldn't be finding you out here."

Her pulse spiked, but she kept her posture straight, her voice even. "I'm just getting some air, sir," she said, standing her ground, though the pit in her stomach was growing. She had heard enough stories to know what kind of man he was, and she'd seen how he treated people he thought were beneath him.

West's lazy grin spread wider. "I read your article. Got it all wrong, didn't you? You don't know a damn thing about this place or people like me."

Her heart raced, but she forced herself to stay calm. She wouldn't let him bait her. "I think you've had too much to drink," she said, taking a small step back, trying to distance herself. Her heel slipped slightly, but she regained her balance, her grip tightening on the champagne glass still in her hand.

West chuckled low, the sound crawling under her skin like a bad omen. "You think you're so clever, don't you?" His voice oozed disdain as he took a step toward her. "You're just a girl playing dress-up, trying to fit in with all the big boys. But you don't know your place."

Cassidy's gaze hardened. "I'm not here to learn it from you," she shot back.

His grin vanished, replaced with something much darker. His eyes narrowed, and his posture shifted — suddenly more aggressive, unsteady but purposeful. He took another step toward her, his breath heavy with alcohol and cigar smoke. "Don't talk back to me, little girl. You might want to show some respect."

Before she could react, his hand shot out, grabbing her wrist with startling force. The pressure of his grip made her wince, and her heart jolted with fear.

"Let go of me," she said, low but firm, the warning clear.

West's grin returned, wider now, as if he were enjoying the game. "I think it's time you learned a lesson." His fingers tensed around her wrist, pulling her a little closer, his breath rancid against her skin.

The anger inside Cassidy flared, but there was a knot in her chest that told her this wasn't just a game anymore. She had no one to rely on but herself.

And this man had underestimated her.

With a burst of adrenaline, Cassidy twisted her wrist, using his own forward momentum against him. Her heel dug into the gravel as she slammed her elbow into his ribs with all the force she could muster. West gasped, stumbling back in surprise, giving her the space she needed to break free. He tried grabbing her again—but she kicked him right in the groin. Hard. Heart pounding, she ran, the hem of her dress catching on her knees as she darted down the shadowed path. She didn't dare look back, her only thought to get away.

All she could hear was his angry grunting behind her.

You can't scream, she told herself. *Don't make a scene. Don't prove them right.*

The lights of the East Room flickered faintly in the distance, but Cassidy turned away from them, plunging deeper into the gardens. She didn't stop running until her lungs burned, until the shadows of the towering trees seemed to swallow her whole.

When she finally stopped, she leaned against a cold marble bench. Her chest heaved, her pulse hammering against her ribs.

She was alone in the dark, trembling, and furious. At him. At herself.

This wasn't the story she had come to tell.

Cassidy's breath came in ragged gasps as she leaned against the bench. Her fingers trembled, her pulse thundering in her ears, when she heard the crunch of footsteps on the path again.

"You little—" Congressman West boomed, closer than she expected. "Where the hell are you?"

Cassidy froze, her heart lurching. He was coming after her.

She stumbled forward, her heels sinking into the soft earth. Her hands fumbled to hitch her dress higher, her movements desperate and clumsy. She tripped on a rock and tumbled down, breaking her fall with the palms of her hands. Crying out, she pushed herself up and kept going. The glow of the White House seemed impossibly far away, the faint hum of laughter and music drowned out by the angry curses of the man chasing her.

"You think you can hit me?" he yelled, slurred with rage. "This isn't over."

Cassidy bit back the whimper threatening to escape her throat. She didn't want to give him the satisfaction of hearing her panic. As she ran, she scanned the shadowed gardens, searching for anywhere to hide, when the faint outline of a row of SUVs came into view.

Security detail. They must have been parked on the far edge of the grounds, barely visible in the darkness.

Her shoes slipped as she darted toward the line of vehicles, her breath hitching as the sound of his footsteps grew louder. *Don't stop. Don't think. Just go.*

She dropped low behind the nearest SUV, her knees scraping against the gravel as she crouched in the shadows. Her lungs burned, the cold air cutting into her throat. She tried to quiet her breathing, to shrink herself into the smallest possible space, but she could hear him, his heavy footfalls slowing as he searched.

"You can't hide from me," he called, his voice jagged and raw. "Come out, and maybe I won't make this worse for you."

She peered under the SUV, her stomach twisting as she saw his dark silhouette pacing closer.

Her options dwindled. If he found her crouched here, it would be over.

No, she thought. *Not here. Not like this.*

Before she could talk herself out of it, she reached for the SUV's door handle. It clicked open, quieter than she'd expected, but her stomach dropped at the faint beep that followed. She froze, waiting for him to hear it.

"What the hell was that?" he said.

Cassidy swallowed her fear and slipped inside, her hands trembling as she pulled the door shut as silently as possible. The interior of the SUV was dark, the smell of leather strong and oddly comforting. She pressed herself into the far corner of the seat, curling up her legs as she tried to disappear into the shadows.

Outside, Congressman West's footsteps drew nearer. She could see his shape through the tinted windows, his movements erratic as he scanned the area.

He lingered there for a moment, breathing heavily, his anger radiating even through the thick glass. Then, with a frustrated grunt, he moved on, his footsteps fading into the distance.

Cassidy didn't move. She stayed curled in the corner, her breath shallow, her body shaking.

Minutes passed, or maybe it was seconds — she couldn't tell. When the silence stretched long enough to convince her he was gone, she allowed herself to exhale, the sound shaky and raw.

But before she could plan her next move, the click of a car door startled her. Cassidy's head snapped up as the opposite door opened, and a man climbed into the SUV's driver's seat.

He wasn't her pursuer. He was tall and broad-shouldered, dressed in a crisp black suit that marked him as Secret Service. And she knew exactly who he was — his slicked back dark hair unmistakable.

Oh no. Oh no, no, no.

The SUV rumbled to life, the low growl of the engine vibrating through the seat beneath Cassidy. Her head shot up, heart hammering in her chest as she realized they were now driving away from the gardens.

She pressed herself lower in the shadows of the back seat, praying he wouldn't glance in the rearview mirror. The last thing she needed was to be caught here, looking like a wreck, and by him of all people.

Duke.

The name alone made her stomach twist.

And now here she was, crouched in the back of his SUV like an idiot, her dress torn at the hem and her palms still stinging from where she'd scraped them on the gravel during her escape.

If he found her…

She squeezed her eyes shut, already imagining the disdain that would harden his sharp features. He'd probably toss her out without a word, disgusted by the very idea of her being here.

The SUV rolled to a smooth stop, and Cassidy held her breath as he spoke into his radio, his voice low and clipped.

"Unit three, I'm heading back to the northwest entrance. Report any movement in the gardens."

Her heart sank. He must've been sent to patrol the grounds after her little escapade. Of course he had. Of all the agents who could have found her, it had to be Duke Armstrong, the man least likely to cut her a shred of slack.

The vehicle eased forward again, the dark gardens slipping past the windows. Cassidy's mind raced. Should she wait until he stopped and try to sneak out unnoticed? Should she confess now and try to explain herself?

Neither option seemed good.

Then Duke's voice startled her out of her thoughts. "You're awfully quiet back there."

Cassidy froze, her breath catching. Had he seen her reflection in the rearview mirror? She stayed perfectly still, her heart pounding so loudly she was certain he'd hear it.

The SUV rolled to a stop again, and she heard the creak of his seat as he turned. "If you're going to hide, at least be better at it."

Her stomach dropped.

Slowly, she straightened, the shadows peeling away from her as she sat upright. Their eyes met in the rearview mirror, his sharp gaze locking on hers with an intensity that made her shiver.

"Evans," he said flatly, his tone devoid of surprise but dripping with disapproval. "You hiding in my car now?"

"No. Escaping. Big Difference."

"Really?" His brow lifted, his expression as unreadable as stone. "Because it looks like you broke protocol, wandered into a restricted area, and snuck into my vehicle...for what? I don't think I want to know."

"This has nothing to do with you." Her cheeks burned. "I wasn't sneaking—I was...escaping."

"Escaping," he repeated, his tone incredulous. "From what?"

She hesitated, torn between telling him the truth and trying to downplay the situation. "I just needed to get away," she said finally, her voice quiet.

His gaze flicked to her torn dress and bloody hands, his lips tightening in a way that made her want to sink into the floor.

He sighed, a heavy sound filled with frustration. "If you were anyone else, you'd already be detained for questioning."

"I didn't mean to cause trouble," she said quickly. "I was just—"

"Trouble seems to follow you, doesn't it?" he cut in sharply.

The words hit harder than she expected, and Cassidy clenched her fists in her lap, hating the way her throat tensed. He didn't even know the half of it, but he didn't have to. He'd already made up his mind about her.

Duke turned back toward the front, his hands gripping the wheel as he said something under his breath she couldn't catch. The SUV began moving again, the tense silence thick between them.

Cassidy bit her lip, staring at the back of his head. She wanted to defend herself, to explain everything, but what good would it do? He wouldn't believe her. To him, she'd always be the naive reporter who didn't belong in the big leagues.

But she wasn't going to give him the satisfaction of breaking down. Not tonight.

Not ever.

Chapter Two

The SUV's tires screeched to a halt, the metallic echo of the parking garage sending a jolt through Cassidy's chest. The vehicle's interior felt like a cold, confining box, the hum of the engine dying, leaving an eerie silence behind. Fluorescent lights overhead flickered in a harsh, clinical rhythm, casting an unforgiving glare on the dark, concrete walls. The sterile environment felt like a cage, each corner sharp and angled, offering no comfort, no escape.

Cassidy gripped the seat beneath her, her breath shallow as her heart hammered in her chest. She hadn't signed up for this. This wasn't part of the plan. But here she was, a prisoner in her own skin, powerless and terrified. She didn't know what he wanted — what he would do next — but the way Duke had looked at her, the coldness in his eyes, sent a chill crawling down her spine.

The door opened without warning, and Cassidy flinched at the sharp sound. Duke stood there, silhouetted against the stark light of the parking garage. His posture was rigid, every inch of him exuding authority, as if he owned this place — and her. He didn't even look at her as he reached for the door handle, his fingers curling around it like it was a command.

"Out," he said, his voice low and clipped. There was no warmth, no kindness — just a demand.

Cassidy's legs shook as she hesitated, struggling to find her voice. But the commanding edge in his tone left no room for debate. She swallowed hard and stepped out of the vehicle, the cold air instantly biting at her skin. The garage's fluorescent lights washed over her, making her feel small and insignificant.

She followed him, her steps uncertain, her knees weak. The sound of his footsteps ahead of her echoed in the hallway like a drumbeat, a constant reminder of his presence, of the authority he wielded. There was no offer of help, no acknowledgment that she was even human. Cassidy tried to steady her breath, but each inhale felt shallower than the last.

They moved through a narrow corridor, the walls unadorned, cold metal doors lining each side. The air smelled sterile, antiseptic, like nothing had been allowed to linger. She caught fleeting glimpses of more uniformed men standing at attention in various hallways. The heaviness of the building was suffocating — everything was too white, too cold, too controlled. The longer she walked, the more she felt like a prisoner, a commodity being dragged along a sterile path she had no power to escape.

When they finally reached the door, Cassidy stopped for a moment. She didn't want to go in. She didn't want to face whatever was waiting behind that door. But Duke didn't pause. He didn't look back. He opened it with a decisive motion and stepped inside.

The office was a sharp contrast to the grandeur she'd seen elsewhere — the White House, with its history and its legacy — this room was sparse, functional. The walls were a dull gray, the carpeting cheap and worn underfoot. A simple desk sat against the far wall, its surface clean and bare except for a few pens and a scattered stack of folders. Behind it, a metal filing cabinet stood in the corner, its drawers ajar, revealing piles of documents stacked haphazardly. The shelves above the desk were lined with binders, but there were no personal touches — no photographs, no mementos. The whole place felt lifeless, designed for efficiency, not comfort.

"Sit," Duke said, his voice again devoid of emotion, as he gestured to the chair in front of the desk.

Cassidy forgot to exhale. She wanted to refuse, to stand her ground, but her legs wouldn't obey. She slowly lowered herself into the chair, her palms clammy as she rested them on her knees. The chair was stiff, uncomfortable, the kind of chair you sat in for hours while you were being interrogated. It felt cold and unforgiving under her, just like the man who stood before her.

Duke didn't sit. Instead, he paced the room, his every movement controlled, calculated. Cassidy could feel his stare on her even when he wasn't looking. She had the distinct impression he was waiting for something — for her to break, for her to react. But all she could do was sit there, her heart pounding in her chest, a mix of dread and confusion swirling inside her.

She tried to speak, but the words wouldn't come. Instead, her throat tightened as the enormity of the situation settled over her. What was he going to do to her?

Cassidy sank into it, her back stiff, her hands clasped tightly in her lap. Duke rounded the desk and sat down, his movements deliberate, his jaw set. He picked up the phone, his finger hovering over the keypad as he glanced at her.

"I'm calling your boss," he said coldly. "He can decide how to handle your mess."

"Don't. You've got this all wrong," she said.

"Do I?" he shot back. "Because you've been here a month, and you've already managed to create a situation that could've spiraled into a security breach. If it had been anyone else but me who found you, do you know how this would look? You'd be out of a job faster than you could blink."

Cassidy clenched her fists, her nails digging into her palms. "I wasn't trying to —"

"I don't care what you were trying to do," he interrupted, his voice sharp. "What I care about is why you were hiding in my SUV, looking like..." His words trailed off as his gaze fell to her hands.

The blood.

Duke's brow furrowed, his eyes narrowing as he leaned forward. "What the hell happened to your hands?"

Cassidy instinctively tried to hide them in her lap, but it was too late. His sharp eyes didn't miss a thing.

"Miss Evans," he said, his voice low and firm, "look at me."

She lifted her head reluctantly, meeting his piercing gaze.

"Tell me what happened," he demanded.

"I—" She hesitated, her throat tightening. "It's nothing. Just...an accident."

"That's not nothing," he snapped, his tone laced with both anger and something else — concern. "You don't just end up with bloody hands after an 'accident'."

Cassidy looked away, her pulse quickening. She couldn't tell him. He'd already made it clear he thought she was trouble, and admitting she'd been attacked would only confirm it.

"I'm fine," she said, her voice barely above a whisper.

"No, you're not."

Before she could protest, Duke stood and disappeared into a small adjoining room. She could hear him placing a call in his cell — to Reed. He returned moments later with a bottle of water, a first-aid box, and a clean white towel.

"Come here," he said, his voice softer but still leaving no room for argument.

Cassidy hesitated, but his expression made her rise and step around the desk. He pulled out the chair beside his and gestured for her to sit.

She lowered herself into it cautiously, watching as he poured some whiskey onto the towel. He grabbed her wrist gently but firmly, drawing her hands closer.

"You don't have to—"

"Quiet," he said, his tone gruff but not unkind.

She bit her lip as he began cleaning the blood from her hands. The whiskey stung, but she barely noticed it. What surprised her more was the care he took, his touch firm but gentle, his movements precise.

Duke worked in silence, his jaw tight, his focus entirely on her hands. He rinsed them with the water, then dabbed at the cuts with a corner of the towel, his brows furrowing every time she winced.

Cassidy couldn't help but stare at him. She'd expected anger, impatience, judgment. But this...this was something else.

22

"Why won't you tell me what happened?" he asked finally, his voice low and steady.

She looked away, her throat tightening. "Because it doesn't matter."

His hand stilled for a moment, and when he spoke again, his voice was sharper. "It matters if someone hurt you."

"No one hurt me," she said, though her voice betrayed her.

Duke's jaw clenched, his eyes flicking to her torn dress and back to her face. "You're lying."

Cassidy pulled her hands free, wrapping them around herself as if to shield against his scrutiny. "I'm not your problem, okay? Just call my boss and get this over with."

He leaned back, his eyes narrowing as he studied her. The frustration in his expression was obvious, but so was the hint of something else—something she couldn't quite place.

"You think I'm just going to let this go?" he asked.

"Yes," she said, her voice wavering. "Because I don't belong here, remember?"

For a moment, Duke didn't respond. He simply watched her, the tension between them thick and unspoken.

Finally, he set the towel aside and stood. "Stay here," he said, his tone firm but lacking the earlier bite.

Cassidy didn't move as he left the room, her mind spinning. For all his anger and disdain, Duke Armstrong had just shown her more care than anyone else in the White House ever had.

And she didn't know what to make of it.

Duke's boots slammed against the polished marble floor of the corridor, each step ringing out like a gunshot in the stillness. His jaw was clenched so tightly his teeth ached from the pressure, and his fists curled involuntarily at his sides. Every nerve in his body was wired with tension, each heartbeat a drumbeat of frustration and fury. The weight of the night — the stakes of everything — pressed down on him, suffocating him with each breath he took.

Ahead, he spotted Thomas Reed rounding the corner, his tall figure cutting through the dimly lit hall like a shadow made flesh. The man had the polished, effortless confidence of someone who had mastered the art of dealing with chaos. As PRN's chief White House correspondent, Reed was as accustomed to the pressure of the political spotlight as Duke was to command. But tonight, Duke's patience was nearing its breaking point.

The moment Reed saw him, his sharp gaze flicked toward him, narrowing slightly. "Armstrong," he said, his voice cool, measured, but with a flicker of caution in his eyes. "Why is my journalist here — alone in this room with you?"

Duke's temper flared, a flash of anger bubbling up, making his chest tighten. He ground his teeth together, trying to keep his cool, but it wasn't working. Not now. Not with her. "Ask her," he growled, his voice low and sharp, like a blade pulled from its sheath. "She's a damn danger to herself and everyone around her." His words were barely contained, each one coming out like it was dragging something raw and unhealed to the surface. "You need to keep Cassidy Evans under control."

Reed's brow furrowed, the wheels of his mind turning, but his face remained a study of practiced neutrality. His lips pressed into a thin line, his posture stiffening. He wasn't about to let Duke off easily. "Care to explain?" he asked, his tone a careful balance of curiosity and challenge.

Duke's jaw tensed further, the muscles in his neck stiff with frustration. He felt a surge of heat, not just from anger but from something deeper—something about Cassidy, something about the way she defied every rule, every expectation. It made his blood boil, and yet...part of him was drawn to her chaos, to the confusion she brought with her.

He jerked his head toward the door of his office, gesturing sharply. He wasn't in the mood for games. "She's sitting in my office, Reed, with torn clothes, blood on her hands, and no goddamn explanation for why she was hiding in my SUV tonight." His voice was tight, strained. He felt every word as it left his mouth. "This isn't the first time she's crossed a line, but it damn well better be the last."

Reed's lips pulled into a thin, hard line. His eyes flickered briefly to the door, then back to Duke, registering the change in his tone, the edge that now ran through every syllable. He didn't say anything—didn't have to—because his silence was its own question.

Duke's pulse throbbed in his temples, his hands balling into fists as he walked toward the door. He reached for the handle and threw it open with more force than necessary. The weight of the room hit him immediately—the thick, musty air, the oppressive silence that seemed to follow him everywhere lately.

As he stepped into the room, Reed followed, the sound of his footsteps distant and faint behind him. But when both men stopped short, everything seemed to freeze. The sight before them was not one either of them had expected.

Cassidy was sitting there, slumped in the chair, her eyes wild and wide. Her breath came in shallow gasps, her shoulders trembling as though she was struggling just to hold herself together. The cold, harsh fluorescent lights above only made the scene more surreal, casting her in stark, unforgiving shadows.

Reed stood beside him, his eyes narrowing as he took in the scene. His jaw clenched, but there was something else in his gaze now — something that, for the first time, seemed uncertain.

"What the hell happened to her?" Reed's voice was quieter now, a sharpness underlying the question, but Duke didn't answer immediately. He couldn't. He was still trying to process the chaos, still trying to make sense of the whirlwind of emotions that had gripped him ever since he first saw Cassidy tonight.

"Why don't you ask her?" Duke said.

Reed crossed his arms as he stared at her. "Cassidy, what the hell is going on?"

She shifted uncomfortably but didn't look away. "I told him — it's nothing."

"Nothing?" Duke growled, stepping closer. "You call bloody hands and sneaking into a secure vehicle nothing?"

Cassidy's jaw tightened, her fingers digging into her palms. "I handled it."

"Handled what?" Reed pressed, his tone sharp but less volatile than Duke's. He shot Duke a glare. "Did he do this to you?"

"No, not him." Cassidy exhaled, her shoulders rising and falling with the movement. "I don't need either of you to fix it, okay? I dealt with it myself."

"That's not an answer," Duke said, his voice dangerously calm.

"I hit him," Cassidy shot back, her voice cutting through the room like a whip.

The silence that followed was heavy and charged.

Reed raised an eyebrow. "You hit him?"

"Yes," she said, her tone firm. "A drunken idiot cornered me in the gardens. He tried to grab me, so I hit him and ran. End of story."

Duke's jaw clenched, and for the first time, he didn't know what to say.

Reed, however, recovered, his lips twitching with something between surprise and reluctant approval. "Well," he said, "I guess I can't fault you for handling it."

Duke's gaze shifted to Cassidy, her defiance masking the vulnerability he'd glimpsed earlier. Despite the chaos she'd caused tonight, he couldn't help but feel a grudging respect. She hadn't broken down. She'd fought back.

But still…

"You should've told someone," he said, his voice quieter but no less firm. "Do you realize how dangerous that was?"

Cassidy stood, meeting his glare head-on. "Do you realize how humiliating it would've been? Everyone already thinks I'm a joke. I wasn't about to prove them right."

The rawness in her voice caught Duke off guard, but he hid it behind a mask of professionalism. Reed, too, seemed taken aback, his expression softening.

"Cassidy," Reed said after a moment, his tone gentler. "Let me take you home. We'll deal with this in the morning."

Her shoulders sagged, but she nodded, clearly too drained to argue.

Cassidy's steps echoed down the hallway as she made her way out of Duke's office, her shoulders tense. The door clicked shut behind her, but the silence that followed felt suffocating.

Duke stood in the office, a storm inside him, but he said nothing. He only watched her leave. That was when Reed stepped forward, his steps heavy with intent.

"You know," Reed's voice was low but thick with judgment, "I don't want to find you alone with her again. Not like this."

Duke didn't respond right away. His fingers tightened into fists at his sides as he turned to face Reed, his jaw set in frustration. He could feel the pulse of anger in his temples, but he bit it back. Instead, he leveled Reed with a look that was both irritated and resigned.

Reed wasn't a man to mince words. He never had been. And Duke knew all too well that this conversation was about more than just Cassidy.

"I don't think you understand how serious this is, Duke," Reed continued, his gaze sharp as he took a step closer. "Your reputation—it follows you. A junior like her doesn't need your...baggage hanging over her. She's working here, not one of your—" Reed hesitated, the words clearly on the tip of his tongue but never quite coming out.

Duke wanted to hit Reed. He wanted to shout that he didn't need anyone telling him who he was, what he was, or what he was capable of. But he didn't. Because that would make him just like Reed—arrogant, dismissive, all the things he hated.

"Stay the hell out of my way," Duke said, his voice low, but filled with an unmistakable warning. He took a step forward, and Reed instinctively backed off, his eyes narrowing, but not without that cold, calculating look that made Duke want to snap.

"Watch yourself," Reed shot back, his tone stiff. "You think you're helping her, but you're not. Just leave her alone." Reed's eyes flicked to the hallway where Cassidy had just disappeared. "She's already finding enough trouble as it is."

Duke's chest tensed. What the hell did Reed mean by that? He wanted to ask, but the words stuck in his throat. He wanted to defend himself, to explain that he wasn't the man Reed thought he was—that he wasn't out to hurt anyone, let alone Cassidy. But the truth was, Reed was right about one thing.

"Just remember, Duke," Reed said, his voice colder now, "stay away from her."

"With pleasure," he replied.

Chapter Three

Monday morning, Cassidy walked through the White House press office, the hum of activity around her fading in and out as she passed rows of journalists huddled over laptops, making calls, or scribbling notes furiously. It was a familiar routine — her first full month on the job, and the atmosphere was a blend of high-stakes politics and quiet tension.

Today, like most days, she felt out of place.

As she walked past the sea of serious faces, her gaze kept drifting to the row of empty desks by the windows, where the real political reporters sat — the ones handling the latest scandals, impeachment rumors, and foreign policy decisions. Cassidy wasn't one of them.

She was a biographer, or at least, that's how they'd pitched her role. "Human-interest piece on the president," they'd said. "A profile of the man behind the headlines." But so far, her article was just a collection of quotes, third-party accounts, and vague observations. It was a half-baked patchwork of facts —

unfocused, unfinished. Not nearly enough for a biographical piece on a sitting president.

Certainly not enough to fill a magazine.

Thomas Reed leaned against the doorframe of his office, his arms crossed, a gruff expression painted across his face. He was a veteran journalist with a permanent scowl that seemed to suggest he didn't have much time for her or her assignment. He didn't even hide it. And Cassidy didn't blame him. What had she really brought to the table? A few photos of the president with his family, a couple of off-the-cuff interviews with staffers who didn't really know him, and a whole lot of guesswork.

"Stay out of trouble this weekend, Evans?" Thomas' voice was blunt, cutting through the quiet murmur of the office.

"Tried to."

"Good. I've been keeping the lawn incident on the hush. With any luck, it will stay that way." He raised an eyebrow, looking up from the stack of papers in his hand. "Where are you on the article?"

Cassidy hesitated, her incomplete article pressing on her chest like a heavy coat. "I've been—uh—gathering insights. People who know him well, you know, staffers, advisors—"

"Right, right," Thomas interrupted, stepping into the room with a deliberate, slow pace. "The president's schedule's tight these days, and you're still waiting on those insights?" His eyes narrowed, a flicker of annoyance passing through them. "I thought you were supposed to be more than just gathering facts. You're supposed to dig deeper, Evans. You're writing a biography, not a press release."

Cassidy swallowed, feeling his gaze. She had been trying. The president had been busy, his schedule packed with post-election strategy, congressional meetings, and foreign policy crises. But even when he did have a few minutes to spare, she was always one of the last people on his list.

"I know," she said. "I just...haven't had a real moment with him yet."

"Yeah, well, those moments won't just fall into your lap." Thomas' tone was sharper now, his voice tinged with the impatience that had become all too familiar to Cassidy. He was. "You're not here to be some passive observer, Cassidy. You need to find a way to force those moments. Otherwise, you're going to end up with a fluffy puff piece that no one takes seriously."

Cassidy winced at the thought. "I don't want that."

"Then you'd better figure out a way to get his attention. You've been here for almost a month, and the president's not exactly making time for you, is he?" Thomas' gaze flicked over her shoulder toward the group of serious reporters clustered around their desks, diving into political strategy with intensity. He lowered his voice, just a little. "You're being buried under the weight of this place, Evans. The longer you sit on the sidelines, the harder it'll be to climb out."

Cassidy's stomach knotted. He was right, and she knew it. The other reporters were handling the big stories—policy, legislation, the president's approval ratings—but here she was, standing on the periphery, hoping for a breakthrough that wasn't coming. "What do you want me to do? I've tried everything."

"Everything?" Thomas raised an eyebrow. "You think trying to squeeze in five minutes with the president between his meetings is enough?" His voice dropped a little, more insistent. "You need to push. Get in the room when it matters. Be bold. Find your angle.

There's more to this president than his slogans. You know that, right?"

Cassidy shifted, her grip tightening on her notebook. "I've tried," she repeated, her voice tinged with frustration.

"You can't just 'try', Evans. You're writing a piece for PRN Media, for God's sake," Thomas said, his voice rough but with an edge of something like pity. "This magazine is not even taken seriously by half the people here. This is our chance to show it's worth something — and give him something in return."

"I know what he wants — to reach the people who don't care about the political scene," Cassidy said, lifting her chin. She tried to muster the same sense of purpose she'd felt when she'd first taken the job. "I've got to make them care about the real man behind all the speeches, the posturing, and the politics."

"Exactly, Evans. And that's why PRN chose you — a fresh journalist without a history of political baggage. The voice of a new demographic."

"But everything I've gotten so far is surface-level. And I don't have anything — anything — that goes beyond that." She almost added that she wasn't sure she could get there, but she stopped herself just in time.

Cassidy felt the familiar sense of frustration rise in her chest, the heat of anger mixed with a cold, deep anxiety. Her article was a mess. The profile was weak, and she knew it. She'd been writing around the president, writing about him in the vaguest possible terms, hoping for a breakthrough that hadn't come. And now the deadline was looming. January first was just around the corner.

"How do I get to him, Thomas?" she asked quietly, her voice tight with her frustration.

Thomas gave her a long look. "You stop waiting," he said, his voice low and direct. "Find a way in."

A moment of silence passed between them, and for the first time, Cassidy felt the full weight of what she needed to do. She wasn't just writing about a president anymore—she was writing about a person. A man who, for all his flaws, had managed to reach millions of people. But she wasn't going to get any closer to understanding him by standing at the edges. She needed to dive in. She needed to take a risk.

She turned to leave, the tension in her chest easing just a little. There it was inside her, some spark of determination she hadn't fully realized was there before. It wasn't enough to just observe anymore. She was going to have to break out of her comfort zone, no matter how uncomfortable it made her feel. She couldn't wait for the president to hand her a story.

She had to take it.

* * * *

It was an ordinary Tuesday afternoon in the White House, and the corridors were buzzing with the usual post-meeting tension. Cassidy stood in the hallway just outside the Oval Office, her palms slick with sweat, heart pounding against her chest. She had to make a move. She had to get real access.

And today was the day.

She knew the president had a busy schedule—meetings with foreign dignitaries, policy updates, and interviews—but there was a sliver of time right before he left for his evening event. If she could just catch him for ten minutes, maybe fifteen, she could get the anecdotes that would bring her story to life.

She had rehearsed this in her head a dozen times. She'd even written out a few questions, ones that didn't sound too obvious or desperate, ones that might spark beyond the routine answers he usually gave to the press.

But as she stood there, waiting for that opening, the reality of her situation hit her like a punch to the gut — she was an outsider in a place where access was as tightly controlled as the security systems themselves.

The door to the Oval Office creaked open and Cassidy's breath caught in her throat. The president stepped out, his usual calm demeanor in place. His security detail flanked him, but he looked up, meeting her eyes. The briefest second of recognition, the faintest flicker of acknowledgment. This was it. Her chance.

"Mr. President," Cassidy called, her voice rising just a bit louder than she intended, cutting through the stillness of the hallway. She hurried to catch up with him, her heart racing in her chest. "Sir, I was hoping to speak with you for just a moment before you head out. For your biography."

The president, already halfway to the elevators, hesitated for only the briefest moment. His eyes flickered toward her, his expression distant, like someone carefully considering whether to engage.

"Miss Evans," he said with a polite nod, almost rehearsed. "I'm actually running late. We'll have to take a rain check."

Cassidy's stomach drew in in disappointment. She had been so sure this was the moment — her opportunity to connect, to do something real. But she could feel it slipping away from her, and the pressure to make this work hit her all at once.

"I'll walk with you," she said quickly, almost too earnestly, the words tumbling out in a rush. "Just a couple of questions. It won't take long, I promise."

Her voice was a little too loud now, shaky with nerves as she tried to push through the distance she felt. But the president's expression shifted, his smile fading as his hand made a subtle motion of dismissal. The veneer he wore was now firm and final.

"I'm sorry, Miss Evans," he said, his tone now more clipped.

Cassidy froze, but before she could even respond, she felt a presence beside her.

In one smooth motion, Duke Armstrong appeared out of nowhere, cutting in front of her with effortless grace. Without saying a word, he gently guided her into a nearby side room, away from the attention of the president and his security detail. Cassidy barely registered the movement before she found herself standing in the small, quiet room, heart still pounding, her mind still spinning.

She turned to face him, her cheeks flushed with the sting of humiliation, frustration bubbling beneath the surface. "What — what are you doing?" Her voice was softer than it had been before, but no less sharp with her confusion.

Duke met her gaze with his usual calm, that cool, unshakable demeanor that always seemed to make her feel smaller. "Christ, Evans," he said, his voice low and controlled. "I saved you."

Cassidy blinked, trying to wrap her mind around his words. "Saved me from what?"

"Suicide."

"You didn't have to do that — "

"It was too fucking painful."

Cassidy's heart pounded harder, but her voice was warm, steady despite the tension. "I just... I just wanted to ask him some real questions. I don't understand why everyone here always feels like they have to play games." She gestured back toward the hallway, the White House itself. "It feels like no one is being real."

Duke raised an eyebrow, his expression unreadable, but Cassidy could feel the weight of his judgment. "Do you know anything about this place? We are talking power, control, and making the right moves at the right time. You think you can just waltz in here, charm everyone with your big, eager smile, and people will just fall in line? You're getting eaten alive."

Cassidy's chest tensed with a mix of frustration and something softer—maybe hope? She didn't know. But she wasn't going to let him win this argument. "I'm not asking them to fall in line. I'm just asking for something real. Why is that so bad?"

"Because this place isn't about real," he said, his voice edged with something close to pity. "This place is about surviving. And if you want to survive, you have to play the game. No one cares about *you*. They care about how useful you are."

Cassidy took a deep breath, fighting the way her heart threatened to crack under his words. She wasn't wrong. She knew she wasn't. But hearing it from him, with all his hardened cynicism, made her feel small in a way she wasn't sure she could handle.

"You're wrong," she said quietly, looking up at him. "And I don't know how to do this any other way."

Duke's gaze lingered on her for a long moment, and for a second, Cassidy thought she saw something— something human—flicker behind his steely exterior. But it was gone just as quickly as it appeared.

"Evans, you never listen. And I can't watch this shitshow anymore."

"You don't get it, do you?" she said, her voice sharp, but trembling with her emotions. "I'm not here to play games. I'm here to get something real. I want to write a story that matters, not a damn piece of political party propaganda. I'm going to get the president to talk to me because I'm going to be real with him. I'm going to be me. That's the only way to break through the noise."

Duke leaned against the doorframe, his arms crossed, eyes narrowed with that familiar, knowing smirk. "You think that's what's going to get him to sit down with you? You think if you're just nice enough, and genuine enough, and...what? Sweet enough? Open up those big, green eyes and eagerly flutter your eyelashes? That's how it works in this world?" His words were almost laced with pity. "No, Cassidy, that's not how it works. That's how it works in some world you've invented in your head. The real world? The one that matters? You want to survive here? You need to be useful."

Her breath caught. She knew he didn't believe in her, didn't believe in her methods. But hearing it— hearing him say it—sent a jolt of anger coursing through her veins. "I am useful," she shot back, her voice barely containing the fire that was threatening to break free. "I'm writing a real story. I'm going to do it my way, not your way."

"What will it take for you to fucking listen." His tone grew serious, almost mocking. "In a month, you'll be begging for a way out. You'll be miserable. You'll quit. And that fluff piece you're so sure you're writing? It'll end up being a joke."

Cassidy felt the words land like a slap. She knew what Duke was doing—he was baiting her. But he was wrong. She was going to prove him wrong.

"No," she snapped, her voice full of defiance. "You're wrong."

Duke's eyes glinted, an amused smile tugging at the corner of his mouth. "I'll bet you anything you want.

You'll be eating your words within a month, probably sooner. You'll come crawling back here, with your tail between your legs. You'll see how life works, Evans."

"I'll prove you wrong. New Years Day. My story will be something real, people will love it, and you'll be eating that crow."

Duke's smirk deepened. "Do you realize you're playing with fire? What's on the line here — your career, your dignity, and your little fantasy."

"I don't care. I'll be fine."

"What do I get if I win?"

Cassidy's pulse quickened at the words. "You want me to thank you? How about a hero biscuit?"

"Careful." Duke's eyes flickered with something — amusement, maybe irritation — but there was no question he wasn't backing down.

The tension between them crackled, their unspoken challenge settling heavily in the room. Neither of them moved as they stood in silence for a moment — Cassidy filled with the steady warmth of certainty, Duke with the cold edge of experience.

Finally, Cassidy spoke, her voice steady. "You need to try my style on for size, Duke. See where it takes you."

Duke's smile twisted, a mixture of admiration and something darker. "That's the opposite of what I'm trying to show you."

"Scared? Where would honesty and realness take you?"

He nodded slowly, the corners of his mouth tugging into a grim smile. "Fine. You're on, but sure as hell — you're going to regret not listening. I'll be there to cut your access badge when you quit."

With that, he turned and walked out of the room, leaving Cassidy standing there, determined, her mind already racing with the possibilities.

This was it. No more playing it safe. No more compromising. Cassidy Evans was going to do this her way—no matter the cost. And she wasn't about to let Duke or anyone else tell her she couldn't.

Chapter Four

Duke adjusted the collar of his nondescript jacket, his gloved hands tucked into his pockets as he scanned the crowd with practiced ease. The chill of the November evening barely registered beneath the thick fabric of his coat. He had long ago learned to ignore the discomfort of the weather — it was a small price to pay for staying unseen in the middle of a protest of this size.

The streets of Pennsylvania Avenue were alive with energy — so loud, so chaotic — that it could have swallowed him whole if he let his guard down. Thousands of voices chanting in unison, their demands rising like waves crashing on a shoreline. Signs and flags danced above the sea of bodies, each one more passionate, more desperate than the last. The slogans ranged from heartfelt pleas for justice to raw, visceral anger, all bound together by the common thread of the conflict in Yemen. The tension in the air was palpable, as if the very atmosphere was charged with the weight of emotions spilling out into the streets.

This wasn't the first protest he had monitored, nor would it be the last, but something about the sense of urgency in the air tonight felt different. The temperature had dropped, but the heat in the crowd was unmistakable. People were on edge. Emotions were running high, fueled by a cause that felt more personal for many than any protest he had seen in years.

He moved through the edges of the crowd, his eyes flicking from one face to the next, always alert, always watching. His posture was deliberately casual, his expression neutral, a part of the scene rather than a looming figure. He nodded at a few familiar faces, police officers and officers from other agencies also blending into the crowd. They were the quiet ones, the ghosts in plain sight—security was everywhere, and nowhere at the same time.

Wyatt and Salem were stationed at separate points along the route, keeping their eyes peeled for any signs of trouble. Duke didn't need to check in with them often—their coordination was seamless, a well-oiled machine honed over countless missions. His earpiece crackled with Salem's voice.

"East corner's clear. TVC protesters are moving toward the Capitol now. No signs of trouble so far."

"Copy that," Duke replied, his voice low and calm, but his gaze still scanning the movement of the masses. He had been in this position long enough to know that the atmosphere could tilt in an instant. One wrong move, one escalation, and things could spiral out of control. That was the key—watch, listen, and never react too quickly.

But then, something shifted. A small movement at the edge of his vision caught his attention—a slight turn of the head, a quick adjustment of the crowd. And then, there it was — a curl of light blonde hair escaping from beneath the hood of a gray sweatshirt. It was brief, fleeting, but unmistakable.

Duke's heart skipped a beat as his mind instantly locked onto the familiar sight. The curl. That particular shade of blonde. It wasn't just the hair — it was the way she turned, the way their profile emerged from the crowd, just enough to confirm what his instincts were already telling him.

"Dammit," he said under his breath.

Cassidy Evans.

Duke's gaze never wavered, tracking her movements through the mass of people. She was close to the edge of the crowd, her pace quickening as the protest began to shift toward the Capitol. He could see the way she was moving — deliberate, yet trying not to stand out. It wasn't a coincidence.

He raised his hand to his earpiece, his voice steady but low. "Salem, I've got eyes on a possible security concern. I'm going to handle it."

There was a pause before Salem's voice crackled back, tinged with confusion. "Understood. Be discreet. Keep us posted."

Duke was already moving, slipping through the crowd with ease, weaving in and out of bodies like a shadow, his eyes never leaving Cassidy. He had trained for moments like this — where keeping his cover was just as important as the mission itself. His pulse was steady now, his instincts sharp. He knew exactly how to read a crowd, how to anticipate the next move, how to blend into the scene.

His jaw tightened as he adjusted his path, weaving through the throng of protesters with ease. He kept his distance, his eyes trained on her as she moved with the crowd. She wasn't carrying a sign, and her hood was pulled low. This was dangerous — reckless. This crowd could crush her. It had gone sideways before.

What the hell are you doing here, Evans?

Duke followed her, his movements keeping him in her orbit without drawing attention. He sidestepped a man holding a poster and edged closer, just in time to hear her voice as she stopped beside a pair of protesters.

"What do you think of the administration's stance on the conflict?" she asked, her tone soft but direct.

Duke's ears perked up. She wasn't shouting, wasn't chanting. She was…interviewing.

The older woman she'd addressed frowned, her grip tightening on the placard she carried. "What stance? They're doing nothing while people are being slaughtered. It's disgusting."

"And you feel that reflects on the president himself?" Cassidy pressed, a small notebook appearing in her hand.

"Of course it does," the woman snapped. "He's the one with the power to stop this. But he won't, will he? Too much money at stake."

Cassidy scribbled something down, then nodded politely before thanking the woman and moving on.

Duke's stomach churned. She wasn't here as a protester — she was gathering intel.

He followed her as she stopped again, this time near a young man holding a sign that read *Ceasefire Now*.

"What do you think the president's priorities should be in addressing this?" she asked him.

The man shrugged, his expression grim. "Not siding with TVC would be a good start."

Cassidy nodded again, jotting his words in her notebook.

Duke's patience snapped. He closed the remaining distance between them in a few swift strides, grabbing Cassidy's elbow and spinning her around to face him.

"What the hell do you think you're—"

Before he could finish, she grinned up at him knowingly, her green eyes gleaming with mischief. Then, to his utter disbelief, she stuck her tongue out at him like a rebellious teenager.

"Evans—"

A sharp crack split the air, followed by a series of rapid pops. The crowd surged in a ripple of panic, and for a moment, Duke's instincts screamed gunfire. His hand went to his concealed holster, his body tense and ready, but he quickly identified the sound— firecrackers. Someone had set them off just a few yards away, sending sparks flying and protesters scattering.

In the chaos, Cassidy yanked free of his grip.

"Cassidy!" Duke barked, his voice sharp with anger, but she was already slipping into the sea of bodies, her hood flying back as her blonde curls caught the light. The protest churned around him, a swirling mass of noise and movement, but all he could see was her. His pulse spiked, a mix of frustration and something darker swirling inside him. She was running. She was alone. In the middle of a damn protest, with no backup, no plan. His stomach twisted with a feeling he didn't have time to unpack.

Dammit, Evans.

He cursed under his breath and pushed into the crowd, his muscles working harder than he'd intended. She was fast—too fast. He hadn't expected that kind of agility from her, the kind of fluid, controlled motion that cut through the crush of bodies like she'd trained for it. His mind flashed to her sprinting down streets, the soft rhythm of her steps, the grace with which she moved.

He gritted his teeth, his jaw clenched so tight he could feel the pressure in his skull. She was getting away from him.

Focus, he snapped at himself. But it didn't stop the instinctive flare of attraction — there was no denying it.

Her figure was a blur ahead of him, a contrast of grace and recklessness. Cassidy Evans, the journalist who somehow always found a way to make things more difficult. His chest tightened with the mix of rage and something else — something darker — that he couldn't untangle. She was out here, no one had her back, and she was treating this like it was some kind of game.

Goddamn it, he thought, as his breathing quickened. He hated the way his body responded to her, even when she made him furious. But right now? He was angry. So angry.

"Evans, stop running!" he shouted, the words ripping from his throat. His heart hammered against his ribcage as he barreled through the crowd, using his size and strength to force his way through. But she didn't slow.

Instead, she sped up, her body slipping effortlessly through the chaos like a swimmer navigating a riptide. She leapt over a low wall with fluid ease, her sneakers hitting the pavement with barely a sound. The adrenaline made his skin burn as he pushed harder, but it wasn't enough. She was getting further away, and his chest tensed with the thought of what could happen if she kept going.

Cassidy slid across the hood of a parked car. She was like a force of nature — wild, fast and free — and for one terrifying moment, Duke wondered if he'd even be able to catch her.

Her figure darted down another side street, disappearing around the corner, and Duke cursed again. He was close now, but she was good. Too damn good. But it only made his pursuit more urgent. She wasn't supposed to be here, and he was the one responsible for making sure she didn't get herself killed in the process. His feet pounded the pavement as he rounded the corner, sweat stinging his eyes, his anger still simmering beneath the surface.

Cassidy's pace slowed as she ducked into a small wooded park. Duke's eyes narrowed as he approached the trees, his breath coming fast now, chest heaving with the effort. The noise of the protest, the shouting and chanting, faded to a faint hum behind him. The cool night air wrapped around him as he stepped into the park, the dark shapes of the trees casting long shadows on the ground. His steps softened on the earth, and he slowed his breathing, instinctively scanning for any movement.

Then, he saw her.

Cassidy was crouched behind a thick oak, her back pressed against the rough bark, chest heaving as she tried to catch her breath. Her blonde curls were wild, her face flushed from exertion, but she didn't look scared. No, she looked defiant, like she thought she could outrun him — or worse, that she could escape.

His temper flared again, hot and sharp. The irritation, the raw, primal need to protect her, tangled with something darker, something he couldn't quite name. He stopped a few feet away, leaning casually against a nearby tree, but his posture was anything but relaxed. His eyes never left her, his fists clenching at his sides, fighting the urge to move closer.

"You're fast," he said, his voice a low drawl, tinged with reluctant admiration. The anger still simmered in his words, but there was no denying the edge of genuine respect in his tone.

Cassidy's head snapped up, her eyes flashing. "And you're persistent," she shot back, her voice sharp, but it wasn't enough to mask the tension in the air between them.

Duke's jaw ticked. "What the hell were you thinking, running off like that?" His voice was low, but there was a dangerous edge to it. "You have no backup, no support. This isn't some damn game."

Cassidy stood up slowly, dusting herself off, but the defiance in her posture remained. "I didn't need anyone," she said quietly, though there was a crack in her voice now, a hint of something that made his chest tighten even more. Was it fear? Or was it frustration—her own version of the wild energy he was feeling?

Duke didn't move, his gaze still fixed on her, burning with a combination of fury and something else—something he wouldn't let himself explore, not yet.

"You should need someone," he said under his breath, but his words were laced with something darker. Something he didn't want to admit even to himself.

Duke tensed as Cassidy crossed her arms and met his gaze. Her defiance, that damn fire, always pushed his buttons in ways he didn't understand. "I can handle myself," she said, voice steady but full of challenge.

He took a step forward, not because he thought it would make her listen but because it made the air between them crackle with something he couldn't quite name. His voice was low, tight with frustration. "You shouldn't have to. Not like this. Do you even realize what could've happened if someone else had followed you? Someone who wasn't me?"

For a brief moment, Cassidy hesitated, just long enough that he saw the flicker of doubt in her eyes. It was gone almost immediately, but it gave him enough to hold onto. "I wasn't in any real danger," she said, her tone a little softer now, but still stubborn.

His jaw clenched. "You don't know that." His voice dropped, softening just a touch, but the intensity in his gaze never wavered. "You're too damn stubborn for your own good."

The words hung between them like a storm cloud, heavy and thick. He couldn't breathe right—couldn't think straight—because the mix of anger and protectiveness gnawed at him. All he could see was her, in front of him, too damn close to something that could blow up in her face. And here he was, unable to stay away.

They stood there in the quiet woods, the sounds of the protest a distant hum in the background. The only thing he could hear was the frantic beat of his own heart, angry and something more—something jagged—coursing through him.

"You don't know anything about me, Duke," she said after a beat, her voice quieter now but still firm. There was something in her eyes—something vulnerable—but she buried it quickly behind her walls.

"I'm starting to," he admitted, his gaze never leaving hers, his voice rougher than he meant. "And what I see is very concerning." The words tasted bitter on his tongue, but he couldn't stop them. What the hell was he supposed to make of her? Of this?

"I'm just doing my job," she shot back, her eyes flashing with irritation, her chest rising with the heat of their argument.

"Your job?" His voice dropped, the sarcasm clear. "Your job is to write a puff piece on the president, not to get yourself caught up in a volatile protest."

Her eyes sparked with defiance, and before she could fire back, she took a deep breath. "This is research," she said, her voice low but full of fierce conviction.

"That's bullshit."

"No," she replied. "It's the truth."

"You got close. Too close."

Cassidy didn't blink. "That's the point."

His chest tightened, his mind screaming at him to pull her away, to get her the hell out of here. This wasn't just about her being in a crowd of protesters. This was about them — about the danger of them being together, of him being out here with her.

He wanted to push her away.

But his body wasn't listening. It never did when it came to Cassidy.

Instead of pulling back, the space between them closed, inch by inch. She didn't move, didn't step back. Her eyes — those green eyes — were locked on his, wide and bright, unguarded.

"What the hell are you trying to prove, Evans?"

Cassidy's lips parted, but she didn't speak.

"You're out of your mind," Duke finally said. "And yet here I am, chasing you down like a goddamn idiot."

His hand moved before he could think better of it. He reached up to the wild mess of curls framing her face. One strand caught his attention, golden under the faint light filtering through the trees. He caught it between his fingers, twisting it and watching as it bounced back into place.

Cassidy didn't say a word, but her cheeks flushed a deep pink, the color standing out against the pale curve of her jaw. Her lips parted slightly, her breath visible in the cold air. She looked up at him, those green eyes of hers wide with something he couldn't quite name — something girlish and vulnerable, yet fiercely alive.

"Evans," he growled, his voice thick with something darker than just frustration. "What the fuck am I going to do with you?"

She swallowed, her throat bobbing visibly as she kept her gaze locked on his. The tension between them was suffocating, thick with anticipation.

He stepped forward, just enough to feel her warmth. His eyes burned into hers, unyielding and intense. The world outside them disappeared for a brief, fleeting moment, leaving just the two of them standing in the middle of the storm they had both created.

"Be honest," he said. "Did you want me to follow you?"

She didn't look away. She didn't back down. And then, the words came, soft but sure, sliding from her lips like they'd been waiting to escape for far too long.

"Yes."

Duke's breath caught in his throat. It wasn't what he'd expected, but it was exactly what he'd needed to hear. The floodgate he'd been holding back suddenly cracked wide open.

"And, do you want me to kiss you?"

For a second, she was still. Her eyes flickered, searching his face for something — maybe for the truth. Maybe for the certainty she'd always seemed to demand of him.

Then, her lips parted.

"Yes."

The word hung in the air between them, fragile and electric, sparking something inside him that he couldn't control. Without thinking, Duke moved. His hand slid to the back of her neck, his fingers tangling in the soft curls there, pulling her closer. The world tilted on its axis as he tilted her head, just enough to bring their lips together.

Her lips carried the cool sweetness of vanilla mint, a flavor that lingered like a secret on the edge of a winter morning.

He kissed her soft at first, slow, like they were both savoring the moment, but then it ignited — fast, reckless, as if they had both been waiting for this. Her lips were warm, yielding, and felt like defiance and chaos. Her hands rose to his chest, and when they made contact, it felt like a jolt of electricity — her touch burned right through the layers of his jacket, igniting a fire inside him that he couldn't put out.

For a man who prided himself on control — on planning, on measuring every move, every word — this was reckless. This was chaos. And every part of him that wanted to stop, to pull away, to make sense of this, was drowned out by the simple fact that he didn't care. Not now. Not here.

She kissed him back, no hesitation, no doubt. Cassidy Evans opened to him — melting into him — and in this moment, she was all that mattered. The protest, the risks, the consequences — they faded in the background. It was just her, just him, tangled together in a kiss that felt like the only thing that made sense in a world that had always been too damn complicated.

Duke's pulse was still racing, but this time it wasn't from the chase or the chaos that had preceded it. It was the kiss. The kind that caught him off guard—too natural, too real, too good to be anything other than raw.

Cassidy's lips were soft but pleading, like she was telling him with every inch of space between them that this—whatever this was—wasn't something she would ever walk away from. And damn it, he wasn't sure he wanted to.

Duke felt a jolt of something unexpected. He hated it. She was warm, intoxicating, and completely unpredictable. He craved it. Her fingers grazed his jawline, tracing the scar that had always been a part of him, and it sent a shiver down his spine.

Cassidy broke the kiss for a second, both of them gasping for air, but neither of them moved away. She blinked up at him, those green eyes of hers shimmering in the dim light, her cheeks flushed, her lips still parted. The teasing gleam in her eyes didn't quite mask the vulnerability beneath. "That honest enough for you?" she said, her voice teasing but shaky, as if she was still trying to steady herself.

Duke tensed. He couldn't tell if it was desire or frustration or both. A slow, breathless chuckle escaped him, his hand still lingering at the back of her neck, reluctant to let her go. "It's a start."

But as the world rushed back in, so did what had just happened. He pulled away, his hands falling to his sides, his pulse still racing in his veins.

She was trouble — more trouble than he'd ever bargained for. She had a way of burrowing under his skin, of making him forget himself entirely. She didn't just shake up his world — she shattered it.

And as much as he wanted to hate her for it, as much as he wanted to scream at her for putting herself in danger like this, there was one thing he couldn't deny.

He didn't regret it. Not even a little.

Chapter Five

Cassidy stood at the kitchen counter, her hands dusted in flour, the soft hum of the oven filling the air, curling around her like a nostalgic embrace. She was preparing her mom's favorite pie — an old family recipe that never let her down, unlike most of her cooking attempts.

She pressed the rolling pin down harder than necessary, the cool, smooth surface of the dough yielding beneath her palms. The resistance was oddly satisfying, the rhythmic motion almost meditative. Still, the simplicity of it only amplified the churn of thoughts swirling inside her head, the growing frustration of how utterly off course her life seemed.

Apple pie should've been a comfort. Instead, it felt like a reminder of everything that had gone wrong. Her life, her choices — each moment a decision she couldn't take back. Even this stupid pie, a Christmas gift for her parents before their trip. A small gesture, a step toward normalcy, but it felt hollow. Like she was trying too hard to hold onto something that was slipping away.

Her mind wandered, as it always did, back to Duke. That damn kiss. She didn't even know why she had kissed him, only that it had felt right in the moment, like the world had clicked into place. But now, standing in her kitchen with the scent of apples and cinnamon in the air, she couldn't help but feel her own impulsivity.

She had bet him, made a joke, thrown out something ridiculous, and kissed him like it was nothing. Like it was just another chapter in the weird, surreal saga of her life.

But it wasn't nothing.

And he hadn't texted her back since. Not once. Not a word. Not even a "What the hell was that?"

Cassidy winced, letting the rolling pin fall still in her hands. She had no idea what she'd expected, really. That he'd come charging after her, demanding to know why she had kissed him? That he'd share some long-winded apology for being a terrible human being? Or was she just waiting for him to act like a grown-up and call her out for being impulsive?

Her phone buzzed on the counter, a notification from a group chat with her parents. She ignored it.

What good was it, anyway?

She dropped her gaze to the pie again.

A small part of her wondered if she should call Duke. If she should do something—anything—to fill the space between them.

But Cassidy knew better than that. She was too much of a mess for him. And if he was done, if he was going to pretend it never happened, then maybe it was time for her to do the same.

With a heavy sigh, she grabbed a cloth and started cleaning up the counter.

"Hey, you okay?" Anne's voice broke through the quiet, sharp but gentle.

Cassidy blinked and looked up. Her roommate was leaning against the doorway, a faint smirk on her face, but her eyes narrowed in that way that meant she wasn't letting Cassidy hide.

"Just baking a pie for Mom." Cassidy shrugged, trying to sound casual, though her mind was still somewhere else entirely. "You coming to dinner?"

"Am I your date?" Anne asked, already grinning.

Cassidy shrugged. "Sure. No. Wait—I was going to grab one of those Secret Service hotties. For balance. To impress my relatives with danger."

"Duke Armstrong?" Anne said it too fast, too loud, like she'd been waiting to say it.

"I don't want to talk about Duke."

Anne, of course, sat down. This was now a hostage situation. "Cass, you need to stop letting him get in your head. Just focus on your job and forget about him. You're here for you, not him."

"But he lied to me," Cassidy said quietly, her gaze dropping to the pie crust, fingers stiff.

Anne's lips pursed. "He was testing you. It's what he does. Probably a game to him."

Cassidy's mind flashed back to that first time she'd met Duke. Her first day. White House press entrance. How he'd introduced himself as 'Jake' and charmed her like…he was just any other guy, like there was nothing at all unusual about him. She'd been so naïve. When she'd realized the truth—when she'd found out who he really was—she'd felt like the rug had been pulled out from under her. A local legend, the kind of guy people warned you about, the kind you were supposed to stay away from. It had hit her like a ton of bricks. He'd played her, like a game, to see how easily he could fool her.

Cassidy closed her eyes for a moment, the sting of that memory fresh. "I thought he was different. I thought maybe we had something real. And then he kissed me...like it meant something. But then it was just another game."

Anne's voice softened. "He's an ass. Forget him."

Cassidy let out a slow breath. "I hate that he's right. I'm just this...naive girl who doesn't fit into his world. I want to show him I'm more than that. I'm more than what he thinks of me."

Anne leaned in, locking eyes with her. "Don't do it for him, Cass. Do it for you. You're not here to fit into his world. You're here to build your own. You don't need his approval."

Cassidy's shoulders straightened, her lips pulling into a tight smile. "Yeah. You're right. I've got a better idea."

"A better idea?" Anne raised an eyebrow. "This doesn't sound good."

Cassidy wiped her hands on a towel. "Don't worry, Anne. You'll come with me."

* * * *

Cassidy shoved her phone back into her coat pocket, fighting the biting December air. The cold gnawed at her skin, her breath visible in short, sharp bursts as she marched down the downtown streets of DC. No message. No reply. She wasn't surprised. Duke never played by her rules, and if she was honest, she was getting sick of waiting for him to.

She glanced over at Anne, whose scarf was wrapped tightly around her neck, her arms crossed in a defensive posture as she followed behind. The city was alive with holiday energy, but Cassidy felt like she was moving through a fog. The Christmas lights strung along the buildings sparkled, but the glow felt distant, a reminder of everything Cassidy couldn't seem to reach.

"Are you seriously dragging me out here for this?" Anne said, her boots crunching against the snowy sidewalk.

Cassidy shot her a sidelong look. "He's going to be here, Anne. Just—trust me."

Anne rolled her eyes, her breath puffing out in a cloud of steam. "Yeah, because waiting for him in the freezing cold for the third time this week is a great plan."

Cassidy's jaw strained, but she refused to let the frustration show. It was bad enough that Anne kept making comments about Duke, but deep down, Cassidy couldn't escape the constant ache in her chest every time he avoided her, every time he shut her out.

She dragged Anne around the corner, passing a row of glittering storefronts as a group of shoppers bustled by. The streets were bustling with people—families, tourists, even a few politicians, their faces hidden behind masks of civility and holiday cheer. But Cassidy didn't care about any of that. She was here for one reason only.

"Duke's not going to show," Anne said, her voice tinged with a mixture of skepticism and concern. "Seriously. He's not even texting you."

Cassidy didn't respond. She had been holding her breath, hoping for a message, any message. But it was almost as if Duke enjoyed making her chase him, enjoyed making her question her worth. Not this time, she told herself. Not anymore.

They rounded the block and found themselves at the entrance of the toy store where the event was being held. The festive decorations glowed bright, casting a soft light on the growing crowd. A massive wreath hung above the door, and fake snow flurries swirled through the air from a nearby machine, settling on the sidewalk like dust. The smell of hot chocolate and gingerbread cookies mixed with the cold scent of the evening. Families huddled together, kids tugging at their parents' sleeves, all waiting for the ribbon cutting.

They stopped at the edge of the crowd, just on the outskirts of the makeshift stage where Torres was about to speak. The atmosphere was electric, filled with the buzz of the media and the flash of cameras. Cassidy's eyes moved over the sea of faces, scanning for one in particular. His.

Cassidy checked her phone again. Six-fifty-seven. No text.

"Any sign of him yet?" Anne asked, half-mocking, half-concerned.

Cassidy shook her head, her gut tightening. She couldn't stop looking at her phone, hoping for some sign that Duke would show up, that he'd finally stop playing his games.

"I don't think he's coming," Anne said again, her voice softer now. "Let's just go home."

Cassidy felt the tightening in her chest again—the familiar sting of doubt. But she swallowed it down. *He'll be here. He has to be.*

Anne let out a long sigh and pulled her scarf tighter, her breath coming out in a frustrated exhale. "You do realize that you're trying to impress a guy who played you, right?"

Cassidy stiffened, but she didn't look at Anne. Instead, she scanned the crowd. Everyone was waiting for Congresswoman Torres to step up to the podium, the big political moment that would make the evening shine. But for Cassidy, none of that mattered. She was here for Duke, and she was determined to prove she didn't need him — no matter how much she wanted him to see her.

"I wasn't trying to impress him," Cassidy said, her voice tight. "I was just showing him I'm not who he thinks I am."

Anne snorted. "Uh-huh. By getting into a pissing contest with one of the most powerful women in the country? I still don't get it."

Cassidy's lips thinned as she finally looked at her friend. "It's not about impressing him. It's about proving a point. He told me I wouldn't win. That honesty and authenticity don't work. So I'm going to prove him wrong."

"By publicly calling out a congresswoman about child labor?" Anne's voice was laced with disbelief. "Cass, that's a suicide mission."

Cassidy's eyes narrowed. "It's not a suicide mission. It's about doing what's right. I'm not just here to play the game. I'm here to make people think. I'm not some naive girl who just goes along with whatever's expected."

Anne shook her head, the hint of a knowing smile on her lips. "You're really going to do this, huh? Well, at least make sure you get your point across without getting arrested."

Cassidy didn't even flinch. "If I get arrested, it'll be for something that matters."

At exactly seven p.m., Congresswoman Torres stepped up to the makeshift podium outside the store, her signature confident smile lighting up her face. The crowd erupted into cheers, and Cassidy felt a surge of adrenaline.

This was it.

She glanced at her phone one more time, hoping for a reply. Nothing.

She scanned the crowd, searching for his sharp features, his commanding presence. But there was no sign of him.

"Good evening, everyone," Torres said, her voice carrying easily over the murmurs of the crowd. "It's an honor to be here tonight to celebrate the opening of this beautiful new toy store—a place that embodies the joy and wonder of the holiday season. This is more than just a store, it's a place where memories will be made, where children's imaginations will soar..."

Cassidy barely registered the words. She was too distracted by the knot of disappointment forming in her chest. She'd been so sure Duke would come. She wanted him to see her standing here, ready to ask the tough questions, ready to take risks for what she believed in.

But he wasn't here.

The minutes ticked by, and as Torres' speech continued, Cassidy's confidence wavered. The cold seeped through her coat, numbing her fingers and toes, but it was nothing compared to the ache in her chest.

When the speech ended and Torres stepped forward to cut the ribbon, the crowd erupted into applause.

Cassidy clapped half-heartedly, her stomach churning with a mix of nerves and disappointment.

"Cass," Anne said gently, placing a hand on her shoulder. "Maybe it's not the right time for this."

Cassidy turned to her, forcing a smile. "It's fine. I'll handle it."

Anne didn't look convinced, but she didn't argue.

Cassidy stayed for a few more minutes, watching as the first customers were let into the store and reporters crowded around Torres for photos and soundbites. She debated whether to approach the congresswoman now or wait for a quieter moment.

But the fire in her chest that had fueled her bold plan was dimming. The truth was, she'd wanted Duke to see her in action. To prove to him — and maybe to herself — that she wasn't just some naive journalist fumbling her way through the big leagues.

But he wasn't here.

And for reasons she didn't want to admit, that hurt more than it should have.

Cassidy wiped her clammy hands on the sides of her coat, her pulse pounding as she edged closer to the congresswoman. The crowd had thinned now that the ribbon-cutting was over, giving her a clearer path. Torres was still surrounded by a few aides and photographers, but Cassidy knew this was her moment.

She took a deep breath, thinking through the words she'd been preparing.

Congresswoman Torres, your support for this company has been criticized given their alleged use of child and forced labor — do you believe this aligns with your values?

She tightened her grip on her notepad, forcing herself to keep moving forward. This was what she'd come here for. Not for Duke, not for anyone else—just for the story.

Her boots crunched against the icy pavement as she weaved through the small knots of people lingering outside the store. Torres' voice carried over the chatter of the crowd, smooth and confident as she spoke to a local reporter about the importance of small businesses and community.

Cassidy's heart was racing now, the adrenaline surging as she closed the gap. Just a few more steps and she'd have her shot.

But before she could open her mouth, a blur of movement caught her attention from the corner of her eye.

"Child labor isn't festive!" someone shouted.

Cassidy barely had time to turn before it happened.

A protester burst from the edge of the crowd, wielding a large can of what looked like red paint or dyed liquid. In one swift motion, they hurled it toward Torres, the liquid arcing through the air like a crimson wave.

Cassidy froze, her mind unable to process what was happening until it was too late.

The red liquid splashed across Torres, drenching her in vivid streaks of crimson. Gasps erupted from the crowd as the congresswoman staggered back, her aides rushing to shield her.

But Cassidy hadn't escaped the blast either.

The liquid hit her square in the chest, soaking through her coat and sweater. The sharp, metallic tang of the dye filled her nose as it dripped down her arms and splattered onto her jeans. She stood there, stunned, her notepad slipping from her fingers onto the wet pavement.

"Get back!" one of Torres' aides shouted, stepping in front of the congresswoman as the protester was quickly tackled by security.

Cassidy blinked, her hands trembling as she looked down at herself. The liquid was cold and sticky, staining her clothes and hands in streaks of red. It clung to her hair, dripping from the ends of her curls.

For a moment, everything seemed to move in slow motion. The crowd surged around her, voices rising in alarm, cameras flashing as photographers scrambled to capture the chaos.

Torres' eyes locked with Cassidy's.

Cassidy opened her mouth, but no words came.

"What the hell just happened?" Anne's voice cut through the din as she pushed her way through the crowd to Cassidy's side. Her eyes widened when she saw the state of her friend. "Oh my God, Cassidy, are you okay?"

Cassidy shook her head, her voice finally breaking free. "I didn't—I wasn't—"

"Get them out of here!" one of Torres' aides barked, gesturing toward security as the protesters surged and the scene descended into chaos.

* * * *

Duke sat in the dimly lit living room of his D.C. condo, a glass of bourbon untouched on the table in front of him. His phone rested in his hand, the screen glowing faintly with Cassidy's message.

Meet me at 7pm. Big new toy store opening. Congresswoman Torres will be there. Trust me, it'll be worth it.

He stared at the text for a moment longer before exhaling sharply. His thumb hovered over the screen, then he pressed delete.

What the hell does she want now?

The kiss replayed in his mind for the hundredth time since it happened, her soft lips, the way she'd melted into him, and the way he'd felt utterly consumed in the moment. It had been a mistake—a reckless, stupid mistake.

She was nothing but trouble, and he had no business entertaining her antics, no matter how magnetic she was.

With a growl, he tossed his phone onto the couch and leaned back, scrubbing a hand over his face.

Focus, Armstrong.

He grabbed the stack of paperwork on the coffee table—incident reports, security protocols, and a background check he'd been reviewing earlier. His eyes scanned the documents, his pen moving methodically as he signed off on a few pages.

But his mind wandered.

The image of Cassidy standing in front of him flashed through his head—her wild curls, her bright green eyes, the stubborn set of her jaw. The way she'd said yes to his question without hesitation, her voice soft but certain.

He shook his head, forcing himself back to the paperwork.

Ten minutes later, he'd read the same paragraph three times without absorbing a single word.

His phone buzzed, and his heart jumped before he realized it was just an email notification. He set the paperwork aside and leaned back in his chair, his gaze drifting to the darkened windows of his condo. The city lights twinkled faintly in the distance, but they only made the silence of the room feel heavier.

He reached for his phone, then stopped himself.

She's a distraction. That's all.

He grabbed his laptop instead, reviewing updates from Wyatt and Salem about the protest coverage. A few minor disruptions, nothing critical. His fingers flew over the keyboard as he sent out a quick follow-up email.

But the pull was still there.

His phone sat on the couch, taunting him.

Finally, at nineteen-fourteen, he let out a frustrated growl and stood. Grabbing his jacket and keys, he headed for the door, muttering under his breath.

"Damn it, Evans."

By the time he climbed into his truck and started the engine, the clock read nineteen-sixteen. The text was long gone, but he still remembered the address.

As he drove toward the toy store, his hands tight on the wheel, he tried to convince himself this was about the bet, about keeping her out of trouble, about the promise he'd made to Reed.

But deep down, he knew better.

Cassidy Evans was in his head, and for the life of him, he couldn't figure out how to get her out.

Duke parked his truck a block away from the toy store, the faint sound of holiday music and chatter drifting through the cold air. Pulling his jacket tighter, he stepped onto the sidewalk, his boots crunching against the icy ground.

The street ahead looked normal enough at first — a typical holiday crowd, with people milling about near the brightly lit storefront. But as he approached, he noticed the tension in the air.

The cheerful hum of the event had been replaced by shouts and a rising commotion.

His chest strained as he quickened his pace. The scene in front of the toy store was chaotic — security guards swarmed, people shouted and pointed, and the crowd surged forward like a restless tide.

Then he saw her.

Cassidy was at the center of it all, her blonde curls unmistakable even under the harsh glow of the streetlights. She was drenched in red liquid, her coat and jeans soaked through, and she wasn't alone. Standing beside her was Congresswoman Torres, similarly covered in the crimson substance, both of them caught in the middle of an increasingly hostile crowd.

Duke's stomach dropped.

Cassidy was trying to move away, her hands raised defensively as she shouted something he couldn't hear. But the crowd around her was growing more aggressive.

He broke into a run, his pulse pounding in his ears.

As he pushed through the edges of the cluster, he saw the moment it all spiraled.

A group of protesters surrounded Cassidy, their anger misdirected. One of them shouted, "She's with them!" Another lunged, grabbing her arm.

"No! I'm not—" Cassidy's voice was panicked, her words cut off as she was yanked backward.

Duke's vision went red.

He didn't stop to think. His body moved on instinct, shoving through the mass of people with brute force.

"Get the hell off her!" he roared, his voice slicing through the chaos.

The nearest protester turned, startled, but Duke didn't give them a chance to react. His fist connected with the man's shoulder, sending him stumbling backward. Another grabbed Cassidy by the other arm, and Duke spun, slamming his elbow into the second man's gut.

Cassidy staggered forward, but before she could fall, Duke caught her around the waist, pulling her against him.

"I've got you," he said, his voice tight with rage and fear.

The crowd pressed in, but Duke didn't care. His only focus was getting her out.

With Cassidy in his arms, he shoved his way through the protesters, his broad frame and sheer determination clearing a path. He didn't stop until they were a block away, back near his truck.

Panting, he gently set Cassidy down on the passenger seat, her trembling form still slick with the red liquid. She was shaking so hard he could feel it in his own hands.

"Are you hurt?" he asked urgently, crouching in front of her and gripping her shoulders.

She shook her head, but her wide, glassy eyes told him she was far from okay.

"Cassidy," he said, his voice softer now, trying to ground her. "Look at me. Are you hurt?"

Her lips parted, but it took her a moment to speak. "No," she said. "I—I don't think so."

Relief washed over him, but it was short-lived. His hands tightened on her shoulders as he looked her over, the red dye staining her skin and dripping from her curls.

"Damn it, Evans," he said, his voice raw. "What the hell were you thinking?"

She didn't respond, her body still trembling.

"Hey," he said, softer this time. "It's okay. You're okay. I've got you."

She looked up at him then, her green eyes wide and shimmering with unshed tears. "They thought I was with Torres," she said, her voice shaking. "They thought I was part of it. I—I didn't even see it coming."

Duke exhaled sharply, pulling her against him without thinking. She didn't resist, her cold, trembling body curling into his chest. His arms coiled around her as he held her close, the red dye from her clothes smearing onto his jacket.

He rested his chin against the top of her head, his heart still racing. The thought of what could've happened if he hadn't come—if he hadn't been there to pull her out—sent a cold wave of dread through him.

This wasn't just reckless. This had been life or death.

"It's over," he said, his voice rough. "You're safe now."

She didn't respond, but her fingers gripped the fabric of his jacket, holding onto him like he was the only solid thing in a collapsing world.

For the first time in years, he didn't feel in control.

Chapter Six

The truck hummed through the city streets, the night air heavy and cold, seeping in through the cracked window. Duke's knuckles were clenched white around the steering wheel, his eyes laser-focused on the road. He could feel the tension in his shoulders, in his neck — every muscle wound so tight it hurt. The weight of what had just happened pressed on him, thick and suffocating. His mind replayed the chaos at the toy store, the frenzied protesters, Cassidy's terrified eyes as she was dragged through the crowd. The memory of her shaking in his arms, vulnerable and lost, gnawed at him.

He wanted to yell at her, to tell her what a reckless idiot she'd been. He wanted to tell her that this whole thing had been a disaster from the start. But the words wouldn't come. The relief that she was still breathing, that she was sitting here at all, felt like a damper on the fire in his chest. He just couldn't bring himself to add more weight to the already thick silence that stretched between them.

The truck hit a pothole with a jolt, and Cassidy flinched, her body jerking against the seat. Duke caught the subtle movement in his peripheral vision, but he said nothing. He couldn't bring himself to. Her face — pale and strained, the remnants of red dye smeared across her cheeks like a grim reminder of what had just happened — stuck with him. Her eyes were fixed on the window, but he knew she wasn't seeing anything outside.

Anne, sitting stiffly in the back seat, broke the silence with a sharp exhale, the sound cutting through the quiet. "This has to be the dumbest thing you've ever done, Cassidy." Her voice was harsh, but underneath it, Duke could hear the concern, the worry that had hardened into frustration.

Cassidy didn't respond. She just sat there, her arms wrapped tightly around herself, as if she could hold the pieces of her together. Duke's grip on the steering wheel tightened, his teeth grinding. He knew Cassidy didn't deserve Anne's anger. Hell, he knew Cassidy didn't deserve anyone's anger. But the reckless, impulsive side of her — God, it made him crazy.

The truck coasted down the quiet streets, snow beginning to dust the sidewalks in the softest, coldest glow. Duke's mind spun in circles, racing through every 'what if' and near-miss. He glanced in the rearview mirror, but all he saw were the sharp angles of Anne's face — staring ahead, lips pursed. Cassidy's reflection, though, was what caught him. Her face was half-lit by the streetlight outside, an almost ethereal glow highlighting the mess of red dye and the fragility that surrounded her.

The truck bumped as he rolled over a crack in the road, and Cassidy flinched again. He saw her try to shrink further into herself. It made him feel like he was losing her somehow, like all the distance between them—every unsaid word, every unanswered question—was stretching farther than he could reach.

Anne said something under her breath, just loud enough for Duke to catch. He couldn't make out the words, but the tone was unmistakable. She was frustrated. And so was he. But Cassidy? Cassidy was just…lost. Quiet, broken in her own way.

The truck pulled up in front of her building—her walk-up, tucked away in the corner of the block like it always had been. The neighborhood was eerily quiet, the dim glow from the streetlights casting long shadows over the freshly fallen snow. Duke cut the engine, and the truck fell into an almost suffocating silence.

"Inside," he said, his voice thick and clipped, a command wrapped in exhaustion.

Cassidy hesitated for a moment, her gaze flicking toward him as if weighing something. His eyes, however, seemed to make the decision for her. She unbuckled her seatbelt and climbed out of the truck without another word.

Duke followed her up the steps, each movement deliberate, but it was Cassidy who was leading the way, her shoulders drawn tight, her footsteps almost inaudible against the cold concrete. She fumbled for her keys, her fingers shaking as she twisted the lock.

Once the door opened, she paused, her back to him. There was something unspoken between them, some tension hanging heavy in the cold night air. She turned slightly, almost as if waiting for him to say something, to break the silence with any kind of reassurance.

"You coming?" Her voice was soft, tentative, almost fragile in the night air.

Duke shook his head. "No," he said, his voice a rough murmur.

Her lips parted, just for a moment, as if she were going to say something — something that might change the silence between them. But it was gone, lost before it ever made it to her tongue. Instead, she nodded quietly, ducking into the apartment without another word.

Duke turned back to the truck, his jaw tightening as Anne climbed out. She gave him a wary look, her breath rising in soft clouds as she pulled her coat tighter around herself, the cold night air biting at them both.

"You wanted to talk?" she asked, her tone guarded but still warm.

"Yeah," Duke said. He stared at Anne for a moment before his eyes flicked to the darkened streets ahead. "What the hell is going on with her?"

Anne sighed, crossing her arms as she shifted slightly. "She's... Cassidy," she said after a beat, her gaze steady but not unkind. "She's stubborn. Impulsive. She wants to do big things. Good things."

"That much is obvious," Duke said, his frustration bleeding through in a sharpness he hadn't meant to show. He took a deep breath, trying to calm himself, but the anger still simmered beneath the surface. "Does she have any idea how close she came to getting seriously hurt tonight? Or worse?"

Anne's lips flattened as she rubbed her forehead, clearly feeling his words. "She doesn't think about that stuff, Duke. She just throws herself into things — headfirst. It's part of what makes her good at what she does. She cares more about getting things done...than being careful."

Duke let out a humorless laugh, the frustration bubbling over. "Good at what she does? She nearly got herself killed over some stunt she thought would prove a point." His hands were gripping the edge of the truck now, like he might rip it off its hinges.

Anne's eyes flashed, a flicker of something defensive in her posture. "You think I don't know that?" she snapped, stepping toward him, lowering her voice. "You think I wasn't scared out of my mind when I saw her covered in red, getting yanked around by a mob? Of course I was scared! But you know what, Duke? This is who she is. She's never going to sit quietly on the sidelines or play it safe. If you don't get that, you don't get Cassidy."

Duke's jaw ticked. Her words were like knives, cutting deeper than he was ready to admit. He stared at her, chest tight, feeling the sharp sting of his own helplessness.

"She's a child," he said finally, his voice quieter but no less intense. "And this city is unforgiving."

"She's a grown woman, and you know that." Anne held his gaze for a long moment, her expression softening as if something about his tone was registering with her. "You care about her," she said gently, almost like a statement of fact, not a question.

Duke didn't respond. He couldn't. His thoughts were a mess—anger, worry, and something else he couldn't quite name—mixing up in his gut. Instead, he just stared ahead, his hand gripping the truck door tighter.

Anne tilted her head, studying him before sighing. "Look," she said, her voice calmer now, almost resigned. "She just needs...well, maybe someone can help her figure out how to stop being her own worst enemy."

Duke let out a short exhale, shaking his head as he let the words sink in. "Who is that someone going to be?"

"Maybe you?"

"She won't listen to me."

Anne laughed—short and humorless, but there was a hint of affection in it. "No. But she'll argue with you. And that's close enough."

Duke let out a huff, a half-smile flickering across his face. "Great," he said, feeling like he was losing the battle before it even started.

Anne took a step toward the door, then paused, glancing back at him with a more genuine expression. "For what it's worth," she said, "thanks for getting her out of there."

Duke nodded stiffly, his hands still tight in his pockets. He didn't have the words for what was simmering inside him, and he wasn't sure he wanted to. Anne disappeared into the apartment, the door shutting behind her with a soft click.

He stood there for a moment, the cold night air biting into him, his shoulders sagging under the weight of everything. His hands were still stained with red dye, the faint smell clinging to his jacket like a reminder of the chaos. He stared at the truck for a moment, then glanced at Cassidy's apartment. His thoughts were a tangled mess of anger, relief, and something else, something he couldn't name.

"Damn it, Evans," he said under his breath, his voice barely audible, as if saying it out loud might make it all easier to figure out. "What the hell am I going to do with you?"

Cassidy stood at the window of her small bedroom, her fingers clutching the edge of the curtain as she peered down at the street below. The red stains on her clothes were starting to dry, the tacky fabric sticking uncomfortably to her skin, but she couldn't bring herself to care.

Her eyes locked on Duke as he stood outside talking to Anne. His broad shoulders were hunched against the cold, his sharp profile illuminated by the faint glow of the streetlights. He gestured with his hands as he spoke, his voice too low to carry up to her window, but the tension in his movements was obvious.

Cassidy winced, heat rushing to her face.

Her amazing plan — to confront Congresswoman Torres, prove her boldness, and win her bet with Duke — had crashed and burned spectacularly. Instead of looking like a fearless journalist, she'd ended up drenched in red dye, mistaken for a protester, and literally carried out of the chaos by Duke himself.

If anyone identified me... She groaned, running a hand over her face.

Anne said something to Duke, her voice sharp enough to cut through the muffled quiet of the night. Cassidy watched as Duke's expression shifted, his mouth pressing into a tight line before he huffed out a visible breath. He looked like the picture of control, even in his frustration — tall, muscular, dark-haired, and steady.

The kind of guy who probably never stumbled through life the way she always seemed to.

Cassidy's gaze lingered on him. There was something infuriating about how composed he was, even after everything that had happened tonight. Like nothing could rattle him.

He was everything she wasn't—cool, smooth, perfectly put together.

And there she was, standing in her stained, dripping clothes, the epitome of chaos.

Anne finally turned, walking back into their walk-up without a backward glance. Cassidy bit her lip, debating whether to move away from the window. But she couldn't take her eyes off Duke, standing alone on the sidewalk now, his broad frame silhouetted against the glow of the streetlights.

Her stomach flipped as his head tilted slightly—and then he looked up.

Cassidy froze, her breath catching in her throat. His dark eyes locked on hers, his sharp features illuminated as if the universe had aligned just to make this moment happen.

Shit.

She stumbled backward, her heart hammering, the curtain falling shut as she pressed a hand over her face. *Great. Just great. Now he knows I was watching him.*

For a long moment, she stood there, frozen in place, willing her heart to slow. But curiosity got the better of her. Taking a deep breath, she edged back toward the window, pulling the curtain aside just enough to peek out.

Duke was still there.

And he was watching her.

Her breath hitched as a smirk tugged at the corner of his mouth. His lips curved slowly, that infuriating, knowing smile that made her want to throw something and melt into the floor all at once.

Then he raised a hand in a casual salute, his dark eyes glinting with amusement.

Cassidy let out a strangled noise, landing on the floor with a soft thud.

Her cheeks burned as she lay there, staring up at the ceiling. "I'm dying," she said to herself, covering her face with her hands. "I'm actually dying."

Her mind replayed the image of Duke's smirk, the lazy, confident gesture of his salute. She groaned, rolling onto her side.

He probably thought she was a complete disaster. And maybe she was.

But as much as she wanted to hate him in that moment, all she could think about was the way he'd held her earlier — strong, steady, like she was the only thing in the world that mattered.

And that smirk.

It was going to haunt her forever.

Chapter Seven

Cassidy sat stiffly in the chair opposite Thomas Reed's desk, her hands clasped tightly in her lap. The cozy warmth of Reed's office—a space lined with bookshelves and decorated with tasteful holiday garlands—did little to ease the knot of dread twisting in her stomach.

Reed leaned back in his chair, steepling his fingers as he regarded her with a stern, almost fatherly expression. "Cassidy," he began, his tone heavy, "you were identified."

She froze.

He continued, "Photos of you, drenched in red paint, are circulating among certain circles. There are...serious questions about what you were doing there."

Her heart sank. "Questions?"

"Yes," Reed said, his voice clipped. "Questions like, 'Is PRN finally going full social justice warrior and attacking politicians now?'"

Cassidy's cheeks burned. "I wasn't involved! I was just—"

"Collecting quotes for a puff piece on the president?" Reed interjected, his tone sharp. "Yes, I know. But the optics, Cassidy. The optics are terrible."

"Am I getting fired?"

"Maybe."

She sank lower in her chair, her gaze dropping to the edge of his desk. She'd been hoping the whole thing would blow over, that the paint would wash out of her coat and her reputation with it. But of course, nothing ever worked out that easily.

"So, what do we do?" she asked quietly.

Reed sighed, leaning forward and folding his hands on the desk. "We need to get ahead of this. Change the narrative. Paint you as an innocent bystander ready to shop for the holidays...who was caught up in the chaos and saved by a heroic Secret Service agent."

Cassidy blinked, her stomach twisting further. "What?"

"Duke Armstrong," Reed clarified. "We're going to spin this as a holiday feel-good story. 'Heroic Secret Service Agent Rescues Journalist from Angry Mob.'"

Her jaw dropped. "You're kidding."

"I'm not," Reed said flatly. "I've already spoken to some people, and we think this is the best way to handle the situation. You'll write a short piece about the incident—nothing too dramatic, just enough to shift the narrative—and we'll start with inviting Armstrong to the PRN holiday party next week as a way to thank him."

Cassidy's stomach flipped. "Wait. You're inviting Duke? To your holiday party? Isn't that...weird?"

Reed raised an eyebrow. "Why would it be weird?"

"Because he's...an ass," Cassidy blurted, unable to come up with a better explanation. "And he's a Secret Service agent. Doesn't that seem...out of place?"

Reed waved a hand dismissively. "Nonsense. Armstrong deserves recognition for what he did, and this will be a perfect opportunity to show that you're both professionals handling the situation with grace."

Cassidy stared at him, horrified. "I've been avoiding him since it happened!"

"Why?" Reed asked, his brow furrowing.

"Because..." She hesitated, struggling to find a reason that didn't involve the memory of Duke carrying her to his truck, holding her tightly, or catching her watching him through the window like a lovesick fool. "It's just...awkward."

Reed sighed, rubbing his temples. "Cassidy, this isn't about your feelings. It's about salvaging your reputation and ensuring this doesn't snowball into something worse. Armstrong is the key to that. You are a victim, not a perpetrator. Be clear that he saved you."

She pressed her lips together, her mind racing. The thought of seeing Duke again, let alone in such a personal setting, made her chest tighten. How was she supposed to act normal around him after everything that had happened?

"You're sure this is the best way to handle it?" she asked weakly, already knowing the answer.

"Yes," Reed said firmly. "I'll reach out to him today, but I need you to be on your best behavior at the party."

She nodded again, standing as he dismissed her. But as she walked out of his office, her mind was a whirlwind of anxiety.

Duke. At the holiday party. Of course, this is my life.

The bright fluorescent lights of the White House hallway buzzed faintly as Cassidy hurried down the polished floor, her notepad tucked under her arm. She was lost in thought, juggling deadlines and edits in her head, when she turned the corner and almost collided with a wall of muscle.

She stumbled back, blinking up—and her stomach dropped.

"Duke?"

He stood there, dressed in his dark suit, his gaze immediately locking onto her. A few of his team members lingered a few steps behind him, their heads turning as they registered her.

Cassidy froze, her heart hammering in her chest. She hadn't seen him since that night outside her apartment, and now here he was, larger than life and twice as intimidating.

"Evans," he said, his voice cool and clipped.

Before she could lose her nerve, she stepped closer, tilting her head toward a side alcove. "Can we talk? Privately?"

One of the agents behind him started to protest, but Duke held up a hand, silencing him. His dark eyes narrowed as he studied her for a moment, then he nodded curtly and followed her into the alcove.

"You've got some nerve interrupting me," he said quietly, crossing his arms over his broad chest.

Cassidy swallowed hard but stood her ground. "I wouldn't interrupt if it wasn't important."

Duke raised an eyebrow, his expression unreadable. "Go on, then. What's so important?"

She hesitated for a fraction of a second before blurting, "Have you received the invitation to Reed's holiday party?"

His eyes narrowed further, the corner of his mouth twitching into something that could have been amusement—or irritation. "Yes. I received it."

Cassidy's pulse quickened. "Have you responded?"

"No," he said flatly.

She fidgeted with the edge of her notepad, and forced herself to meet his gaze. "Are you...planning to come?"

He paused, his sharp eyes searching her face as if weighing his next words carefully. "Do you want me to come?"

The question caught her off guard, and her breath hitched. She opened her mouth to respond, but Duke stepped closer, his presence filling the narrow space between them.

"Answer honestly," he said. Voice dropped. Calm. Firm. "Remember the terms of the bet."

Cassidy's face burned, and she looked away for a moment, staring at the polished tile beneath their feet. When she finally spoke, her voice was quiet but steady.

"Yes," she admitted. "I want you to come."

His eyebrows lifted slightly, but he didn't say anything, waiting for her to continue.

Cassidy exhaled sharply, frustrated with herself. "I don't know why, okay? Maybe because it's going to be awkward enough as it is, and having you there makes it...less awkward. Or maybe because..."

She trailed off, biting her lip.

"Because?" he prompted, his tone calm but insistent.

Her gaze snapped back to his, and she found herself caught in the intensity of his dark eyes. "Because you saved me, and I haven't even thanked you properly. And maybe because I'm just..." She struggled to find the right words. "Because I don't know what I'd have done if you weren't there."

Duke tilted his head slightly, his expression softening for the briefest of moments before his mask of cool professionalism slipped back into place.

"Well," he said finally, his tone unreadable. "That's honest, at least."

Cassidy huffed, crossing her arms. "So? Are you coming or not?"

He studied her for a long moment, then smirked faintly. "You'll find out."

Before she could press him further, he straightened and stepped back, gesturing toward the hallway. "I've got a job to do, Evans. Try not to cause any more trouble before the party."

And with that, he turned and walked away, his men falling into step behind him.

Cassidy watched him go, her chest tight and her cheeks flushed. She still didn't know why it mattered so much if he came to the party—but deep down, she couldn't shake the feeling that it mattered a lot more than she wanted to admit.

Chapter Eight

The office buzzed with Friday morning energy, the kind Cassidy had come to expect this close to the holidays. Staffers, festively dressed to impress, hovered near their phones and glanced up at the giant screen at the front of the room, processing last-minute updates. Cassidy sat in the center, notebook open, pen ready — focused, but already feeling the pull of the distractions just outside the door.

Duke was there too, standing at the back like a silent sentinel, his posture rigid, his eyes scanning every face in the room, assessing. He was there to shadow her today — extra security following the protests, they said. His presence hung heavy, like an unspoken rule she couldn't ignore. She could feel it even as she tried to focus on the briefing.

He wasn't looking at her because he wanted to — he was assessing her, as always, trying to figure out if she was going to make trouble.

Fine, she thought, adjusting the papers in front of her. *Let him watch.*

This meeting wasn't just important—it was pivotal. Cassidy had spent weeks preparing for this pitch, crafting her argument and digging into stories that deserved attention. It wasn't the kind of work that usually got recognition in the political machine of the White House, but Cassidy knew it mattered.

"Cassidy," her boss, Thomas Reed, said, snapping her out of her thoughts. "You're up."

She stood, her heart racing, but she kept her face steady as she moved to the head of the table. Her notebook felt heavier in her hands as all eyes turned to her, including Duke's from the back of the room.

"Thank you," she began, her voice steady despite the pulse pounding in her ears. "I've been working on a piece about federal disaster relief in small towns— places that often get overlooked in the larger conversations about policy."

Her voice warmed as she spoke, weaving the human stories she'd gathered into a tapestry that demanded attention. She talked about a family who'd lost their home to flooding, about a single mother who'd fought to rebuild after a tornado wiped out her town, about how bureaucratic delays left people waiting far too long for help that sometimes never came.

As she spoke, the room shifted. The distracted glances stopped, phones were lowered, and attention sharpened. Cassidy felt the shift like a tide turning in her favor, and it bolstered her confidence.

She glanced at Reed, who was nodding slightly, his expression unreadable but not dismissive.

Then her eyes flicked to the back of the room, to Duke.

He was watching her. Not the way he usually did — assessing, guarding, waiting for her to misstep. His arms were crossed, his dark eyes fixed on her, his expression inscrutable but focused. For once, she didn't feel like he was waiting for her to fail.

She continued, her voice growing stronger as she detailed her proposal — a series of articles that would spotlight these overlooked stories and push for reforms. "We need to stop thinking about disaster relief as a one-size-fits-all solution," she said. "These communities need tailored support, and the only way to get it is to make their stories impossible to ignore."

When she finished, the room was quiet for a beat, and Cassidy's heart lurched in the silence. Then, a few nods, murmurs of agreement. Reed cleared his throat, breaking the spell.

"Strong pitch," he said simply. "Let's move forward with it."

The relief hit her like a wave, but she kept her expression steady, offering a polite nod as she returned to her seat.

The meeting wrapped up quickly after that, and Cassidy busied herself gathering her things, avoiding looking toward the back of the room. But as the other staffers filed out, she felt him approach.

"Cassidy."

She turned to find Duke standing closer than she expected, his expression softer than she'd ever seen.

"Nice work in there," he said, his voice low, almost careful.

She blinked, startled by the compliment. "Thanks."

"You made them listen," he added, his gaze steady. "That's not easy in a room like this."

There was no sarcasm, no skepticism. Just honesty.

Cassidy hesitated, unsure of how to respond. "You sound surprised."

Duke tilted his head slightly, his lips quirking in the faintest hint of a smile. "I shouldn't be."

The air between them shifted, and Cassidy felt her chest tighten. He wasn't just seeing her work — he was seeing *her*. The fire, the determination, the way she cared too much and tried too hard. For the first time, it didn't feel like he was judging her for it.

"I told you authenticity wins," she said softly, her voice a mix of challenge and vulnerability.

Duke's expression flickered, something warm and unreadable passing through his eyes. "Maybe you're right," he admitted quietly. "But, you didn't win."

She opened her mouth to respond, but the intensity of his gaze silenced her. The moment stretched, taut and electric, until Duke finally straightened, his professional mask slipping back into place.

"Let's get you out of here," he said, his tone back to its usual clipped formality.

But as he turned and walked toward the door, Cassidy couldn't help the faint smile that tugged at her lips.

* * * *

Later that afternoon, the town hall meeting was about to start — another round of speeches. The president's end-of-year remarks were on the agenda, and while Cassidy wasn't exactly looking forward to the speeches, she knew it was part of the job. She'd be there, whether she wanted to be or not.

When the doors to the East Room finally opened, she filed in with the others, exchanging polite nods with a few colleagues before finding an empty seat near the middle. The room buzzed with anticipation, the low murmur of conversation barely registering until her eyes found him.

Duke stood near the back wall, his broad frame cutting through the dim light like a figure carved from stone. His face was hard to read, but his presence was undeniable—commanding, silent, but impossible to ignore. He wasn't looking at her, but somehow, it didn't matter. She felt the pull of him anyway, like an invisible current drawing her in.

Don't look at him.

Her mind screamed the command, but her eyes betrayed her, flicking toward him again and again, as if they had a mind of their own. Every time she caught sight of his profile—his jaw set, his posture rigid—her chest tightened. She hated how much space he took up in her thoughts, how easily he could unravel the walls she'd worked so hard to build.

Focus. Just focus on the speeches.

But the words from the podium felt distant, muffled by the pounding in her ears. Her gaze kept drifting back to Duke. His presence was a weight in the room, pulling at her like a magnetic force. When their eyes met, even for a fraction of a second, it was a gut punch. Damn it—that look—brief, but intense. It burned her. She couldn't look away.

She couldn't take it.

Without thinking, she stood, nearly knocking over her chair. Reed shot her a quick, confused glance, but she said something about needing a break. No one questioned her, which made it easier to slip away. She made her escape down the quiet hallway, her pulse pounding in her ears.

Cassidy turned down a dimmed hallway and hid behind a massive floor-to-ceiling Christmas tree. She leaned against the cold wall behind the tree, her hand pressed to her chest as she tried to steady her breathing. *What the hell is wrong with me?* Her thoughts spun in frantic circles. *Why does he get under my skin like this?*

Her fingers curled into fists, her nails digging into her palm. The answer was too tangled, too complicated to face. He was everything she shouldn't want. Too cold. Too controlled. Too…damn tall. And yet, there it was. That pull. That magnetism.

She toyed with a decorative snowflake on the tree. She felt anything but festive. She felt like quitting.

It was infuriating. It made her feel like a stranger in her own skin. She wasn't supposed to care about him — she wasn't supposed to want him to notice her, to make her feel…something. Yet here she was, unable to shake the feeling that the closer she got to him, the more she was losing control.

And she hated it.

"Running away again?"

The deep, familiar voice startled her, and she spun around to see Duke standing a few feet away. She'd never seen anyone approach her with so much… intensity.

"I'm not running," she said sharply, crossing her own arms in defiance. "I just needed a minute. Alone."

"Sure," Duke said, his tone dry as he stepped closer. "Because avoiding things has always been your style."

Cassidy's eyes narrowed. "What do you want, Duke?"

He sighed, his shoulders relaxing slightly. "I want you to stop pushing yourself into trouble because of some stupid bet."

Her jaw set, her chest burning with frustration. "The bet isn't stupid."

"It is," he shot back. "It's reckless, and it's dragging you into situations you don't need to be in."

"Oh, I see," Cassidy said, her voice trembling, though she wasn't sure if it was from anger or something else entirely. "Why do you care?"

"This isn't about caring," Duke replied, his voice calm but taut, as though every word was measured.

Cassidy stepped closer, her green eyes blazing. "Then why?"

"It doesn't matter."

The dismissiveness of his tone hit her like a slap, and she stopped in her tracks, her chest tightening. "Or I don't matter?"

That got him. Duke froze, his jaw tightening as her words hung in the air between them. The flicker of something raw passed across his face, and for a moment, she thought he might say something real.

"That's not what I meant," he said finally, his voice rough but quiet.

"No?" Cassidy challenged, stepping even closer, her heart pounding now. "Because that's what it feels like. Every time you look at me like I'm some naive kid who's out of her depth. Every time you try to shut me down instead of seeing what I'm capable of."

Her voice broke, and she hated herself for it, for the vulnerability that bled through her words. But she couldn't stop. Not now.

"Cass…" Duke was softer now, almost pleading. He ran a hand through his hair, his frustration visible in every sharp line of his face.

"No," she interrupted, trembling. "Just tell me. Tell me why you're like this with me. Why you can't seem to decide whether you want to push me away or — "

He moved before she could finish, closing the space between them in one long stride. With a low growl, he grasped the back of her head, tangling his fingers in her curls, and with the other hand, gripping her waist, he pulled her to him.

"Because you matter very much," he said. And then his lips met hers again.

The kiss stole her breath, silencing every word, every thought, every argument she had left. His mouth was firm, insistent, and utterly consuming, his hand tightening in her hair as though he couldn't bear to let her go. His grasp around her waist was like he was holding something much more dangerous, something that required control — control that, for once, seemed to be slipping away from him.

Cassidy's body melted against his, her hands clutching at the front of his shirt as the heat of him burned through her. It was dizzying, overwhelming, the kind of kiss that left no room for doubt. It wasn't just the way he was kissing her. It was how he was doing it. Each dance of his tongue with hers seemed deliberate, determined, as if kissing her was the only thing keeping him sane.

He broke away just enough to whisper against her lips, his breath hot and uneven. "You matter more than you should. More than I can handle."

She stared up at him, her chest heaving, her lips tingling from the force of his kiss. She shifted uncomfortably, her heart racing for reasons she wasn't ready to admit. The vulnerability in his dark eyes was so stark, so raw, it made her heart twist painfully in her chest.

"Duke…" she started, her voice barely a whisper, but he shook his head, his hand still tangled in her hair.

"Don't," he said, his tone rough. "Just…don't."

And then he kissed her again, slower this time, his lips softer, his touch less frantic but no less consuming. This kiss wasn't about silencing her — it was about showing her everything he couldn't say.

"I wish you wouldn't do this to me." She broke the kiss, confused. Her chest was heaving, the taste of her still on his lips.

His hands lingered on her waist, as if reluctant to let her go, cursing himself under his breath.

"You matter," he said again, his voice trembling slightly. "More than you know."

For a heartbeat, neither of them moved. Cassidy's pulse quickened, her cheeks flushed, his stare hitting her like a sudden wave. He wasn't smiling, but there was something there — something dark and dangerous. Something she wasn't sure she could handle.

Chapter Nine

"Dammit, Cassidy," Duke said, running a hand through his hair, stepping away from her as if the space could calm the chaos swirling inside him. The heat of her touch still burned on his skin, a cruel reminder of how easily she unraveled him. "This is wrong. I shouldn't have —" He stopped, jaw clenching, his gaze flickering to the side. "You deserve better than this. Better than me."

"Enough," she said, her voice cutting through the storm of his self-recrimination. "Why don't you stop following me into corners — easy, right?"

"You don't get it," he shot back, his frustration flaring, words sharper than he meant. "You've been reckless, Cassidy."

She tilted her head, eyes flashing. "How unsafe can I be if I have the Secret Service following me?"

His fists clenched, the pressure rising in his chest. "You don't know who I am or what I'm capable of."

She flinched, but her chin lifted in defiance. "You make it sound like you're some big, bad wolf."

"You don't understand," he growled, the words coming out rougher than he wanted. "You're playing a game you don't know how to win."

"I have to try," she said, her voice rising with a fire that mirrored his. "Play the game — they say."

Her words hit him like a punch to the gut. He stared at her, eyes dark and conflicted, his jaw working as he tried to contain everything inside him. Finally, the words came out in a clipped, icy tone. "I shouldn't be humoring this. The bet's off."

"No," she said, stepping forward with an intensity that left him breathless. "You don't get to decide that."

"You have no idea," he said, voice rising again, the frustration spilling over. "I can't —"

"You can't what?" she interrupted, her voice trembling with a mix of fury and something deeper. "You can't deal with me proving you wrong? That being real, being honest, being me can actually work?"

"Being a naïve lamb doesn't work in the lion's den."

"Good thing lions don't actually eat lambs."

Duke opened his mouth to respond, but the words stuck in his throat. She was too much — too strong, too relentless, too damn stubborn for him to process. And it scared him more than he wanted to admit.

Her voice softened, but the anger still simmered beneath it. "You think this is about me, but it's not, is it? It's about you. You're scared. Scared I'll prove you wrong. Scared that I'll show you it's okay to let people in. To let me in."

"Let you in? No, no —"

"Right, because I'm not good enough for you?"

His chest burned, her words cutting deeper than he cared to admit. She saw right through him. He didn't want to let her in. He didn't want to be the man she thought he was. He wasn't worthy of her belief, of the risk she was so willing to take.

"Go back to your corner and watch me win...from the sidelines," Cassidy's voice was low now, but trembling with emotion.

She turned, her steps steady, but he could see the tightness in her shoulders, the pain she was trying to hide. Duke stood frozen, his fists clenched, heart pounding in his chest, his eyes dark with emotions he couldn't—or wouldn't—name.

* * * *

The vintage store smelled faintly of lavender and old leather, the racks of clothing arranged in an artful chaos that only a regular shopper could navigate. Cassidy sifted through a rack of dresses, the delicate fabrics swishing with every flick of her fingers. Velvet, sequins, lace—she couldn't tell if she was finding treasures or relics.

"You are such a manic arts kid," Anne said, plopping down on an overstuffed ottoman in the corner of the store. She crossed her arms and grinned. "I mean, look at you. Do you ever buy mainstream labels?"

Cassidy rolled her eyes, pulling out a deep burgundy dress with an asymmetrical hem. "I'm not a hipster," she said, holding the dress up to herself and studying it in the mirror. "I buy normal things."

Anne snorted. "You literally dragged me into a vintage store for a holiday party outfit. You're one step away from quoting obscure poetry at me."

Cassidy ignored her, disappearing into the nearest changing room with an armful of dresses. Behind the curtain, she struggled with the first one — a too-tight sequined number that made her feel like a walking disco ball.

"No," she said, peeling it off and tossing it aside.

One by one, she tried on each dress, but nothing worked. One was too loose, another too fussy, and the third clung in all the wrong places. Frustration bubbled up as she pulled on a navy sheath dress that looked drab and unflattering.

"I'm doomed," she said through the curtain.

"You're being dramatic," Anne replied. "But seriously, are you going to find something before this place closes? Because I'm starving."

Cassidy sighed, leaning her forehead against the cool wall of the changing room. "I don't even know why I'm trying so hard. It's just a stupid party."

"A stupid party with a stupidly sexy secret service agent who may or may not show up," Anne shot back. "Hmmm..."

Cassidy opened her mouth to protest but stopped when the curtain fluttered slightly. She turned, startled, to find a small, older woman standing there with a familiar smile and a garment draped over her arm.

"I think this is what you're looking for, dear," the woman said, her voice soft but confident.

Cassidy blinked, confused. "I didn't see that on the racks."

The woman just smiled, handing over the dress. "Try it on."

Before Cassidy could say anything else, the woman turned and walked away, disappearing into the maze of racks.

Cassidy hesitated, then held the dress up. It was dark green velvet, the fabric rich and soft in her hands. The silhouette was simple but elegant, with a deep neckline and a cinched waist. It practically said holiday magic.

She slipped it on, the fabric gliding over her skin, and stepped in front of the mirror. For a moment, she barely recognized herself. The dress clung to her curves in all the right places, the deep green bringing out the brightness of her eyes and the blush in her cheeks.

"Whoa," she said.

"Cass? Are you alive in there?" Anne called.

Cassidy drew in a breath and pulled the curtain aside, stepping out into the store.

The reaction was immediate. Conversations stopped, heads turned, and a collective gasp rippled through the room.

Anne's jaw dropped. "Oh my God. Cassidy."

"What?" Cassidy asked, her voice tight as the unease started to creep in. "Is it bad?"

Anne stood, shaking her head slowly. "No. It's... You're... I've never seen you look like this. You're elegant. Stunning."

Cassidy's stomach fluttered as her reflection caught her eye in one of the mirrors. *Elegant. Stunning.* Words she wasn't used to hearing, let alone seeing for herself.

She smoothed her hands over the velvet, her throat tightening. The dress felt like a fairy tale, but the attention made her feel exposed, vulnerable.

Anne stepped closer, her voice softer now. "Cass, you look amazing. And if Duke shows up, he won't be able to take his eyes off you."

Cassidy's stomach knotted. "And if he doesn't?"

Anne paused, then gave her a pointed look. "Then you walk into that party like you own the damn room and make him regret it."

Cassidy tried to smile, but the unease lingered. She couldn't stop herself from wondering.

Will he show up?

Chapter Ten

The bar was a riot of noise and movement, the kind of energy Duke knew how to crush. Laughter bounced off the walls, glass clinked in time with the music's thump, and the lingering scent of cheap perfume and spilled beer filled the air. It was a scene. He thrived here, always had.

He leaned back in the booth, arm draped casually over the worn leather, watching the scene unfold around him. Salem and Wyatt were doing their usual thing, trading jabs and jokes, while a small group of women crowded them, hanging on every word like they were hanging on the edge of a cliff.

"You're quiet tonight, bud," Wyatt said, lifting his beer with a grin. "The man, the legend, keeping us all guessing."

Duke let his eyes flicker up for a moment, a smirk curving on his lips, but it was half-hearted, like everything else about him these days. "Just enjoying the show."

Wyatt laughed, elbowing the blonde next to him. "See that? Armstrong doesn't even have to talk to be the most interesting guy in the room."

The blonde giggled and leaned into Duke's space, her fingers trailing lightly along his arm. He didn't flinch, but neither did he lean into her. It wasn't about her. It never was.

"Come on," she purred, her voice sultry, leaning closer. "You can't just sit there looking all broody. Say something."

Duke picked up his whiskey, taking a slow, deliberate sip before setting it back down, watching her expectantly for a moment before he answered. "I'm good."

Her smile faltered for just a second, and after a moment, she shifted her attention to Salem, who was already more than willing to entertain her. Duke didn't care. He didn't care about her, or the others, or the attention that followed him like a shadow. It was all just noise.

Wyatt gave him a sidelong glance, lifting his beer to his lips. "You sure you're not sick? Or secretly married? You're usually halfway to the dance floor by now."

Duke exhaled, his gaze drifting over the crowd, the laughter and chatter blending into a dull hum. "Just relaxing."

Wyatt shrugged, returning to the group with a bemused look, but the moment passed, and the conversation moved on without him.

Duke let the noise wash over him, his eyes flicking over the room with practiced indifference. A couple in the corner, cozy and content, laughing easily as they shared a plate of fries. The woman's hair was mussed from the night, her laughter unpolished and real, her smile open in a way Duke rarely saw anymore. The guy beside her leaned in with ease, brushing crumbs from her sleeve like he'd done it a thousand times.

Duke's fingers tightened around his glass, a sharp jolt of something running through him, but it was gone as quickly as it came. He didn't dwell.

"You ever think about what comes next?" The question slipped out before he could stop it, quiet but cutting through the thick air like a blade.

Wyatt looked over, his brow furrowed. "Next? Like your next assignment? Or next drink?"

Duke's lips twitched, a dry smirk pulling at the corners of his mouth. "Something like that."

Wyatt rolled his eyes. "Man, you already know the answer. Somewhere with a hell of a view and fewer responsibilities than here." He grinned, but it faded when Duke didn't take the bait. "What's up? Something going on?"

"Nothing," Duke said too quickly, the lie hanging in the air heavier than it should've. "Just got some rough news today."

Wyatt raised an eyebrow but didn't push it. Salem was already deep into another ridiculous story, the women laughing along like it was their first time hearing it.

Duke's phone buzzed on the table, lighting up with a message. He glanced at it—didn't even bother to read it—and slipped it back in his pocket. It buzzed again. He growled and pulled it out. A calendar reminder linked to Thomas Reed's email invite.

Holiday Party
Location: Reed Family Home
Time: 8:00 PM

It was nineteen-thirty now. He hadn't RSVPed. He hadn't planned to.

He scrolled through the email again, his jaw tightening at the bolded line near the bottom.

We'd love to recognize your heroic actions last week and thank you in person.

The blonde next to Wyatt leaned in, her voice cutting through the clatter. "You're such a mystery, Armstrong. Why don't you tell us what's on your mind?"

Duke turned his head slightly, his gaze cool, unreadable. "Not much to tell."

Heroic actions, he thought with a snort, swirling the ice in his glass. He hadn't felt particularly heroic dragging Cassidy out of a mess she'd gotten herself into. Reckless, stubborn, trouble — those were better descriptors for her.

As if on cue, a woman sauntered over to the table. Blonde, tall, all curves and fake smiles. Duke recognized her immediately — Alyssa, a fling from months back.

"Duke," she purred, leaning down and pressing a kiss to his cheek. "Long time no see."

He leaned back slightly. "Alyssa."

She perched on the edge of his chair, her hand brushing his arm. "You've been avoiding me."

"I've been busy," he said flatly, pulling his arm away and glancing at his watch.

"Too busy for an old friend?" she teased, her tone dripping with forced sweetness.

Duke's irritation flared. Everything about this moment felt wrong. The noise, the meaningless flirtation, the empty conversations around him. And Alyssa—fake, insincere, reminding him of everything he was trying to leave behind.

He was done.

He stood abruptly, causing her to stumble slightly. "Excuse me," he said, his tone clipped.

Without waiting for a response, he grabbed his coat and phone, heading for the door.

"Where you going, Armstrong?" Wyatt called after him.

Duke didn't answer. He was already halfway to his truck.

It was twenty-hundred by the time he pulled up to the Reed family home. The house glowed warmly against the crisp night, strings of white lights outlining the roof and a wreath hanging on the door. Through the windows, he could see the soft flicker of candles and the golden glow of a chandelier.

He stepped out of his truck, glancing down at his dark jeans and sweater. He hadn't thought to change.

Great, he thought. *This'll be fun.*

As he walked to the door, he could already hear the hum of conversation and laughter inside. The faint scent of roasting turkey and cinnamon wafted out as he stepped into the entryway, greeted by a cheerful host who took his coat.

"Mr. Armstrong!" Thomas Reed's voice boomed from across the room. The crowd quieted slightly, heads turning as Reed approached with a broad smile.

"You made it," Reed said, clapping him on the shoulder. "We were just about to start dinner."

Duke suppressed a groan as he followed Reed into the dining room, the hum of conversation resuming behind him.

The space was warm and inviting, the long table set with fine china and lit by a centerpiece of glowing candles. Reed's wife and teenage children greeted him politely, their smiles genuine. Around the table sat reporters, editors, and a handful of other familiar faces from the paper.

But one face was missing.

Duke scanned the room as Reed guided him to a seat. The whole place was cozy, festive, perfect for a family gathering.

And Cassidy wasn't there.

Reed leaned closer, his voice low. "Relax, Armstrong. Enjoy the evening."

Duke nodded stiffly, sitting down as the first course was served.

He wasn't sure what was worse — the fact that he felt so out of place here, or the fact that the one person he'd expected to see wasn't here at all.

The soft hum of conversation in the dining room barely registered as Duke sat back in his chair, the amber glow of the chandelier casting long shadows across the polished table. He toyed absently with the edge of his napkin, twisting it between his fingers, his jaw tight, and his mood as sour as the wine he was supposed to be savoring.

Across the table, Sven — some wannabe hipster in a slim-fitting cardigan and way-too-perfectly styled hair — leaned forward, gesturing wildly as he talked about some obscure artist or band Duke didn't care about. His voice had that obnoxious, over-enthusiastic quality, like he thought everyone around him was hanging on every word.

Duke's fingers tightened around his glass, the wine sloshing as he held it in his hand. But his focus was elsewhere — his eyes kept drifting, scanning the room for Cassidy.

He hated how badly he was waiting for her, but he wouldn't admit it. Instead, he listened to Sven's self-important ramblings about some indie music festival he'd just returned from, the words washing over him without leaving any trace. His attention wavered again, back to the door, back to that impossible-to-ignore hope that she'd walk in at any moment.

And then she did.

The chatter around him dulled to static, his focus narrowing on the doorway as Cassidy appeared.

His jaw ticked, then went slack.

That dress.

The dark green velvet clung to her in a way that made it impossible to look anywhere else. The neckline dipped just enough to be enticing but still elegant, and the fabric hugged her waist and hips like it had been tailored to her body. Her blonde curls framed her flushed face, and her bright green eyes scanned the room with an almost hesitant energy.

She looked stunning. No, that wasn't the right word. Unreal. The kind of woman who made every head in the room turn without trying. And judging by the sudden quiet murmur that spread through the table, he wasn't the only one noticing.

He forced himself to sit up straighter, his expression carefully neutral as she stepped farther into the room. Reed greeted her warmly, clasping her shoulder with a grin before leading her toward the table.

"Cassidy," Duke said, keeping his voice polite as she passed him. He tipped his head in acknowledgment, trying not to let his gaze linger too long.

"Duke," she replied, her tone even, though the faint pink in her cheeks deepened. She didn't pause, moving toward her seat halfway down the table.

Duke's eyes followed her despite himself, his pulse quickening as she gracefully sat down near a group of younger men. One of them, Sven, a tall guy with dark-rimmed glasses and an annoyingly trendy beard, immediately stood to greet her.

"Cassidy!" Sven said, his voice warm and familiar. He leaned in, pulling her into a deep hug that lingered far too long for Duke's liking.

Duke's teeth clenched.

Sven laughed, saying something Duke couldn't hear, and Cassidy smiled in response. She seemed at ease, her laughter ringing out as she settled into her chair.

Duke barely registered the conversation happening around him at his end of the table. His gaze kept drifting back to her, to the way she seemed to light up the room, to the way that hipster douchebag leaned closer as he spoke to her.

The napkin in Duke's hand crumpled.

"Armstrong," Reed's voice broke through his thoughts, and Duke turned his head sharply.

"Hm?" he replied, trying to mask the irritation simmering beneath the surface.

"I was saying," Reed continued, his tone amused, "it's good to have you here tonight. I hope you're enjoying yourself."

Duke forced a tight smile. "Yeah. It's great."

But his gaze flickered back to Cassidy, and his mood darkened further as the hipster leaned closer, gesturing animatedly about something while Cassidy nodded, clearly engaged.

Relax, Armstrong, he told himself, though the knot in his chest didn't ease.

The warmth of the room, the festive atmosphere, the glowing candles—all of it grated on him now. All because of one woman.

Cassidy turned her head then, her gaze briefly meeting his from across the table. Her lips parted, her expression unreadable, and for a moment, the rest of the room seemed to fade.

Duke quickly looked away, grabbing his glass of water and taking a long sip.

He was here to be polite, to make an appearance, to salvage her reputation—not to get distracted by how damn incredible she looked. And definitely not to let himself get worked up over some guy who clearly didn't know how to keep his hands to himself.

But as the dinner went on, Duke couldn't stop the flicker of possessiveness stirring in his chest.

The dining room glowed with soft, golden light, the warmth of the candles and the twinkling Christmas tree in the corner wrapping Cassidy like a cozy blanket. Reed's family home was everything she'd imagined—classic and inviting, filled with personal touches. A garland wrapped around the staircase banister, stockings hung by a stone fireplace, and a faint scent of cinnamon and pine drifted through the air.

Dinner had just begun, and Cassidy felt herself relax as the first course was served—a light but decadent butternut squash soup with a drizzle of crème fraîche and toasted pumpkin seeds. She sipped it slowly, savoring the balance of flavors. Across the table, glasses clinked as Reed raised a toast to "another year of great stories and even greater camaraderie," earning a round of cheers.

Seated next to her was Sven. He covered music and the arts for the paper, and Cassidy had always appreciated his sharp wit and offbeat taste in stories.

"This soup is incredible," Sven said, leaning in slightly. "Almost makes up for the hit my ego takes every time I walk into a room full of Pulitzer nominees."

Cassidy laughed, setting her spoon down. "I'm not a Pulitzer nominee, so you're safe around me."

"Yet," Sven corrected, his grin widening. "I've read your pieces, Cassidy. You've got the kind of voice that sneaks up on people and stays with them. Don't sell yourself short."

Her cheeks flushed, and she glanced down at her plate, letting the compliment settle before changing the subject. "Have you been to that new gallery on H Street? The one with the pop art installations?"

Sven's eyes lit up. "Oh, the one that has the neon room with the mirrored walls? Loved it. Felt like stepping into a Bowie fever dream."

Cassidy nodded, her enthusiasm building. "Exactly! And the abstract pieces in the back — did you see the one that looked like a shattered cityscape? It reminded me of..."

As they talked, Cassidy found herself caught up in the easy rhythm of the conversation. Sven was passionate, funny, and genuinely interested in what she had to say. It was refreshing to relax and be herself, especially after the chaos of the past week.

The second course arrived — roast duck with a cranberry-orange glaze, accompanied by rosemary potatoes and haricots verts. The richness of the meal paired perfectly with the glasses of red wine being poured by Reed's teenage son, who had been pressed into service as a waiter for the evening.

Cassidy took a sip of her wine, laughing as Sven recounted a disastrous attempt to review an experimental jazz performance. But as she glanced across the table, her laughter faltered.

Duke was watching her.

He sat near the head of the table, his broad shoulders hunched as he picked at his plate. His dark eyes followed her movements, his expression unreadable but sharp, like he was calculating something.

She quickly looked away, focusing back on Sven, who was now gesturing animatedly about an obscure music exhibit.

"So, do you think you'll check it out?" Sven asked, leaning closer, his voice warm and inviting.

"Definitely," Cassidy replied, smiling. "It sounds incredible."

But as Sven leaned in, his elbow resting on the table between them, she couldn't ignore the prickling sensation of Duke's gaze. She chanced another glance his way and caught the faint tightening of his jaw as Sven said something that made her laugh.

Why does he look pissed? she wondered, trying to suppress the flutter of nerves in her chest.

"Hey," Sven said, nudging her slightly. "You."

She blinked, startled. "Sorry. What was that?"

Sven chuckled, shaking his head. "I asked if you'd want to grab coffee next week and compare notes on those exhibits. Unless you're too busy writing the next great human-interest piece."

"I—"

Before she could answer, her gaze flicked back to Duke. His fork was still in his hand, but he wasn't eating. Instead, he was leaning back slightly, his dark eyes boring into her with a mixture of annoyance and something else she couldn't quite place.

The energy in the room felt warmer and brighter, filled with laughter and clinking glasses, but between her and Duke, it was taut as a wire.

"Cassidy?" Sven prompted, his smile easy but curious.

She forced herself to smile back, ignoring the heat rising in her cheeks. "Coffee sounds great."

Sven beamed, raising his glass in a toast. "To art and caffeine."

Cassidy clinked her glass with his, but her attention drifted again, her pulse quickening as Duke finally looked away, his expression shadowed.

Why does he care who I talk to? she wondered, her fingers tightening around her wine glass.

Chapter Eleven

The Reed family retired the holiday party to their heated patio, the hum of conversation and the glow of string lights creating a festive, intimate atmosphere.

Cassidy stood near the fire pit, her glass of mulled wine warming her hands as she laughed at something Sven had said. The tension she'd carried for weeks had finally started to ebb.

Savannah Hatton entered with her usual entourage—Joan and Claire—three women who moved with the practiced ease of those accustomed to taking up space. They were sharp and sleek, predators entering their territory, and Cassidy knew right away that their presence wasn't a coincidence.

The weight of their gaze fell on her like a shadow, and Savannah's smile was wide, almost too wide, the kind that never reached her eyes. Her eyes glittered with a mix of amusement and something more calculating. As they approached, Cassidy's stomach twisted.

The President's Bodyguard

Savannah's voice slid through the noise of the crowd, smooth but laced with an edge. "Cassidy," she said, her tone dripping with sweetness that Cassidy knew all too well. "Enjoying yourself?"

Cassidy forced a smile, her pulse quickening despite herself. "It's a lovely party."

Savannah tilted her head, letting her dark eyes linger on Cassidy a moment too long. "Lovely indeed. Must be a nice change of pace for you," she said, her voice carrying the faintest hint of condescension.

Joan and Claire stood on either side of her, like shadows, their eyes cold but unreadable.

Savannah swirled her drink in her hand, her lips curling as she glanced over Cassidy's shoulder, surveying the room with the same air of superiority she always wore. "It's been an eventful few weeks for you, hasn't it? Quite a...splash, from what I've heard."

Cassidy's stomach clenched, but she forced herself to meet Savannah's gaze, unblinking. "I'm not sure what you mean."

Savannah's laugh was soft, almost too smooth. "Oh, come on now. The protest, the paint, the sudden rescue by a certain agent? It's been quite the story, hasn't it?"

"And not exactly professional," Joan added, her voice as cold as Cassidy's blood started to feel.

Claire sipped her wine, eyeing Cassidy with a look that was both dismissive and curious. "I suppose it's all part of the learning curve. Finding your place, figuring out what kind of journalist you want to be. Or dream to be." The words were a sneer wrapped in a smile.

Cassidy's cheeks burned, the sting of their words settling deep. She wanted to snap back, to demand they mind their own business, but she kept her jaw clenched and her expression neutral, letting the insults roll off her.

Savannah leaned in slightly, her voice shifting to something more intimate — and far sharper. "But take care, Cassidy. This is a tough business. Not everyone gets to stay, especially those who don't know what they're doing."

The words cut deep, more than any of them realized. Cassidy's chest tightened painfully, her hand gripping her glass so tight she thought it might shatter. She opened her mouth, but the words wouldn't come.

"Excuse me," she said, her voice quiet but steady, a tightness wrapping around her throat.

Savannah's gaze tracked her every move as Cassidy stepped back, the sound of her low, mocking laugh trailing behind her like smoke. "Of course. Don't let us keep you."

Cassidy didn't wait for them to say anything more. She turned, slipping through the crowd, her vision blurring as she made her way through the house. The laughter and chatter seemed to fade, leaving nothing but the echo of her own thoughts.

Her breath hitched in her throat, each step carrying the weight of their words. The sting of their insults gnawed at her, twisting in ways she didn't want to admit. She needed a place to breathe, somewhere no one could see her crack. Least of all Duke.

Her footsteps quickened, and she finally found a door ajar at the end of the hallway. Cassidy slipped inside.

The room was dark, save for the pale moonlight that filtered through the curtains, casting a soft glow on the polished surface of a grand piano. She leaned against the frame, pressing a hand over her mouth, willing the tears not to fall.

But they did anyway.

She didn't want to cry. Not here, not like this. She didn't want to give Savannah — or anyone like her — the satisfaction of seeing her break. But the words still stung, sinking in deeper than she cared to admit.

* * * *

Duke's eyes never left Cassidy all night, but he kept his distance — kept quiet. He was too aware of the people around her, too damn aware of the fact that no one else seemed to care.

She had been laughing earlier, vibrant, carefree — her usual fire lighting up the room. Then Savannah had shown up. Duke had seen it immediately. The way Cassidy had stiffened, the way her laugh had faltered the second those women entered.

He'd watched it all — how the smiles had turned thin, how the air around them had grown cold. He'd seen the flicker of hurt in her eyes, just for a moment, before she'd masked it with a tight smile and slipped away.

He had no choice.

He immediately followed.

Duke moved through the crowd, his pulse spiking as he noticed no one else following her, no one else checking in on her. They were all too wrapped up in their own little worlds. Too caught up in their pretentious social game to notice that Cassidy was unraveling right in front of them.

That's what made his blood boil.

He pushed out of the crowd, making his way toward the house. His steps were quick, deliberate, just enough to stay behind her without alarming her.

Cassidy was already moving through the halls, her pace picking up. She wasn't walking away to be alone — she was running from something. From them. From the moment.

Duke followed. Silent. Close enough to sense the shift in her energy, too far to stop her. She slipped around a corner, and he hung back, making sure no one noticed.

No one was coming after her. He was the only one.

She pushed open a door, stepping inside.

Duke didn't hesitate. He moved to the door, pressing his palm against the wood. The faintest crack of light spilled through the space, and he slipped inside, shutting the door quietly behind him.

The room was bathed in moonlight, the piano gleaming in the center, its polished surface untouched by the chaos of the night. But Cassidy? She was against the far wall, her body hunched as if trying to shrink into herself. Her arms were wrapped tightly around her, like she was holding herself together.

Her shoulders trembled, the movement so slight, so fragile, Duke could feel it even from across the room. His chest burned at the sight.

No one was watching her. No one but him.

The anger roared inside him — at Savannah, at the others, at himself — but mostly at the way Cassidy looked so damn broken, trying to hide it behind the wall she'd built between herself and the world.

He took a step forward. And then another.

Cassidy didn't hear him approach, didn't look up as he reached her. His hand hovered by her arm, unsure whether she'd pull away, but he didn't care.

It was just him and her in that room now.

"Cassidy," he said quietly.

She flinched and tilted her head up as her wide, tear-bright eyes met his in the dark. "Duke," she breathed, her voice a mixture of surprise and frustration. "What are you—"

"You bolted," he said simply, stepping closer. "You always run when it's bad."

Her lips parted, but she didn't reply. She turned her head away, wiping quickly at her cheeks as if she could erase the evidence of her tears.

"I'm fine," she said.

"You're not."

Cassidy let out a short, humorless laugh, shaking her head. "What, are you following me now?"

"Yes," he admitted without hesitation. "Because every time you run, it's trouble. So, here I am."

Her gaze snapped back to him, her brows knitting together in irritation. "I don't need you to babysit me, Duke."

"But, I'm here," he said, his tone softening. "Talk to me."

Cassidy's shoulders sagged slightly, her defiance crumbling as she looked away again.

"Those women," he said carefully, watching her reaction. "They were out of line."

She let out a shaky breath, her voice barely above a whisper. "I don't care what they think."

He said nothing.

She glanced at him, her expression wavering between irritation and vulnerability. "What does it matter? They're probably right."

Duke's jaw set. "No, they're not."

Cassidy blinked, her surprise breaking through her sadness for a moment. "You don't even know what they said."

"Doesn't matter," he said, his voice firm. "They don't know you. Not really."

Her breath hitched and she looked away again, her fingers brushing against the piano as if grounding herself.

His chest strained, the sight of her vulnerability hitting him like a punch. Before she could react, he was pulling her into his arms.

She stiffened at first, but then she melted against him, her hands gripping his sweater as a shaky breath escaped her lips.

"It's okay," he said softly, one hand smoothing over her back, the other cradling the back of her head. "You're okay."

She shook her head against his chest, her voice muffled and trembling. "No, I'm not. I—"

"Stop," he interrupted gently, his lips brushing the crown of her head. "You don't have to explain anything. Just breathe."

Cassidy's fingers curled tighter into his sweater, and he felt the rapid thrum of her heart against him. He tilted his head down, her curls brushing his cheek as he resisted the overwhelming urge to do more—to press his lips to her hair, to kiss away the tears on her cheeks.

She deserved comfort, not complications.

After a moment, her breathing slowed, and she pulled back slightly, just enough to look up at him. Her green eyes shimmered with unshed tears, her expression raw and unguarded.

"They hate me," she said, her voice breaking. "They think I'm a joke."

"No," Duke said firmly, his hands tightening on her shoulders. "They're wrong."

"You don't know that," she said, her gaze dropping. "You didn't hear what they said —"

"You're not a joke, Cassidy," he continued, his dark eyes locked on hers. "You're smart, you're brave, and you care more about your work than half the people in that room combined. You're winning the bet."

Her breath hitched, and she blinked up at him, her expression wavering between disbelief and something softer. Her eyes searched his, and he let her see everything — his belief in her, his frustration at how she let those women get under her skin, and the barely restrained pull he felt every time she was near.

He leaned in slightly, just enough to feel her breath on his skin. Her lips parted, and for a heartbeat, he thought about closing the distance, about giving in to the instinct to kiss away her worries.

But he stopped himself, his grip on her hands tightening slightly. "You're amazing, Cassidy. Don't let anyone make you forget that."

Cassidy barely registered the room anymore, the moonlight filtering through the curtains, the faint gleam of the piano in the shadows.

All she felt was Duke — his arms strong and steady around her, the warmth of his body against hers as she let herself lean into him. She wasn't supposed to need this. She wasn't supposed to need him. But in that moment, she couldn't bring herself to pull away.

"Cass," he said, his voice low and rough, sending a shiver down her spine.

She tilted her head to look up at him, her breath catching at the intensity in his dark eyes. There was something raw there, something she hadn't seen before, and it made her heart pound in a way that had nothing to do with the tears she'd been crying.

Before she could speak, he leaned in, his lips capturing hers in a kiss that stole the air from her lungs.

Cassidy froze for half a second, her mind racing, before her body responded instinctively. Her hands slid up his chest, clutching at the fabric of his sweater as he deepened the kiss, his mouth moving against hers with a hunger that made her knees go weak.

"Duke," she said when he pulled back.

"You drive me crazy," he said, his voice rough and thick with emotion.

Before she could reply, his hands shifted, one sliding down to her thigh. He hitched her leg up against his hip, his fingers gripping the soft velvet of her dress as he pressed her back against the wall. The cool surface against her spine only heightened the heat spreading through her body as his mouth found hers again, this time fiercer, more possessive.

"You don't know what you're doing to me," he said against her lips, his voice a low growl. "That dress..." His hand tightened on her leg, his other hand cradling her jaw as his thumb brushed her cheek. "You're a damn vision."

Cassidy's breath hitched, her hands fisting in his sweater as his lips moved to her neck, the roughness of his stubble sending sparks skittering across her skin.

"Duke," she said, her voice trembling with a mix of desire and disbelief.

He pulled back just enough to meet her gaze, his dark eyes burning with something she couldn't quite name. "I didn't like seeing you with him," he said bluntly, his jaw tight. "That guy. Sven. I didn't like it."

Cassidy blinked, her head spinning. "Sven? He's just—"

"I don't care who he is," Duke interrupted, his voice rough. "I don't want to see you with anyone else. Not like that."

Her heart raced, her breath coming in shallow gasps as she stared at him. "Why?" she asked.

"Because," he said simply, raw and possessive as his lips crashed into hers again.

The kiss was hotter this time, more desperate, as if he was trying to brand the truth of his words into her. Cassidy's mind reeled, but she couldn't think, couldn't do anything except cling to him as he consumed her completely.

But somewhere in the haze, a thread of uncertainty pulled at her.

His hands were sure, his kiss was claiming, but there was something else in the way he held her—something conflicted.

He pulled back again, his chest heaving as he pressed his forehead to hers, his eyes closing briefly. "You're trouble," he said, his voice tinged with frustration. "You're going to make my life hell."

Cassidy swallowed hard, loosening her grip on his sweater. "Duke…"

His thumb brushed against her cheek again, his touch softer now. "This shouldn't be happening. But you…" He shook his head, his lips quirking in a faint, humorless smile. "You're so damn sexy."

Cassidy's heart ached at the honesty in his voice, everything unsaid pressing down on them.

"Is this more than just attraction?"

Cassidy's breath came fast, her chest heaving as Duke leaned back slightly, the tension between them thick enough to cut. Her hands trembled as they hovered near her sides, still desperate to reach for him again. But the look in his eyes—raw, conflicted, and burning—rooted her to the spot.

She swallowed hard, her voice shaking when she spoke. "Do you have feelings for me?"

Duke froze.

"No," he said flatly, though the word carried none of the conviction she'd expected.

Cassidy tilted her head slightly. "You have to answer honestly, Duke," she said softly but firmly, the reminder of their bet hanging heavily in the air. "The bet."

His nostrils flared as he exhaled sharply, his hands clenching at his sides. "Cassidy…"

"Be honest," she pressed. "Do you have feelings for me?"

Chapter Twelve

Duke's jaw worked as if he were physically biting back the words. But when he finally looked at her, the carefully constructed mask he always wore seemed to crack.

Feelings?

"Yes," he said, rough, almost torn from him. "Yes, I have something for you. For the first time...it feels real."

Before Cassidy could respond, he closed the distance between them, his hands cupping her face as his lips found hers again.

This kiss was different. It was fiercer, hungrier, and Cassidy melted into it without hesitation. Her arms wrapped around his neck as his body pressed hers firmly against the wall.

Duke groaned low in his throat, the sound vibrating against her lips as his hands slid down her sides, gripping her waist before moving lower. The velvet of her gown bunched under his fingers, and she gasped as he hitched her leg up against his hip again, his body pinning hers in place.

"You drive me insane," he said against her lips, his voice thick with frustration and want. "This dress, the way you looked tonight… God, Cassidy."

Her fingers tangled in his hair, pulling him closer as he kissed her again, his mouth hot and demanding against hers. One of his hands moved to her shoulder, his fingers trailing over the soft fabric of her gown before slipping the strap down. The velvet slid easily, baring her breast to the cool air, and Duke's breath hitched as he pulled back slightly.

"You're beautiful," he said, his voice hoarse as his fingers brushed over her bare skin. "You're so damn real. You have no idea."

Cassidy's cheeks flushed, but the heat in his gaze made her feel bolder than she ever had before. She ran her fingers through his hair, holding him to her as she rocked her hips against him. Duke groaned, sliding his hands down her breasts and back up again, his touch firm but reverent. He returned to her mouth, kissing her deeply, his body pressing hers further into the wall as his control wavered. The fire between them burned hotter with every second, every kiss, every touch.

Here he was, in the middle of her boss's home, standing like a man who had all the time in the world, his warm, rough hands wrapped around her waist as if she were the most important thing he'd ever have. He hitched her up higher against the wall, holding her entire weight with ease. He kissed down her neck, fierce and with intent, and found her breast with his mouth. He ran his tongue over her nipple, playing with the sensitive bud.

Cassidy felt her pulse quicken, her breath catching as she watched him. He moved slowly, appreciating and mummering prayers to her. He didn't rush it.

The air felt heavier. Time seemed to stretch. Cassidy's eyes followed the way his lips parted as he pulled her breast from his mouth. The tip of his tongue flicked out for just a second, catching the bud, and the sight—damn it, the sight—made her entire body tense with something unfamiliar.

He worked his way back up her neck, kissing and tasting her. Holding her against the wall, he slid his other hand up her thigh, underneath her dress. She opened her hips as he slid higher, playing with the edge of her panties. He kissed her slow, deliberate, easing the tension from her in ways that had nothing to do with just physical relief.

Finally, he slid underneath her panty and to the hot slit of her pussy. "This is where I want to be," he said. "Right here."

Every stroke of his fingers made her body hum with something else. She moaned into his kiss as he moved in slow, steady circles on her clit, and with each press of his thumb, Cassidy felt herself becoming more aware of something—more than the heat spreading through her skin, more than his fingers seeming to know exactly where she needed it. Something between them thickened with every passing second as he brought her closer to the edge.

She bit down on her lip, trying to not to scream as he pumped his fingers into her, curling just right.

"Like that?" he asked, his voice a low growl.

Cassidy swallowed hard, her heart racing a little faster than she would've liked. "Yeah," she managed to say, her voice coming out softer than she intended. "Oh God."

His eyes met hers, and for a brief moment, it felt like the whole world had gone still. She saw something flicker in his gaze, something that made the air between them electric, charged in a way she wasn't sure how to interpret. His thumb pressed onto her clit, harder this time, and Cassidy's breath caught.

"Come for me, Cass," he said, his voice like gravel, sending a strange shiver through her.

Cassidy bit her lip, fighting the odd mix of fascination and something else that simmered just below the surface. The way he worshipped her...the slow draw of his mouth, the subtle movement of his jaw as he played his tongue against hers and worked her clit. She was coming, falling over the edge. She moaned his name into his mouth. He grinned in satisfaction as he felt her release, collapsing into him.

Cassidy barely had time to catch her breath, her back still pressed against the wall, when the door creaked open.

Duke stepped away from her like he'd been burned. Hands off. Face blank. Damage control.

Thomas Reed stood in the doorway.

His gaze swept over the scene—Cassidy flushed, her hair askew, dress rumpled. Duke two steps away, expression shuttered.

The tension in the room turned glacial.

"Reed," Duke said evenly, his posture snapping to professional. "It's not what—"

"Get the fuck away from her."

Reed's voice was quiet. Controlled. And lethal.

Cassidy flinched. "Thomas, it's not—"

Reed didn't look at her. "Don't. Don't defend him."

Duke's jaw twitched, but he didn't move.

"I trusted you," Reed said, taking a slow step forward. "I went to bat for you. I helped bury that last mess. Because I thought—hell, I don't know what I thought. That you made a mistake. That you cared. That it wouldn't happen again."

Cassidy's brow furrowed. "What are you talking about?"

But Reed was already closing in, eyes locked on Duke like he was dissecting him. "You think I didn't notice the pattern? The interns. The press aides. A diplomat's fucking wife. And now her."

Duke stiffened.

"Thomas," Cassidy tried again, voice rising. "You're out of line—"

"No, Cassidy. He is." Reed turned to her, finally. "You know don't know what happened back then? Because Duke couldn't keep his dick to himself and blew up the life of a woman with two kids and a dangerous husband."

Cassidy's breath caught.

"She was the one who got raked through the mud," Reed continued. "But Duke? He came out fine. Shiny badge, Presidential family, a sad little photo of him looking mournful in *The Post* when people's lives ended because of his affair. And I—" He laughed bitterly. "I helped manage that narrative. I made sure he looked redeemable."

Cassidy looked at Duke. "Is that true?"

Duke didn't answer.

"Is it true?" she said again, sharper now.

Reed's voice turned venomous. "It wasn't just one time. It was a habit. A goddamn habit. You chew them up, Armstrong. You make them feel special, like they matter. Then you vanish. Or worse, you let them take the fall."

Duke's fists clenched, but he stayed still.

Cassidy stared at him like she didn't recognize him anymore.

"Not her," Duke said finally, his voice raw. "This isn't that."

Reed exploded. "That's what you said last time. And the time before that. I'm not letting my staff be another fucking casualty in your redemption arc."

"Fuck you." Duke stepped forward, voice low. "You don't know shit."

Reed's reply was a fist.

The punch landed hard—fast and clean. Duke staggered, caught himself against the wall, wiped blood from his mouth with the back of his hand.

Cassidy gasped. "Stop it! Both of you!"

Reed's chest heaved. "He doesn't care about you, Cassidy. Get the fuck out of this while you can."

She turned to Duke. "Tell me he's wrong."

Duke didn't meet her eyes.

"Duke," she said again, quieter. "Please."

Still nothing.

And that silence? It said everything.

Cassidy stepped back like she'd been hit, too.

"Don't," Duke said finally. One word. Choked.

Then he walked out. No defense. No denial. Just…gone.

The door clicked shut.

Cassidy stood there, breath shallow, the air still vibrating with everything unsaid.

Reed looked at her, face softer now. "I'm sorry."

She shook her head. "You don't get to be the good guy in this either."

He blinked.

"I don't need protection. I need the truth."

She pushed past him, wiping tears away before they fell. Her voice cracked as she added, "You should've told me who he really was."

Chapter Thirteen

The White House was a blur of holiday cheer — twinkling lights, wreaths hanging from every doorway, the scent of pine in the air — but none of it reached Cassidy. The festive energy that hummed through the halls felt like a sick joke against the knot of anxiety twisting in her stomach. Everything around her sparkled with warmth, but inside, she was freezing, numb.

A week had passed since the holiday party, but it might as well have been a lifetime. She hadn't seen Duke. Not once. Which, in itself, was remarkable — because when it came to Duke, he was everywhere. Or at least, he had been. Now, there was nothing. No texts. No calls. Just silence. The kind of silence that made it clear — she was nothing more than an afterthought. A mistake he'd made once, and now wanted nothing to do with.

She gripped her laptop tote tightly as she stood in the West Wing lobby, staring at the holiday decorations she couldn't bring herself to appreciate. A cup of cocoa, hot but tasteless, warmed her hands, but not much else. The holiday cheer around her felt like a distant echo. She was a spectator in her own life — separate, untouchable. The buzz of conversation and laughter swirled around her, but it was all muffled, out of reach.

Her thoughts spiraled uncontrollably. She replayed every moment with Duke over and over in her mind — the way his hands had felt on her skin, the heat of his kiss, the rawness in his voice when he'd confessed that she mattered. And then, the crash. The brutal sting of Reed's punch, the venom in his words, the way Duke had taken the blow without a single protest, without defending himself. Cassidy's chest twisted as the memory replayed with relentless clarity.

"Evans," Reed's voice jolted her back to the present. He stood beside her, looking down with his usual blend of authority and familiarity. "You okay?"

She forced a smile, but it felt brittle. "Of course."

He nodded, satisfied, and turned his attention back to the room just as the president entered the room. The shift was immediate — conversations quieted, heads turned.

He carried a box of wine bottles and gift cards, handing them out personally as he made his rounds. Cassidy knew the ritual was meant to feel warm and personal, but she couldn't shake the anxiety bubbling beneath her skin.

Her breath caught as the president approached, his sharp, charismatic smile directed at Reed first.

"Thomas," President Armstrong said warmly, shaking Reed's hand. "Another incredible year. You and your team have done fantastic work."

"Thank you, sir," Reed replied, his posture straight and confident.

The president's gaze shifted to Cassidy, and his smile softened, more curious now. "And here we are — Miss Evans."

Her heart thudded painfully, but she managed a nod, extending her hand. "Yes, Mr. President."

"And how is my biography coming along?"

"Great," she lied.

"I'm looking forward to seeing your final story," he said, shaking her hand with a firm grip.

Cassidy blinked, her anxiety spiking. "You are?"

"I am," he said, his tone pleased. "I've seen a teaser from Reed. So far... insightful, well-written. Perhaps, there are a few tweaks I'd like to make — nothing major — but I think we can add a little more context before it comes out next week. A few points I think the public will appreciate."

Her cheeks flushed, but the unease didn't fade. "Of course, sir. I'm happy to make any adjustments."

"Great, we have work to do." He nodded, satisfied, before tilting his head slightly. "What are your plans for the holidays, Cassidy? Staying in town?"

She hesitated. "Not much, really. My family's on a trip, so I'll just be at home. Here in DC."

The president laughed, a deep, genuine sound that carried over the low murmur of the room. "Sounds like a quiet holiday."

She nodded, her smile faint but polite.

"Well," he said, glancing at Reed before turning back to her, "if you're free, come join my family at our retreat for a day. We're heading to Evergreen Lake Lodge in the Blue Ridge Mountains. We can work through the final edits."

Cassidy's stomach dropped. "That's incredibly kind of you, sir, but I don't think—"

"She'd love to," Reed interrupted, his hand firm on her shoulder.

Cassidy's head snapped toward him, her eyes wide. "I—"

"It's a wonderful opportunity, Cassidy," Reed said pointedly, his gaze locking with hers.

The president smiled, apparently satisfied. "Good. My staff will send you the details." He paused and nodded to Reed. "Reed, you might as well come too."

Cassidy stood frozen as the president moved on, shaking hands and handing out gifts to the rest of the room.

She turned to Reed, her voice low and sharp. "Why would you do that?"

"Because it's good for your career," Reed replied bluntly. "Do you have any idea how rare this is? Being invited into the president's inner circle? You don't say no to that, Cassidy. And I'll be there, don't worry."

Her chest hurt, the weight of everything hitting her. "I don't want to go," she said, her voice trembling.

Reed's expression hardened slightly. "This isn't about what you want. It's about what's good for you. You represent the paper now. The brand. And after everything, you need this."

Cassidy flinched at his choice of words, her mind flashing back to the confrontation in the piano room. Reed's anger. Duke's quiet acceptance. The way she'd felt caught in the middle, helpless to stop the damage.

"Everything," she repeated softly, the word laced with bitterness.

Reed's gaze softened slightly, but his tone remained firm. "Trust me, Cassidy. This is how you move forward."

She nodded mechanically, though her heart screamed otherwise.

There was no way she was going to go.

* * * *

Later, the East Room buzzed with the kind of excitement only the last hour of the year could bring — everyone was ready to shut down, head out the door, and escape to their holiday plans. The chatter, the clinking of glasses, the easy laughter — it was all the same familiar buzz of the year's final moments, the exhaustion of endless meetings and relentless work replaced by a collective sigh of relief.

Cassidy stood near the edge of the room, a glass of champagne in hand, the bubbles flat in her glass as she took a sip. The golden glow of the Christmas lights, the lush garlands, the festive energy in the air — it should've been comforting, but all it did was amplify the nervous tension in her chest.

She didn't want to be here. Not after everything with Reed, not after Duke had all but disappeared. She hadn't expected it to hit her this hard. The pain, the confusion — it should've been a distraction, but standing here, surrounded by people humming with excitement about the holidays, made her feel more isolated than ever. She'd spent the past few days pretending everything was fine, plastering on a smile like she wasn't holding it together.

And then, as if on cue, the door to the East Room opened and the crowd stilled, cheer slipping away like a curtain dropping. The president had arrived.

Cassidy's stomach dropped as President Armstrong made his way to the front of the room, his stride purposeful and commanding, the crowd parting automatically to make room for him. She found herself pushed forward with the tide, her heart sinking as she was jostled into a more central position.

"Thank you all for being here," the president boomed, warm yet firm. He looked every bit the man who'd weathered several political firestorms since his re-election, his smile polished and genuine. "This year has been extraordinary. We've faced challenges, celebrated victories, and none of it would have been possible without the dedication of the incredible people in this room."

A round of applause erupted, echoing off the walls, and Cassidy clapped along with the others, the sound hollow in her ears as her mind wandered. She was not really listening, her thoughts caught in a whirlwind of memories—Duke's retreat, the tension between them, the way Reed's punch had shaken everything.

But as the applause died down, Cassidy noticed something shift in the room. The president's smile flattened just a fraction, the air hanging with an unspoken tension as he adjusted his grip on the podium.

The president continued, "As we close out the year, I want to take a moment to recognize someone whose service and sacrifice have been an integral part of this administration."

Cassidy blinked, her attention sharpening.

"This man has been a rock for our security operations, both here and abroad, and I'm proud to announce his promotion to head of security operations in Erbil, Iraq."

Her chest tightened, her breath catching in her throat.

President Armstrong smiled, gesturing to someone behind her. "Duke Armstrong, please step forward."

Cassidy's stomach dropped.

Erbil? Iraq?

The crowd applauded as Duke marched up, his broad shoulders impossibly straight as he approached the president. The room swam around Cassidy, her mind racing as the president continued to speak about Duke's new post—a five-year deployment to oversee operations in one of the most critical and volatile regions for American interests.

Five years.

She barely registered the rest of the speech, her pulse roaring in her ears as she watched Duke shake the president's hand. The two men exchanged words she couldn't hear, the president clapping him on the back before they turned to face the cameras.

Duke's expression was calm, stoic, his professionalism unshaken as the cameras clicked.

He knew. The thought hit her like a punch to the chest.

He had to have known. And he hadn't told her.

Cassidy's hands trembled, her champagne glass threatening to slip from her grip. She couldn't stand there, couldn't watch as Duke posed for photos, his departure already settling over the room like a shroud.

She turned abruptly, bumping into someone and muttering a quick apology as she stumbled toward the nearest exit. Her heels caught briefly on the edge of the carpet, and she barely managed to right herself as she fled the room.

The cool air of the hallway hit her like a slap, but it wasn't enough. She kept moving, her chest tight and her eyes burning as she made her way through the White House, the festive decorations blurring in her peripheral vision.

When she finally reached the front doors, the cold December night greeted her like a lifeline. She stepped outside, gasping for breath as she descended the steps, the sound of her heels echoing in the quiet.

How long had he known?

The question clawed at her, tearing through the haze of shock and hurt. Of course he'd known. He had to. A deployment like that didn't come out of nowhere.

Why didn't he tell me?

Her throat closed in as she stepped onto the sidewalk, her hands clutching her coat as the wind bit through her. She didn't know where she was going — she just knew she couldn't stay. Not after hearing that he was leaving.

He hadn't told her.

And that hurt more than anything else.

* * * *

The White House was nearly silent, its usual hum of activity replaced by the stillness of the holiday shutdown. Most of the staff had left hours ago, leaving only a skeleton crew and the faint twinkle of Christmas lights strung across the grounds outside. Duke leaned against the edge of a hallway, his gaze drifting to the faint glow spilling from a partially open door.

He didn't know why he followed her. Maybe it was the way she'd disappeared from the festivities earlier, her absence gnawing at him like a splinter. Or maybe it was the unresolved tension between them, the way her words still echoed in his head. *You don't think I matter.*

He pushed the door open gently, the soft creak revealing a darkened room lit only by the reflection of outdoor Christmas lights. The room itself was small and intimate, probably a sitting room no one used anymore. Cassidy sat curled on a bench by the window, her profile illuminated by the faint glow of red and green. Her knees were drawn up, arms wrapped around them as she stared out at the lights.

She didn't look at him, but he could tell by the way her shoulders stiffened that she knew he was there.

"Shouldn't surprise me anymore to see you running off," he said quietly, his voice low and rough as he stepped inside and closed the door behind him.

"But it does surprise me that you keep following me," she replied, her tone soft but edged with weariness.

"Someone has to," he said, leaning against the doorframe.

"I should be glad it's you?"

"I wouldn't say that."

She turned her head slightly, her green eyes catching the light as they met his. "What do you want, Duke? To apologize?"

The question hung in the air, heavier than it should have been. He pushed off the door and walked closer, his steps slow, deliberate. When he stopped, he was just close enough to see the tension in her face, the faint glimmer of something raw in her eyes.

"You," he said finally, "look like you're about to fall apart."

Cassidy exhaled a shaky breath, her gaze dropping back to the window. "I'm fine."

"You're not."

She laughed softly, a bitter sound. "And you're the expert on holding it together, right?"

His jaw set. "I didn't say I was."

"No," she said, turning back to him. "You don't say anything, Duke. You just brood in corners and follow me around like you're waiting for me to implode."

He didn't respond, his silence only deepening the tension in the room.

The worst part had come. The real part.

She said, "Why didn't you tell me?"

"I couldn't," he said, the words clipped.

"Liar," she said, her tone laced with a mix of frustration and sadness. "What happened to honesty, huh? Isn't that what the bet was about?"

"I guess I lost."

"You never wanted to win. Not really."

Duke's chest caught on fire as Cassidy stood and stepped toward him, the room seeming to shrink around them. His eyes drank her in, the curve of her body moving with an athletic grace that made his throat dry. Her dress clung to her in all the right places, accentuating her slim waist and the swell of her breasts. God, those breasts—they made his mouth water. He forced himself to breathe, but it didn't help.

Her golden hair had fallen loose from where she'd pinned it earlier, one soft curl tumbling over her cheek. Without thinking, he reached up, his fingers brushing it away, the silky strand catching the light like a whisper of sunlight. Her face was so close now, pert and sweet, her cheeks dusted with that perfect flush, like she'd just come in from the cold.

A Christmas angel, he thought absurdly, his heart pounding harder. That's what she looked like—an angel with cheeks as rosy as ripe apples and eyes so bright they put the firelight to shame. They were green, the exact shade of fresh pears, and so vibrant it was almost startling. He'd heard once that green was the rarest eye color in the world.

She was the rarest, he realized.

It wasn't just her beauty — it was the way she was so unapologetically herself. Sweet and fierce, soft and strong, all at once. There was no pretense with her, no guarded walls. She stood before him with that mix of vulnerability and defiance that left him shaken, unsure if he wanted to shield her from the world or stand back and let her conquer it.

"Cassidy," he said, his voice low and hoarse.

She tilted her head slightly, her lashes so thick they cast shadows against her cheeks as she blinked up at him. The corner of her lips curled, that little smile that was both innocent and utterly maddening, and he felt the last of his restraint unravel.

"You're..." He shook his head, his hand lingering near her cheek. "You're something else, you know that?"

Her brows lifted slightly, a teasing challenge lighting her gaze. "Good something or bad something?"

His fingers brushed her jaw, trailing down to her chin as he held her gaze. "The best something," he said, his voice rough with sincerity.

And then, because he couldn't hold back any longer, because she was so damn rare, so unapologetically herself, he leaned in to kiss her like it was the only thing that made sense in the world.

But he never found her lips.

She pulled back.

"Tell me what happened," she interrupted, her voice breaking. "Tell me why you never texted me back. And why you keep looking at me like you want to say something but never do. Tell me why you are suddenly being shipped off and why no one seems to care."

"Because...because it doesn't matter," he said, his voice low and rough. "Nothing I say is going to change anything."

She flinched, his words hitting her square in the chest.

Duke took a step back, his gaze flickering to the window as if searching for something in the darkness beyond the lights.

"Duke," she said softly, her voice pleading now. "You hurt me. That's what matters. You played me and you don't even care."

"I do care."

"Act like it."

His chest ached at the sincerity in her tone, at the way she looked at him like she already knew he was breaking. He wanted to tell her, wanted to lay it all out—the deployment, the five years, the distance that felt like a death sentence. But the words caught in his throat, his fear of what they'd mean for both of them locking him in place.

"I'm sorry," he said finally, his voice barely above a whisper.

Her face crumpled slightly, and she shook her head, stepping even closer. "You're embarrassed...about me."

"That's not it," he said. "It's not about you."

"Then what is it?" she demanded, her frustration boiling over.

"Because if I let you in, it'll make leaving harder," he said. "Isn't it obvious? This was never meant to be a thing. I just can't fucking stop myself when I'm around you. I just want to grab you and kiss you and make you—" He stopped himself, taking a deep breath.

Cassidy's lips parted, but no words came out.

"I have to go," he said quietly, the words barely audible. "You don't understand."

And then he turned and left.

Chapter Fourteen

It was a great way to kick-off the holidays—heartbreak.

Cassidy drove with no destination in mind, the lights of DC fading behind her as the highway stretched out into the dark. Her bag sat in the passenger seat, hastily packed with whatever she could grab in the blur of her decision to leave town. Snowflakes danced in the glow of her headlights, the soft rhythm of their fall doing nothing to calm the storm raging in her chest.

She didn't even know where she was going. Anywhere but there—the White House, DC, the scene that had chewed her up and spit her out, that had let her believe, for one fleeting moment, that she had something.

Her hands gripped the steering wheel tighter as her thoughts spiraled. The last month had been a slow unraveling, but today had been the breaking point. Duke's departure. Reed's revelation. The realization that she'd been fighting so hard for something that might not even matter.

Authenticity wins. She'd repeated that mantra to herself every day since making the bet with Duke, but now it felt like a cruel joke. Duke was leaving for five years, banished for reasons she could barely wrap her head around, and she was left behind to pick up the pieces of whatever they had almost been.

She wanted to yell, to cry, to hit him for not telling her sooner.

Her mind churned with too many emotions to name. Anger, sadness, frustration. Duke was leaving, disappearing into a new post halfway across the world, and she wouldn't see him again. The month she'd spent trying to prove herself, trying to prove to him that being herself could win anyone over — including him — suddenly felt meaningless.

He won.

The thought hit her hard, a bitter realization that made her chest ache. She wasn't making it to the end of the month. She didn't belong here. And, worst of all, she didn't even have the energy to keep fighting.

Congratulations, Duke. You were right.

The snow fell heavier as she drove farther from the city, the roads quieter and darker. She didn't care. She pressed the gas harder, letting the hum of the engine drown out her thoughts.

Her phone buzzed in the cupholder, lighting up with a notification. She glanced down, her breath hitching when she saw the name.

Duke.

She snatched the phone and threw it into the back seat, the screen going dark as it hit the floor. "Not now," she said, her voice cracking. "I can't deal with you right now."

The highway blurred past, the white lines blending with the snow. She wasn't even sure how far she'd gone—an hour, maybe two. She passed signs for small towns she didn't recognize.

By the time Cassidy pulled into the rundown truck stop, the tears had dried, but the ache still gnawed at her chest like an empty stomach. She parked her car under the flickering neon sign that buzzed weakly against the dark, snow-laden night. Her breath fogged up the windshield, and she sat there for a moment, staring out at the parking lot where the only movement was the occasional plow truck pushing the snow into towering drifts.

This wasn't the escape she'd imagined. But it was all she had.

She grabbed her bag from the passenger seat, the chill of the car biting at her skin as she stepped out, her boots crunching on the gravel. The wind hit her face like a slap, stinging her cheeks as she pulled her coat tighter. Inside, the warmth hit her with a stale, greasy slap—a mix of diesel fumes, fryer oil, and burnt coffee that lingered in the air.

The waitress barely glanced up as she slid into the barstool, her apron squeaking as she dropped a menu in front of Cassidy without a word. The low hum of the television mixed with the clatter of a plate being slammed onto the counter. There was a flickering light above her head, casting long, erratic shadows on the chipped linoleum floor.

Cassidy didn't need to look around. She knew the type—truckers with rough hands and hollow eyes, a few locals nursing beers and shooting the shit about weather and politics. It was all noise, and Cassidy didn't care. She just wanted to sit and blend into the background.

She dropped her bag by the stool and slid the strap off her shoulder. The bar was surprisingly quiet for a holiday evening, everyone too tired or too drunk to put up a front. She turned her gaze toward the window. Snow fell in slow, thick flakes, covering everything in a soft, white veil. The cold, dark night beyond felt like a better place than here, and Cassidy wished she was anywhere else but stuck in this cheap hole-in-the-wall.

She tapped her fingers aimlessly on the counter as she watched the snow swirl, her mind too busy to focus on anything for long. The last few weeks — hell, the last month — flashed before her eyes. *The bet. The stupid bet.* The arguments, the unspoken things she had pretended not to notice. The kiss that had meant nothing to him. The way his words had stung, but the silence after felt worse. She remembered the look on his face the last time they spoke, the one where she knew she could break him if she tried.

She was alone. For the first time in a long while, she had no idea what to do next.

The waitress slammed a plate in front of her. Apple pie. The crust was soggy, the filling too sweet and too tart, but she didn't care. She dug in with a fork, the sweetness of it cloying in the back of her throat as she chewed mechanically. What else was there to do? The holidays weren't exactly going as planned. Hell, nothing had gone as planned.

Her phone buzzed in her pocket. She glanced at it, barely registering the message. It was a work email — something about a press release for the holiday season.

She swiped past it, not caring. And then another one popped up.

Subject: Holiday Retreat Details

Cassidy felt her heart skip. She stared at the subject line for a long beat, her finger hovering over the screen. She didn't want to open it. But she did. The email from the secretary had the coordinates for the president's private retreat in the Blue Ridge Mountains, the words somehow cheerful in contrast to her mood— *We look forward to seeing you there!*

Cassidy snorted, a bitter laugh slipping from her lips. *Yeah, I bet you do.*

She stared at the map, the pin marking the location of the retreat nestled in the mountains. It looked serene. Remote. Peaceful, even. Everything that DC wasn't.

For a second, she considered it. Running there, into the quiet, into the trees, leaving all of this behind. But she quickly shut that thought down. She didn't belong there. Not with the president's family, not with whatever posh guests would be gathered around the fire, sipping their wine and laughing about their fancy lives. Christmas was two days away. And she had nowhere to go.

This wasn't the way it was supposed to be. The holidays, the time for family and connection, had always been an afterthought for her. The loneliness, the chaos, the rush to escape—this was what it had always been. It had always been running, pretending she wasn't broken, pretending she didn't care about anything, least of all him.

But as she sat there, nursing her pie, she wondered if maybe she didn't have to keep running. Maybe it was time to stop.

Maybe she should go.

Cassidy shoved her phone into her pocket, the cold, metallic feel of it grounding her as she stood, her muscles stiff from sitting too long. The truck stop had a strange sort of quiet around it now, as if the world itself was taking a deep breath before the rush of another day. She barely glanced at her bag before she tossed it over her shoulder, the weight of it comforting and familiar.

The waitress, standing behind the counter, looked up as Cassidy approached, her tired eyes softening just a little at the sight of Cassidy's approach.

"Leaving already?" the waitress asked with a half-smile.

"Yeah," Cassidy said, returning the smile with a flicker of warmth. She reached into her wallet and pulled out a couple extra bills, slipping it onto the counter.

The waitress's eyes widened as she looked down at the bill, then back at Cassidy. "Thank you," she said, her voice soft with surprise. "You really didn't have to."

"I know," Cassidy said, her smile growing more genuine now. "But I wanted to. Merry Christmas."

"Merry Christmas," the waitress echoed, and Cassidy could see a subtle shift in her posture, a lightness in her expression.

Cassidy made her way toward the door. As she passed through, she noticed a small family sitting at a table near the exit — a father with a young son, probably around five or six, their laughter ringing through the room as the boy excitedly pointed at the Christmas tree in the corner.

"Look, Dad! It's like a real-life Christmas tree," the boy said, his face lighting up with awe.

Cassidy couldn't help but smile as she slowed her steps. She wasn't sure what drew her to them — maybe it was the pure joy on the boy's face, or maybe it was just the sudden warmth in the room that had nothing to do with the heating system.

"Hi there," she said, crouching down to the boy's level. "That's a pretty amazing tree, huh?"

The boy's face lit up even more, if that was possible. "Yeah! It's so big! Look at all the lights!"

"It sure is," Cassidy said, smiling at him. "You must be really excited for Christmas."

"I am!" he replied, his voice full of the kind of unrestrained happiness only a kid could have. "I hope Santa brings me a big toy truck."

Cassidy laughed. "I bet he will. I bet he's already got it all packed up and ready to go."

The boy's eyes widened, and he looked at his dad, his voice dropping into a conspiratorial whisper. "Do you think Santa knows I've been really, really good this year?"

Cassidy turned to the father, who chuckled softly. "He knows," he said with a wink. "Santa keeps a list, you know."

"Good," the boy said seriously, his small hands folding together as he turned his attention back to the tree.

Cassidy smiled, her heart light as she straightened up. "Merry Christmas," she said to the father, who nodded and returned the wish with a smile.

"Merry Christmas," he said, and Cassidy could hear the warmth in his voice as if it were meant just for her.

She turned to leave, her spirits buoyed by the brief, unexpected moment of connection. For the first time in what felt like forever, the world seemed a little less cold, a little less heavy. She stepped out the door, the snowy night welcoming her back like an old friend.

She slid into the driver's seat of her car, her hands wrapping around the steering wheel with purpose. The engine rumbled to life, and the soft hum of the car beneath her fingertips felt like the first sign of control she'd had in days.

She pulled out of the parking lot, the tires crunching over packed snow, and her eyes flicked to the glowing GPS on her dash—but she didn't need it. She knew exactly where she was going.

The Armstrong lodge.

Not to chase Duke. Not to beg. But because she needed answers that only that place could give her. She'd let herself be yanked around by emotion and memory, by whispers and half-truths. Not anymore. That house had history—his, the family's, maybe even hers now. If she was going to write this story, if she was going to survive it, she needed to walk straight into the heart of it. Into the house where Duke Armstrong went to disappear.

Let him try to hide. She was done hiding, too.

* * * *

Cassidy gripped the steering wheel tightly as the winding mountain road narrowed. The GPS chirped at her with precise, disembodied directions.

Outside, the mountains stood stoic and silent, snow clinging to the pine branches like breath held too long. The sun was slipping behind the peaks, casting shadows that stretched like warning signs across the windshield. The world out there was serene. Inside her car? Absolute chaos.

Cassidy hadn't packed with clarity — she'd packed like someone fleeing a crime scene. One boot, then the other. A sweater that still had the tag on it. A duffel bag crammed with random clothes and half of her essential toiletries, like she'd been dared to prepare for both a weekend getaway and an emotional breakdown. Matching socks hadn't even made the shortlist. Formality? She left that folded on the floor with the rest of her dignity.

The president's family lodge. It sounded fictional, like something out of a tabloid or a Netflix drama. A place with golden halls and buried secrets.

When the estate finally emerged from the trees, Cassidy's breath caught. The lodge was a sprawling, majestic structure of dark wood and stone, standing like a fortress against the mountains. Twinkling white lights dripped from the eaves, weaving through the bare branches of surrounding trees, and wreaths of deep green adorned every window. The grounds were blanketed in a thick layer of snow, pristine and untouched except for the soft imprints of footsteps leading to the front door. The distant sounds of laughter and music carried faintly on the wind — merriment drifting from the ice rink where children zipped by, their blades cutting through the smooth surface of the frozen pond.

Cassidy parked her car, the tires crunching over the icy gravel as she hesitated before stepping out. The evening air bit at her cheeks, and she pulled her scarf tighter around her neck. Her fingers brushed against the cold metal of the car door as she grabbed her bag, but it felt strangely heavy in her hands, like a weight she couldn't quite shake. She took a deep breath, trying to steady herself, and walked toward the front.

The stone walkway leading up to the lodge was lined with flickering lanterns and evergreen garlands, their deep green needles dusted with snow. It was idyllic—too perfect—and she couldn't shake the feeling that she was intruding on something far too grand for her to be a part of.

"Here we go—just a relaxing holiday with the president," she said under her breath, the snowflakes drifting down in soft, delicate patterns against her coat.

Before she could gather her nerves, the door swung open, revealing a warm, welcoming figure standing in the doorway.

"Miss Evans!" The voice was smooth and graceful, instantly putting Cassidy at ease. Caroline Armstrong, the First Lady and Duke's aunt, smiled brightly at her from the threshold. Her dark hair was swept into an elegant updo, the strands glimmering in the soft light spilling from the lodge behind her. She wore a shimmering golden dress that caught the light just so, its fabric catching Cassidy's eye. It was a look of quiet opulence—refined, understated, and entirely fitting for the home she stood in.

"Welcome!" Caroline said with an openness that made Cassidy feel, if only for a moment, like she was no longer the stranger in the room. "I'm so glad you made it! It's a little quieter than I'd hoped, but we're almost ready to start the festivities. A few others are still on their way, but most of the family's here."

Cassidy stepped forward, feeling suddenly self-conscious under the weight of the moment. She let out a soft exhale and gave Caroline a hug, trying to maintain the appearance of confidence despite the storm of nerves inside her.

"Thank you for having me," Cassidy said, the words sincere but tinged with the unease she couldn't quite hide.

"It's so good to see you!" Caroline replied warmly, her voice carrying a genuine sense of affection. She placed a hand on Cassidy's shoulder, giving it a reassuring pat. "I hope you're ready to dive into the madness of it all."

Cassidy managed a small smile, but the flutter in her chest only grew. "Oh, I'm sure it'll be a lot of fun. I can't wait to see what the Armstrongs do when they aren't running the country."

Caroline laughed, her eyes twinkling as she leaned in, as if to share a secret. "That's the spirit! And don't worry—we'll make sure you feel at home here. I'll introduce you to everyone. They're all a bit…much, but you'll fit right in."

Cassidy nodded, her throat tight, but somehow the warmth in Caroline's voice was enough to soften the edges of her anxiety. Still, as she stepped inside, the gilded glow of the lodge enveloped her, and the moment settled back in.

The interior of the lodge was everything Cassidy had imagined and more. The grand foyer stretched high into vaulted ceilings, the beams above exposed and dark, adding an earthy, rustic elegance to the polished opulence of the room. A massive stone fireplace crackled and roared with fire in the center of the room, sending a warm, amber glow across the polished wood floors. The scent of pine, cinnamon, and freshly baked cookies wafted through the air, creating a feeling of home — comforting and entirely out of reach for someone like her.

Cassidy's eyes drifted over the crowd, but the awe she had felt when first walking into the grand lodge quickly faded. The Armstrong family was everywhere — polished, powerful, and impossibly perfect. They looked like a living, breathing political dynasty, each figure impeccably put together — tailored suits, designer dresses, perfectly coiffed hair — and Cassidy felt small. Too bright. Too out of place. Her simple black dress and unruly hair felt like a stark contrast to the effortless elegance around her.

Her chest thumped as she moved through the sea of strangers, each one seemingly more confident, more poised than the last. She could feel their eyes on her — polite smiles, sharp glances, quiet murmurs that drifted through the air like whispers. *Who is she? Why is she here?* she could almost hear them ask.

"Cassidy."

The voice cut through her thoughts, sharp and familiar. She turned quickly, a flash of recognition in her eyes, only to find Thomas Reed approaching her with an expression she couldn't quite decipher. It was a mixture of relief and wariness, like someone walking on fragile ground.

"You made it," he said, his tone thick with a careful effort to sound casual. His smile was tight, though, more out of habit than genuine warmth.

"Yep," Cassidy replied, forcing a smile of her own. "I'm here. For better or worse."

Reed let out a dry chuckle, his smile flickering for just a moment. "Try for better," he said, giving her a pointed look. "And try not to cause any trouble, Miss Evans. The president's hoping to keep us all on the same page through the New Year, if this works out."

Cassidy nodded stiffly, her stomach tightening in response. She could feel the entire room bearing down on her. "Noted," she said, her voice hollow as she glanced around the room.

Reed's voice continued in a quick, practiced cadence, running through the schedule for the weekend — dinners, outings, family traditions. Cassidy nodded along mechanically, but her mind was elsewhere. She wasn't listening to him. She was scanning the crowd, searching for one familiar face.

And it wasn't anywhere in sight.

At his own family's Christmas.

The thought made her stomach churn as she searched the crowd again, trying to ignore the way her pulse quickened at the absence of the one person she hadn't been able to shake from her mind. The warm glow of the lodge, the laughter that echoed in the background, all of it was still there, but it felt like a mask — a polished, carefully constructed mask. Behind it was something sharp, jagged, and unfamiliar — the same ache in her chest that had been there since the last time she saw him.

Her mind kept replaying the punch. Reed's fist. Duke's face. The kiss that had seemed like it might be the start of something beautiful, only to be shattered in an instant. All of that for nothing, she thought bitterly. All of that and now...

Duke hadn't said a word to her after that night. Not one. He'd just turned and walked out, leaving her with broken trust.

A part of her wanted him to stay away. Another part of her, the one that was still holding on to the thread of hope, couldn't shake the feeling that he would appear soon enough. It was inevitable. She would have to face him eventually.

And when she did, she wasn't sure which version of him would show up. The man she'd kissed, or the man who'd let her go without a second thought.

* * * *

Dinner wasn't just a meal — it was material.

Cassidy had barely settled into her seat at the end of the table when the president's sister, Lila Armstrong Sinclair — elegant, ageless, and terrifying in the way only political royalty could be — rose to her feet with a crystal glass in hand.

"All right, everyone," she said with a warm, polished smile that belonged on a campaign poster. "Before the wine starts speaking for us, let's take a moment to welcome a few familiar and not-so-familiar faces."

A chorus of polite laughter followed, the kind Cassidy was learning to recognize as the Armstrong version of a warning shot.

Lila gestured elegantly up the table. "Senator Mills, always a thrill. Claire and Joel, I admire the commitment to showing up even with the twins melting down before dessert. Harris, we'll skip the gap year jokes — for now. Elaine, thank you for running the entire family while the rest of us pretend we're busy."

Soft laughter. The kind that floats just above suspicion.

"And of course," Lila continued, placing a well-manicured hand on Cassidy's shoulder with the flair of a magician revealing a new act, "we're delighted to have Cassidy Evans with us tonight."

Every head turned in her direction. Every smile tightened. Suddenly Cassidy noticed the two empty seats beside her all the way down at her end of the table.

"She's the journalist writing an article on the president," Lila added, voice lilting with the kind of warm amusement that carried consequences. "So try not to say anything you wouldn't want appearing in print."

A few laughs. A few uncomfortable glances. One very pointed toast in her direction.

"And, Cassidy," Lila said with a slight tilt of her glass, "this is my nephew Ethan—who has, miraculously, arrived mostly sober and wearing shoes. A win for all of us."

Ethan, seated directly across from Cassidy, smirked as if the night had just gotten interesting.

"A pleasure," he said, eyes fixed on Cassidy with an interest that wasn't subtle and absolutely wasn't professional.

Cassidy smiled, the way you smile at a fire alarm that hasn't gone off yet.

Ethan Armstrong looked like the kind of guy who had peaked in the final round of a college fraternity beer-pong tournament and just...stayed there. Effortlessly handsome in a way that felt like it had been passed down with the family yacht, he wore a tailored sweater and high-end jeans like they were casual afterthoughts— *Oh, this old thing? Just something I keep around in case of polo.*

And just like that, the meal began. The knives hadn't touched the food, but they were already out.

Cassidy scanned the room as conversations sparked and laughter flowed like wine. Every gesture, every offhand remark, every sideways glance between the Armstrongs—it all meant something. These weren't just relatives around a table. They were legacy holders, power shapers, the quiet architects of the president's image.

She watched the way Duke's aunt gently corrected someone's story, the way his cousin slipped into political anecdotes like he'd been born on a campaign trail. It was all useful. Every moment peeled back a layer of their world and where the president came from—what shaped him, who protected him, how much of him had been choreographed before he ever stepped into the spotlight.

It was the kind of feast that felt like something straight out of a holiday special, all festive and full of promise. But Cassidy could hardly appreciate it, her stomach twisting as she poked at the edges of her food, the roast beef and mashed potatoes far less satisfying than they should have been.

The atmosphere around her felt so perfect—too perfect. The Armstrong family was everywhere, cousins, aunts, uncles, all laughing and talking in low voices, their conversation flowing easily. Some of them had the same dark hair, the same gray eyes.

It was then that a small voice interrupted her thoughts.

"Can I sit next to you, Cassidy?" A little girl with wild curls and big brown eyes tugged at the sleeve of her dress.

Cassidy turned to find Abigail, one of Duke's younger cousins, standing there with a shy smile. Cassidy's heart softened immediately. "Of course, sweetie," she said, patting the seat next to her.

Abigail beamed and climbed up, her small hands fidgeting nervously with the edge of her dress. Cassidy couldn't help but smile back as the little girl settled in, her energy infectious. She was only seven, but she seemed like a little grown-up, with her polite mannerisms and mature way of speaking.

"Is the food good?" Abigail asked, her eyes wide with curiosity.

Cassidy nodded. "It's really good. Do you like mashed potatoes?"

Abigail scrunched up her nose. "I like my mashed potatoes, not these ones," she said, pointing to the mound of creamy potatoes on her plate. "They're too soft."

Cassidy laughed, shaking her head. "You're a tough critic, Abigail."

Abigail smiled proudly, showing off a tiny gap in her front teeth. Then, without warning, the little girl leaned forward in her chair to reach for her juice. As she did, her elbow nudged the glass, sending a stream of cranberry juice spilling over the edge and onto Cassidy's lap.

"Oh no! I'm sorry!" Abigail's eyes widened in horror.

Cassidy looked down at her lap, the red stain barely noticeable in the fabric of her black dress. Then she saw Abigail's face—wide-eyed and panicked—and something inside her softened.

"It's okay, Abigail," Cassidy said, smiling. "Don't worry about it. We can't even see it."

"But I spilled it on you," Abigail said, her voice tiny, almost on the verge of tears.

Cassidy leaned over, giving her a wink. "It's really okay. No harm done. And you know what? This just gives me a great excuse to get up and get a napkin."

Abigail's face brightened. "You're not mad?"

"Not at all," Cassidy said, laughing. "I'm sure I'll spill something worse on myself soon."

Abigail gave a sheepish grin, and Cassidy could see that her earlier nervousness had faded. As she excused herself to get a napkin from the nearby sideboard, she started to feel just a little more comfortable. Cassidy dabbed at the stain, and as she looked up, she found herself surrounded by the sounds of laughter, the clinking of silverware, and the low murmur of conversation. The Armstrongs were in their element, relaxed and at ease in this luxurious setting. But here, with little Abigail beside her, Cassidy couldn't help but feel a flicker of warmth, the feeling that maybe—just maybe—she was starting to belong.

When she returned to the table, Abigail squeezed her hand. "I'll be extra careful next time."

Cassidy smiled, feeling her heart lighten a bit. "I know you will," she said, ruffling the little girl's hair. "And now we have a funny story to tell."

As the evening wore on, Cassidy's tension started to loosen just a little—she could feel her shoulders defrosting, her grip on her fork relaxing, even laughing here and there, as though life wasn't an ongoing dumpster fire. But of course, all good things come to an end. And in this case, it came in the form of dessert.

"So, you've been working with Duke," Ethan said, leaning in with that *oh, I know* look, the kind that made Cassidy's stomach do a backflip. "What's that like?"

Cassidy froze for just a second, her brain doing a quick inventory of things she wanted to say, none of which involved the actual truth. *What's it like working with the guy who broke my heart so badly, you could probably still feel the cracks two counties over? Oh, it's fine. Really fine. Totally fine.*

"It's...fine," she said, making the word come out like it had been dredged up from the bottom of a lake.

"Just fine?" Ethan pressed, grinning like he was about to win a prize. "You hate him yet?"

The question landed like a punch. Cassidy could feel heat creeping up her neck and into her cheeks, a perfect cocktail of frustration and shame bubbling just below the surface. How could she answer without giving away too much? How could she not reveal that the man was the emotional equivalent of a tornado that had destroyed her life in about ten minutes, only to leave without even a sorry?

"He's a legend, all right," Joel said, leaning back with a grin that screamed 'I know more than you think'. "But you definitely don't wanna be on the wrong side of him, that's for sure."

Cassidy swallowed hard, the sarcasm rising up in her chest like bile. *Right. Because nothing says legend like an emotionally unavailable, self-absorbed heartbreaker.* But she didn't say it, because saying it out loud might have meant she was still — *ugh* — thinking about him.

"Man's a legend," Ethan agreed. "Even Joel thinks so."

Cassidy fought the urge to throw her glass of wine in his face. "Can we stop saying legend?" she snapped, her knuckles turning white as she gripped her fork with the intensity of someone trying to keep themselves from throwing a plate.

The table went quiet for just a second, before all the cousins turned toward her. She immediately ducked her head and forced a smile, because God forbid she be the weird one at the table.

The food in front of her was exquisite. Too exquisite, actually. The mashed potatoes were so smooth they could've been whipped cream. The turkey was golden and perfectly roasted. The honeyed carrots could have been grown in some magical garden that only the rich and powerful got to visit. The gravy? Rich and spiced. It was enough to make her stomach churn, only it wasn't the food—oh no, it was the conversation.

"I don't really have any stories," she said, as flat as she could manage. "We work in different areas."

She felt that sentence immediately. It was the most boring thing she could have said. But at least it didn't involve any personal revelations that would make her sound like a soap opera.

"Smart answer," said Ethan, his eyes narrowing suspiciously. "A real politician's response."

Cassidy nodded absently, wishing she could melt into her chair like a puddle of well-buttered mashed potatoes. She felt like a fraud. She didn't belong here, with these people who seemed to understand Duke. To idolize him. She could barely keep the bitterness out of her throat as the conversation about him continued. He was everywhere. He was the ghost at the table. The one everyone said about while she was just…stuck with it.

"Yeah, a real legend," she said under her breath, stabbing at a carrot like it had just insulted her.

And then, as if summoned by her thoughts, she saw him. Not Duke, of course, but someone like him. One of the cousins, dark and imposing with those same sharp gray eyes that felt like they could pierce right through her. Cassidy fought the urge to make an obscene gesture. His presence was a reminder of everything she couldn't have, everything she shouldn't want. And yet, there it was.

She shifted her attention to her plate, her gaze darting nervously around the table. She could feel the conversation swirling around her, but it was as if her own personal soundtrack was playing in her head. Did he ever care? Did I mean anything? Was I just a blip in his day, another conquest to check off before he moved on?

The questions echoed, too loud to ignore, drowning out even the polite chatter of the Armstrongs. But she wouldn't — couldn't — let herself give in to it. Not here. Not in front of these people. Not in front of him.

So, instead, Cassidy put down her fork, forced a smile, and focused on something much more important — not crying in front of a bunch of strangers who didn't know the first thing about the wreckage Duke had left behind.

After dinner, the Armstrongs and their guests gathered near the towering Christmas tree in the lodge's main room, their laughter and chatter a soft hum that filled the space. The tree, a masterpiece of sparkling ornaments and glimmering lights, cast a gentle glow across the room, bathing everything in a warm, golden hue. The scent of pine mingled with the sweet bite of cinnamon and the faint smokiness of the fire crackling in the hearth, the heat from the flames a stark contrast to the biting mountain cold just beyond the windows. The room buzzed with energy — comforting, festive, and yet, to Cassidy, it all felt like a world apart.

She stood against the wall, cradling her glass of mulled wine a little too tightly, the warmth of the drink slipping over her tongue in slow, spiced waves, but it did little to thaw the tension that knotted in her chest. The wine was sweet, like liquid Christmas, but it felt hollow — a Christmas card with no message. She scanned the room, watching the Armstrongs — their perfectly pressed suits, their polished smiles, their effortless confidence. They moved like a unit, a living, breathing machine of wealth and power, each conversation a dance of inside jokes and shared history, and Cassidy felt herself on the outside, a stranger to their warmth.

Her gaze slid to the fire, the embers crackling as they gave off a fleeting burst of heat before settling back into their steady glow. Every inch of the room felt out of reach. Even the air, thick with the scent of pine, felt as though it belonged to them.

Cassidy's pulse jumped at the president's voice before she even saw him.

"Thomas, my friend, so glad you could join us this evening."

It carried across the room effortlessly — warm, commanding, impossible to ignore. Reed offered a polite smile that didn't reach his eyes.

"Always a pleasure," he said, flat. "Nothing says festive like federal policy over whiskey."

The president chuckled, lifting his glass like a man who already knew the room was his. "But what we're really waiting on is that story. We'll see it before the January doom polls, won't we?"

Cassidy's stomach clenched.

The story.

Months of research. Quiet interviews, subtle observation, staying late at press briefings just to catch a passing glance or offhand comment. She'd built the scaffolding, yes — but this holiday, this curated, intimate access to the inner circle, was supposed to be the final chapter. The payoff. The close.

And every free moment, she was working on it — editing by the fire, scribbling notes on napkins, rewriting transitions in her head between conversations. But the closer it got to being real — being read — the more her chest tightened. These weren't just sources. They were subjects. Gatekeepers. Judges.

Cassidy was just about to slip away, the evening pressing down on her, when Ethan stepped into her path, blocking out the soft glow of the Christmas tree. The flickering lights from the tree caught in his dark hair, casting shadows that seemed to make his presence even more imposing.

"Hey, you," Ethan said.

Cassidy didn't miss the glint in his eyes — the kind that said he knew exactly how attractive he was, and that he weaponized it like a seasoned hobbyist.

"*Hola*," she replied, forcing a smile. She quickly tried to escape into small talk. "Enjoying the party?"

Ethan shrugged, but his eyes never left hers. "Can't complain." He reached into the bag hanging at his side and pulled out a bottle of whiskey. "But I think it could be better if you tried this." He held up the bottle, its label sleek and elegant. "Special batch. Aged twelve years. Part of the Armstrong tradition. When in Rome..."

Cassidy hesitated, the glass of her mulled wine still in her hand. She wasn't a whiskey person, not really — not after everything. The thought of drinking anything stronger made her stomach churn a little. She took a deep breath, trying to smile politely. "I'm good, thanks. Really. I should get to bed."

Ethan's smile only widened, and he leaned in closer, his presence almost magnetic. "Come on, don't be a spoil sport. It's only ten. One drink won't hurt. Besides, after working with my folks all month, you deserve it."

He uncorked the bottle with a satisfying pop, and the rich aroma of whiskey hit her before he even poured it.

His smile was smooth, a little too smooth. Too practiced. He leaned in with the charm turned up to eleven, the kind of grin that made women say *"I know better,"* and then immediately forget it.

He wasn't just flirting — he was circling.

"Bottoms up," he said, handing her a glass and taking the mulled wine from her.

She didn't want to cause a scene, so she relented.

"I'm sorry, Ethan." She tried again, firmer this time. "I am really beat."

But Ethan was relentless, his tone more playful than apologetic. "Oh, come on, Cassidy. Just one. It'll be fun, promise."

Cassidy gripped the glass, the liquid shimmering up at her like a dare. She was about to make another attempt to back away when a voice sliced through the conversation, low, cold, and familiar.

"She said no."

Cassidy froze. Her heart slammed into her chest as she turned, and there he was. Duke. Standing in the doorway to the grand room, framed by the flickering firelight, his broad shoulders blocking the entrance like a force of nature. His jaw was tight, his eyes narrowed, burning with a heat that made Cassidy's pulse stutter. He didn't even look at her. Not once.

"Enough," Duke said, his voice low and dripping with venom. "Leave her alone."

Ethan blinked, clearly startled, his face shifting from surprise to irritation in an instant. He opened his mouth, but Duke was already turning away, walking off with quick, purposeful strides, his back tense and muscles rippling beneath his shirt. Not a single glance in Cassidy's direction. Not even a second of acknowledgment.

"And that's my cousin for you," Ethan said with a bitter chuckle. "Cheerful lad."

Cassidy was left standing there, frozen, her hand still clutching the glass. Her mind raced — What the hell just happened?

He arrived — *when*?

One thing was for sure — she hadn't expected him to be so…possessive.

Overprotective.

She wanted to scream.

* * * *

Cassidy slipped out of the front hallway, her breath quickening as she rounded the corner toward the entry foyer. Her hands were already fumbling for her scarf when a quiet voice spoke up behind her.

"Heading out?"

She turned to find one of the lodge staff offering her coat with a polite smile. The woman didn't ask questions. Just held the wool neatly by the shoulders and gave Cassidy the briefest look of understanding —

as if she'd seen other guests, other women, who'd needed air between champagne toasts.

"Thanks," Cassidy murmured, pulling the coat around herself, wrapping her scarf tighter with slightly shaking fingers.

She had one hand on the heavy door handle when it opened behind her again.

"You always leave parties early?" Ethan's voice.

Of course.

Cassidy stepped outside without answering, letting the blast of icy air shock her system. Her boots crunched softly on the stone as she walked off the porch and around the lodge's side path, toward the edge of the forest line where shadows overtook the curated landscaping.

She was nearly out of sight when she heard him again, just behind her.

"Cassidy, hey—" Ethan's voice was low and laced with that drunk-but-smooth thing he did. "Don't walk away. Not yet."

"I'm not walking away," she said without turning around. "I'm walking outside. Alone."

"You're always alone," he said, catching up to her, his breath misting in the cold. "Even in a room full of people. Kind of your thing, huh?"

Cassidy exhaled slowly, willing herself not to say what she wanted to. Get bent probably wouldn't go over well with Aunt Lila.

"I'm here to work, Ethan."

"Sure you are," he said, grinning like a man who'd never once been told no in a meaningful way. "But come on, I see the way you watch everyone. You're not just reporting. You're feeling it. All of it. I think maybe you like being inside the machine more than you let on."

Cassidy turned, fixing him with a flat stare. "Are you drunk?"

Ethan's smile widened. "Are you single?"

Her laugh was sharp and humorless. "Oh my God."

He stepped closer. Not threatening — playful, in that infuriating Armstrong way. "I'm just saying...it's a big house. Lot of empty space. You don't have to spend the night alone."

Cassidy blinked. "Ethan, I would rather sleep in a snowbank and let the wolves eat me, slowly."

And right on cue —

"Ethan James Armstrong."

Aunt Lila's voice cut through the night like glass cracking under pressure. Cassidy turned to see her standing at the edge of the porch, her coat wrapped tight, expression icy enough to make the moon flinch.

Ethan straightened like a boy caught smoking behind the chapel. "Aunt Lila — "

"Inside. Now. It's time for the reading."

He blinked. "The what?"

"The Armstrong holiday tradition," Lila said crisply. "You know, the one your grandfather created before you were born and that we do every year? The one you're late for?"

Ethan looked back at Cassidy, gave her one last grin — this one duller, like a charm switch had finally shorted out — and sauntered off with his hands in his pockets.

Lila didn't look at Cassidy. She just tilted her head slightly. "I do hope you're not writing him too kindly."

Then she disappeared back inside.

Cassidy retreated into the darkened side path. She didn't know how long she walked, but with every step, she felt everything inside her slowly loosen. The crisp cold was biting at her cheeks, but it felt good — alive, in a way the warmth of the lodge never could. She was alone here, with only the sound of her own breathing.

She made her way down the winding path toward the lake. It felt like the right place to be — somewhere far from the noise, from the expectations, from him. Even the thought of Duke caused a tight knot in her stomach, but she forced it down. She wasn't here to think about him. She was here to breathe. To clear her head. To escape.

Cassidy drew in a long, steady breath, letting the icy air fill her lungs, watching her breath plume into the dark. The world was still and silent, the stars above like pinpricks in the deep, endless sky. Here, in this frozen world, she could forget for a moment. Forget about the pressure, about the forced smiles, about Ethan and his relentless charm. Forget about everything but the peace that came with the solitude.

The lake stretched out before her, dark and silent, the surface glittering with frost. Cassidy stood at the edge, gazing across the frozen water, her eyes unfocused. The icy expanse seemed endless, a reflection of how small and insignificant she felt in this moment, this strange, in-between place. The snow had softened the world, making it feel like a dream, like she was walking in the quiet middle of the night, suspended in a moment that wasn't real and couldn't be held onto.

Tomorrow was Christmas Eve. She should've been excited, caught up in the holiday spirit. But instead, all she could feel was the day pressing against her, the expectations, the forced cheer.

She wanted to go home. But that wasn't possible, was it? Not now. She couldn't escape this.

Her hands were cold now, too cold to feel, and she stuffed them into her coat pockets, feeling the emptiness there. There was no one to talk to. No one who would understand the mess swirling in her chest, the tangled knot of emotions that had formed ever since Duke had walked away without a word, without an explanation.

Cassidy blinked up at the sky, the moon glowing soft above her. Snowflakes kissed her cheeks, her lashes. Everything was quiet — too quiet, as if the world itself had given up trying to speak.

Maybe it *was* all a dream. Maybe tomorrow, when the sun rose, everything would be clearer. Maybe she could find a way to pull herself out of this numb, foggy place and make sense of what had happened, what was happening. But for now, all she could do was stand there, looking at the moonlit lake, feeling her breath mix with the cold air, and wishing for a life that wasn't so heavy.

The snow fell around her, soft and light, and she felt it settle on her shoulders, the weight of it gentle. It was peaceful here, in the stillness. But peace didn't mean contentment. It only meant silence. And silence never fixed anything.

It never made the hurt go away.

Cassidy turned away from the lake and started walking along the path leading back to the lodge. But before she could take another step, she heard it — the crunch of boots in the snow, slow and deliberate.

She didn't need to turn to know who it was.

"There's my favorite runner." His voice, deep and familiar, sliced through the stillness.

"And that makes you my favorite follower," she said, her voice sharper than she intended. She started walking again, getting away from him.

"Maybe *least* favorite now." He followed behind.

"No." It came out sounding defensive, brittle, but she couldn't help it. She was tired of the game. Tired of the pretending.

"Liar." His voice had that familiar edge of frustration, the one that always seemed to linger when they talked. The one that made everything feel like it was just on the verge of snapping.

Cassidy could feel the burn in her throat, the heat of anger building. "Why are you here? To annoy me, I'm guessing?"

"Yes, I live to annoy."

"You do seem keen on wasting my time." She shot, spinning on her heel to face him.

Which was a mistake.

Duke halted, now silhouetted against the pale glow of the snow-covered trees. His hands were shoved deep into his jacket pockets, his face shadowed but still striking in the moonlight. He looked every bit the part of the man who had built walls around himself and kept everyone — including her — at arm's length.

For a long moment, neither of them said anything. Cassidy just stared at him, feeling everything that had gone unsaid between them.

"Try to answer honestly — why do you actually always follow me?" she asked quietly, her voice trembling slightly. "Because every time I go for air, I have a shadow. And that's you."

Duke didn't answer immediately. He just looked at her, and for the first time in what felt like forever, Cassidy saw something flicker in his eyes — hesitation, maybe. A vulnerability he was too stubborn to show.

"I...can't stay away," he said finally, his voice rough. "I like being with you. And that's the simple truth."

Cassidy's breath hitched, her chest tightening with an emotion she couldn't place. The hurt, the anger, the confusion — all of it swirled together inside her, until she couldn't keep it in any longer.

"I wish you told me the truth," she said, her voice cracking. "From the beginning."

His jaw set, but he didn't look away. "You wouldn't believe me. No one else did."

She exhaled sharply, shaking her head. "Try me. I'm a good listener. Journalist, remember?"

Duke's eyes flickered to the ground. He opened his mouth, closed it again, and when he finally spoke, his voice was low — barely above a whisper.

"Well, let's start with the fact that I'm being deployed," he said, and it felt like a weight had dropped onto her chest. "To Erbil. My flight out is on Boxing Day, which means I have two days left to say goodbye to my family."

"So I've heard." Cassidy's stomach dropped, and she opened her mouth, but the words caught. "Seems sudden."

"Got that right."

"So, why?" she asked. "Why now? What happened?"

He exhaled sharply, and the cold air turned his breath into visible clouds. When he spoke again, it was with a bitterness that made Cassidy's heart ache.

"Because the president wants me gone. Out of sight, out of mind. The Armstrong name doesn't need me to stick around."

"Something happened."

"Yup."

"What?"

Duke looked up at her then, his eyes filled with something that she couldn't read. "Another simple truth. I screwed up," he admitted, his voice rough, like he was forcing the words out. "And now everyone sees me as that guy. The guy who couldn't keep it together. The guy who tarnished the family name. And some mistakes are too big to forgive."

"What did you do?"

"Does it matter? I'm wild. I do bad things. I'm selfish and I'm a fuck-up."

Cassidy took a step closer to him, her heart aching at the rawness in his voice. "Duke, that's not you," she said.

His face was shadowed, his gaze distant. "I don't like this person everyone seems to think I am."

"No." Cassidy stepped closer, her voice strong despite the way her heart was breaking. "I don't see you that way."

"How do you know? You barely know me."

"I just know."

He looked at her, his gaze haunted, his past pressing down on him like a physical force. "I don't know how to fix any of it," he said. "I don't know how to be the person you think I am. The person you want me to be."

Cassidy's breath caught, and she reached out, her fingers trembling as she touched his arm. "I wish you'd tell me more."

He closed his eyes briefly, as if her words were too much to bear. And for the first time, Cassidy saw it—

the vulnerability that he had buried deep inside, the hurt that was driving everything.

"The way this works—when you take an oath. I'm loyal to my uncle. And, I've gotta be a big boy now and take my lumps."

"Five years in Iraq," she said softly. "Seems harsh. Can't you fight it?"

"Not a chance."

"Can you change anything?"

Duke's chest rose and fell with uneven breaths, and finally, he met her eyes again. "You make me want to be better," he said, his voice thick with emotion. "That's the only thing I can change."

"I could wait," she said. "For you to find your way back."

"No, I wouldn't ask that. Don't even say it."

"But I—" she started.

"No," he interrupted. "Don't. It will only make this harder. Let me walk you back."

He offered her his arm, which she took.

Under the moonlight, with the snow falling gently around them, it was the first time honesty came first.

Duke led Cassidy down the winding path back to the lodge, the distant glow of its windows barely visible through the trees. The moonlight spilled over the snowy landscape, and the air was still, save for the faint rustle of the breeze and the sound of their footsteps. Cassidy clung to his arm, her fingers curled around his jacket sleeve, and for a moment, neither of them spoke.

The silence wasn't heavy or awkward—it was a quiet understanding, a space where their words lingered without needing to be said. Cassidy's heart ached as she walked beside him, her chest tight with what they hadn't figured out yet, and what time seemed so determined to steal from them.

The snow fell in soft whispers around them, the world hushed and cloaked in silver. The lodge was still a fair walk away, only the faintest glow of its warm lights visible through the snow-draped pines.

Duke glanced down at her, his dark eyes flickering with something she couldn't quite name. "You're shivering," he said, his voice a gruff murmur that sent a ripple of warmth through her.

"I'm fine," Cassidy started to protest, but before she could finish, he slipped his arm free and shrugged off his coat. He draped it over her shoulders in one swift motion, the heavy weight of it settling around her like an embrace.

The scent of him—leather, pine, something raw and distinctly Duke—wrapped around her, making her breath hitch. She tugged the coat tighter, the warmth of it sinking into her skin. "Better," he said, his voice low, almost reverent.

Cassidy tilted her head up, her gaze tracing the hard lines of his profile. The sharp angle of his jaw, the faint shadow of stubble, the tension etched into the corners of his mouth. "Do you always carry the weight of the world on your shoulders?" she asked softly, her words breaking through the quiet like a thread of light.

Duke let out a low laugh, though there was no humor in it. "It's part of the job."

"No," she said, her voice firm but gentle. "It's part of you."

He stopped abruptly, turning to face her. The moonlight caught his face, illuminating the raw emotion in his eyes. Cassidy's breath caught as she saw it — something unguarded. It was a side of him he rarely let anyone see, and it made her chest tighten.

For a moment, she thought he might speak, let her in completely. Instead, his hand rose, his fingers brushing a stray curl from her cheek. The touch was achingly tender, his knuckles grazing her skin as if he were memorizing the shape of her face. When his hand lingered, she leaned into it without thinking, her heart thundering in her chest.

"I wish I could promise you something," he said, his voice barely above a whisper. "Something more than this. But I can't."

Cassidy's throat collapsed, her gaze locked on his. "What if you could?" she said. "Would you?"

His lips curved into a faint, almost broken smile. "I've never made those types of promises before — but something about you..." He trailed off, his thumb brushing her cheek.

"I feel it too," she admitted, her hand rising to cover his where it rested on her face.

Duke's eyes darkened, his breath catching. "You're the opposite of me. And I like that. I think I need that. I've started realizing...wouldn't I be a better man if I were a little more like you?"

Cassidy's heart fluttered, a bittersweet smile tugging at her lips. "Well, how nice of you to say."

His lips twitched in response, the smallest hint of humor breaking through his intensity. "That night I watched you talking about art museums with Sven," he continued, his voice rough with emotion. "It just hit me...why didn't I ever do that with you? Why didn't I take you on a proper date?"

She raised an eyebrow, her smile growing. "Because I annoyed you?"

"You're the opposite of annoying," he said, his voice low and heated. "Thrilling, yes. Maddening, sometimes." His hand shot up, threading into her hair, pulling just enough to tilt her head back, his breath ghosting across her mouth. "I always wanted a girl who'd get my blood pumping and didn't buy into my bullshit."

"You always wanted a girl who went undercover at protests?"

"And ran from me faster than I could catch her."

His eyes raked over her face—lips, cheeks, eyes, back to lips—and lingered there like he was fighting something primal.

"What do you really want?"

"I don't know," he said, voice tight and gravel-edged. "I've been trying to stay away from you since the moment you walked into that goddamn briefing room. You don't even fucking know what you're doing to me."

Cassidy's breath came in shallow bursts. Her skin lit up under his touch. "Then stop watching," she whispered. "Start doing."

And that was it. That was all it took.

He kissed her like a man starved—hard and full of heat, like he was finally really marking her as his. He was fierce and hungry, his hands gripping her waist, her back, her hips like he didn't know what to touch first. He wanted it all. She gasped against him, and he deepened the kiss, tongue sliding against hers, a low groan vibrating from his chest into her body like a threat and a promise.

She moaned into his mouth. He didn't stop—didn't ask—just kissed her harder, one hand in her hair, the other splayed across her lower back, pressing her flush against him. She could feel everything—his heat, his need, the full weight of him anchoring her in place like the world might end if he let go.

"I want you so fucking bad it hurts," he said, in between flicks of his tongue. "But if I keep touching you..."

"Then don't stop."

He stared at her like she was the thing that would ruin him. Like he wanted to be ruined.

But then—his hand slid from her waist. His body pulled back, just barely. Barely enough to make her ache from the absence.

"I can't. Not like this. Not yet."

The air felt colder without him against her. She blinked, dazed, lips still tingling, heart still racing.

"Let me walk you back."

Cassidy nodded, jaw tight, breath still unsteady.

They walked side by side, the space between them humming with everything they hadn't finished. Everything they'd just started.

And everything that was going to burn.

When they reached the porch steps, Duke slowed, his hand brushing hers like he wasn't ready to let her go.

Cassidy turned to face him, the cold air tightening around them, the heat between them lingering like static.

He took her hand—not just held it, but really held it, like it meant something—and brought it to his lips. The kiss he pressed to her knuckles wasn't soft. It was reverent. Final. Like a man saying goodbye to something he never truly got to have.

His eyes found hers, unreadable and intense. The kind of look that made time feel like it was holding its breath.

"You're everything I didn't know I needed," he said, low and wrecked. "And I hate that I can't give you more."

Cassidy's throat clenched. Her fingers curled tighter around his like they could anchor her there forever. "You already did," she murmured, barely trusting her voice.

He let go slowly, like his body didn't want to obey the command.

Then he stepped back — into the dark, into the cold, into the space between them that now felt unbearably vast.

Cassidy turned before she could shatter, slipping inside and closing the door behind her with trembling fingers.

She didn't look back.

But she felt him out there, still watching. Still burning.

And she knew...this wasn't the kind of goodbye that ended anything.

Not really.

Chapter Fifteen

Christmas Eve

The scent of fresh coffee and cinnamon filled the sprawling kitchen as Cassidy hovered near the edge of the counter, clutching a steaming mug. She tried to stay out of the way, her gaze darting toward the Armstrong family as they moved with easy grace, exchanging polite laughter and quiet conversation.

She felt like a trespasser in their holiday tableau, an interloper amid the polished perfection. The kind of family that didn't just hang ornaments — they curated heirlooms. The kind that hosted Christmas in a mountain retreat so flawless it looked like a holiday movie set.

Cassidy shifted uncomfortably as she overheard snippets of their conversations. Most of it was harmless chatter about the schedule for the day — a snowshoe trek, lunch by the firepit — but her ears caught the occasional murmur that sent her stomach twisting.

"...interesting choice to bring her here."

"...isn't she that journalist? The one hanging around Duke?"

"She's...unconventional."

Unconventional. The word stuck like a thorn. Cassidy kept her head down, pretending to sip her coffee as the whispers pricked at her nerves. She told herself she didn't care what they thought, but the tightness in her chest said otherwise.

"Good morning."

She looked up to find Ethan standing in front of her, a charming smile on his too-perfect face. Dressed in a trendy fitted sweater and high-fashion ripped jeans, he had the effortless confidence of someone who had never been told no in his life.

"Morning," Cassidy replied cautiously.

"So, Miss Cassidy," he said, his smile widening. "The infamous journalist. Miss writer-extraordinaire."

She tensed at the words, but Ethan didn't seem to notice. He leaned casually against the counter, his eyes sparkling with interest.

"I read your article on the disaster relief efforts," he continued. "Really impressive work. The kind of thing that gets people talking."

"Thank you," Cassidy said, trying to gauge his sincerity.

"So," he said, leaning in slightly, "how does a journalist like you end up spending Christmas with us mere mortals? Really, how did this happen?"

She forced a laugh, keeping her voice light. "I think it was a scheduling mix-up."

Ethan chuckled, but his eyes lingered on her for a beat too long. "Well, I told Aunt Lila last night—we're lucky to have you. Duke's lucky, too."

Cassidy's smile faltered. "What do you mean?"

Before Ethan could answer, a new voice cut through the room.

"Ethan."

Cassidy turned to see Duke standing in the doorway, his dark gaze fixed on his cousin. He didn't move, but the tension in his stance was palpable.

Ethan straightened, his grin undeterred. "Morning, Duke. Just getting to know your lady friend."

"Good," Duke said flatly. "Now you know her. Move along."

The chill in his tone made Cassidy's cheeks flush, though she wasn't sure if it was embarrassment or anger. Ethan, however, seemed entirely unfazed.

"Well, Miss Cassidy," Ethan said, turning back to her, "if you need anything while you're here, just let me know. Perhaps a walk or a drink. I'm happy to entertain you."

"Thanks," Cassidy said, her voice clipped.

"Some people say I am the most entertaining cousin, if you don't count stories about Duke, that is. The legend."

Ethan gave her one last smile before strolling out of the kitchen, leaving her alone with Duke. The tension in the air was thick enough to cut.

"You don't have to scare everyone away," Cassidy said, setting her mug down with more force than necessary.

Duke's brow furrowed. "Ethan's not everyone."

"What's that supposed to mean?" she snapped, crossing her arms.

"It means he likes to collect things," Duke said, his voice sharp. "And right now, he's decided you're interesting."

Cassidy pressed her lips together, unwilling to make a scene.

"You don't know him," Duke said, stepping closer. "I do."

She opened her mouth to argue, but the sound of voices from the hallway stopped her. She caught the words "Duke" and "Cassidy" and felt her stomach twist.

"...of course, it's him again."

"Can't stay out of trouble, can he?"

"She's not exactly helping his case."

The words were low, but they cut deep. Cassidy looked away, her chest tightening. She didn't need to turn around to know who was talking.

"Don't listen to them," Duke said quietly.

She forced a laugh, bitter and hollow. "Easy for you to say. You're used to it."

Duke flinched, the words hitting harder than she'd intended. For a moment, the anger drained from his face, replaced by something rawer.

"I know what they think of me," he said, his voice low. "But that doesn't mean they get to decide who you are."

Cassidy looked at him, the tension between them crackling like static. "And what about you, Duke? Who gets to decide who you are?"

For a moment, he didn't answer. His gaze dropped, his jaw tightening as if he were holding something back.

"That's not the same," he said finally, his voice rough.

"Isn't it?" she pressed. "Because from where I'm standing, it seems like you've already let them decide."

The silence between them was deafening, her words hanging heavy in the air. Duke looked at her, his expression unreadable, before stepping back.

"I'll see you later. Be good," he said quietly, turning and walking out of the kitchen.

Cassidy stared after him, her chest aching with a mix of anger and something she couldn't quite name. She wanted to chase him down, to make him see what she saw.

* * * *

The sound of soft laughter and the clink of teacups echoed through the lodge's sunlit sitting room. Cassidy sat perched on a plush armchair, her notebook balanced on her knee, trying not to feel out of place. The Armstrong women—led by the president's wife, Caroline—had invited her for morning tea. She wasn't entirely sure why, but the invitation had come with a tone that didn't leave room for refusal.

Caroline Armstrong was a force of nature. Poised, elegant, and effortlessly commanding, she had a way of making even small talk feel significant. Cassidy had expected her to be distant, to look at her with the same polite disinterest as most of the family. But instead, Caroline had spent the better part of the morning drawing Cassidy into the conversation, asking pointed questions about her work at PRN and her perspective on the president's administration.

"You've been very quiet, Cassidy," Caroline said. "What do you think about all this?"

Cassidy blinked, caught off guard. "About…what, exactly?"

Caroline smiled faintly. "Everything. The policies, the stories you cover. You're in the thick of it, aren't you? Surely you have opinions."

Cassidy hesitated, glancing around the room. The other women were watching her, some with faint curiosity, others with thinly veiled skepticism. She could feel their expectations, the unspoken rules of how she was supposed to behave.

But then she thought about the families she'd interviewed, the small-town struggles she'd fought to bring to light, the pieces she'd written that had almost been buried under politics and red tape.

"Well," Cassidy said, her voice steadying, "I think the policies coming out of the administration are strong in theory. But they're not always reaching the people who need them most."

Caroline tilted her head, intrigued. "Go on."

Cassidy leaned forward slightly, her notebook forgotten. "Take disaster relief, for example. Federal funding is crucial, but the process to access it is so bogged down in bureaucracy that by the time it reaches small towns, it's too late. These communities are left to fend for themselves. And when the media does cover it, it's always a quick story about devastation, not a follow-up on how these people rebuild — or don't."

The room was silent, the women's eyes fixed on her. Cassidy's cheeks burned, but she pressed on.

"That's why I focus on human stories," she said. "Not just the numbers, but the lives behind them. It's not always flashy or headline-worthy, but it's real. And it's what matters."

Caroline's smile widened, a glint of approval in her eyes. "You have a way with words, Cassidy. No wonder the president wanted you on his team."

Cassidy flushed. "Thank you, Mrs. Armstrong."

"Call me Caroline," she said, setting her teacup down with a decisive clink. "And tell me, are you working on anything now?"

Cassidy hesitated. "We'll, I've really just been focused on my big piece going live on New Year's Day. It's…it's only focused on the president, actually. The story has become sort of a reflection on his journey and what his leadership has meant for the country. It's interesting because I don't think we've ever had such a personal account of a president before. It's incredible he's allowed us such access."

The other women exchanged looks, murmuring softly, but Caroline's gaze remained fixed on Cassidy.

"I'd like to see it," Caroline said. "You have the draft? We have been eager to see it."

Cassidy's heart skipped. "Of course. I mean, I'd be happy to share it, but if you don't mind, it's still an early draft…and not edited or finalized."

"That's what I'd expect," Caroline said, her smile turning sly. "That's why he invited you and Thomas, after all. To smooth out the final narrative."

Cassidy nodded, trying to tamp down the rush of nerves. This was it—the opportunity she'd been waiting for.

Chapter Sixteen

Christmas Eve family traditions — a foolproof recipe for keeping things peaceful and drama-free.

That was pretty much all Cassidy could think of as she sat on the edge of the lake, fumbling with the laces of a borrowed pair of skates. The frozen lake sparkled in the afternoon light, surrounded by twinkling garlands strung along the trees. The festive atmosphere was straight out of a postcard, with steaming mugs of cider set up on tables near the firepit and holiday music floating from hidden speakers.

Cassidy tugged her scarf tighter, watching as the Armstrong family glided across the ice. They moved with an elegance that made it look effortless, as if they'd been born wearing skates. Caroline and the president skated side by side, their movements synchronized and graceful. Younger cousins zipped across the ice, their laughter ringing out as they wove between the more sedate skaters.

Cassidy felt a pang of unease. She wasn't terrible on skates, but she wasn't exactly graceful either. Still, she wasn't about to sit on the sidelines and look like she didn't belong. Not today.

"You coming, Cassidy?" Caroline called from the ice, her smile warm and encouraging.

"Absolutely," Cassidy said, forcing a grin. She finished lacing up her skates and stood, wobbling as she stepped onto the frozen surface. The ice was smooth but unforgiving, and it took all her focus just to keep her balance as she shuffled forward.

She made it a few feet without falling and allowed herself a small victory smile. Not so bad.

That thought lasted approximately five seconds before Ethan Armstrong skated up to her, his movements annoyingly fluid and confident.

"Looking a little stiff there, Cassidy," he teased, circling her like a shark. "You need to loosen up. Relax."

"I'm relaxed," she lied, focusing on keeping her knees bent and her weight centered.

"Doesn't look like it," Ethan said, skating backward in front of her. "Here, I'll help." He reached out, grabbing her hands before she could protest and pulling her forward at a speed she definitely wasn't ready for.

"Ethan, don't—" Cassidy started, but the words were lost as she stumbled, her skates scraping awkwardly against the ice.

"Come on, trust me," Ethan said, laughing as he pulled her into a wide arc. "It's easy. Just lean into it."

Cassidy shot him a glare, but before she could respond, Ethan let go, skating backward with a cocky grin. "See? You're fine."

She wasn't fine. She wobbled dangerously, her arms flailing as she tried to regain her balance. "Ethan, stop messing around," she snapped.

Ethan just laughed and picked up speed, circling her again. "You've gotta loosen up, Cassidy. You're way too tense."

"I'm not tense," she said through gritted teeth, focusing on staying upright. But her legs were already screaming from the effort, and Ethan's unpredictable movements weren't helping.

He sped past her again, this time closer, and Cassidy flinched as his arm brushed hers. The sudden contact threw off her balance, and she felt herself tipping forward.

"Ethan!" she yelled, panic flaring as she tried to catch herself.

But it was too late—she was twisting backward and falling.

Duke saw the fall coming a split second before it happened.

He moved without thinking.

By the time Cassidy hit the ice, Duke was already there, his skates carving into the frozen surface as he slid to her side. He crouched down, his hands reaching for her shoulders, his heart pounding harder than it should have.

"Cass," he said, his voice low and urgent. "You okay?"

She nodded quickly, her cheeks flushed with embarrassment and cold. "Yeah. I'm fine."

But Duke didn't let go. His hands stayed on her shoulders as he glared up at Ethan, who stood a few feet away, grinning like none of this mattered.

"Back off, Ethan," Duke said, his voice low and dangerous.

Ethan raised his hands in mock surrender, his grin fading slightly. "Relax, Duke. It was just a joke."

"It's not funny," Duke snapped, his dark eyes narrowing. "She's not here to be your entertainment."

Ethan opened his mouth to argue, but the look on Duke's face stopped him cold. "Fine," Ethan said, backing up. "Whatever. Didn't know you were so sensitive."

Duke ignored him, his focus shifting back to Cassidy. He pulled her to her feet, steadying her as she wobbled slightly.

"You good?" he asked, his voice softer now.

Cassidy nodded again, her gaze flicking up to meet his. "Yeah. Thanks."

For a moment, neither of them moved. The world around them faded, the laughter and chatter of the Armstrong family distant and muted.

"Stay close to the edge," Duke said finally, his voice quiet but firm. "If you're not comfortable, you don't have to be out here."

Cassidy straightened, her chin lifting slightly. "I'm fine, Duke. I can handle it."

He hesitated, his chest tightening. Her determination was part of what drew him to her, but it also made her vulnerable. And if there was one thing he couldn't stand, it was seeing her hurt — by Ethan, by the family, by anyone.

He stepped back, dropping his hands reluctantly. "Be careful."

Cassidy nodded, a faint smile tugging at her lips as she skated toward the edge of the lake.

Duke stayed where he was, his eyes following her as she moved, her balance slowly returning. He knew the family was watching. They saw what he did, even if they didn't say it out loud.

Duke wasn't just the screw-up anymore. Not today.

And yet, watching her smile as she skated along the edge, Duke couldn't bring himself to regret stepping in. Not now. Not ever.

* * * *

The Armstrong family dining room had been transformed for the evening's final celebration before Christmas Day — a casual holiday gathering filled with twinkling lights and festive warmth. Snacks and drinks were laid out across the long oak table, an inviting spread of savory bites and holiday treats. Near the fireplace, the family lounged in cozy clusters, their laughter and conversation filling the open space with a buoyant energy.

Duke leaned against a far wall, his broad shoulders resting against the dark wood paneling, his hands shoved deep into his pockets. He kept his gaze steady, watching the scene unfold without stepping into it. This was how he always navigated family events — on the edge, observing but never participating. It was safer that way.

His reputation clung to him like a shadow, unspoken but always present. Few in the room were willing to look past it, least of all his cousins.

Especially not Ethan.

Duke's jaw clenched as his eyes tracked Ethan across the room. The younger man sat in the center of the action, leaning back in a chair with his arm slung casually over the backrest. His laughter rang out, loud and grating, as though he wanted the whole room to notice him.

Duke's ears pricked when he caught snippets of the conversation. Ethan's grin was too sharp, his voice tinged with a condescension that set Duke's teeth on edge. He saw the way Ethan's gaze flicked toward Cassidy, lingering too long as he said her name, his words punctuated by a pointed chuckle.

Cassidy stood a few feet away, unaware of the attention she'd drawn. She was laughing with Caroline near the fireplace, a glass of champagne in her hand. She wore a simple red dress that hugged her in all the right places, her golden curls catching the light like strands of spun gold. Duke couldn't tear his eyes away from her, the warmth of her smile lighting up the room in a way that made his chest ache.

But Ethan's gaze lingered too long, his grin turning sly as he leaned toward one of the cousins, whispering something that made them laugh. Duke's patience snapped.

Pushing off the wall, he crossed the room with measured steps, his gaze locked on Ethan. The chatter and laughter seemed to fade as his focus narrowed, the tension in his body coiling tighter with every step.

"Ethan," Duke said, his voice low but carrying an edge that silenced the younger man mid-laugh.

Ethan looked up, his grin faltering for a split second before he plastered it back on. "Duke," he said, leaning back in his chair with exaggerated ease. "Enjoying the festivities?"

Duke's eyes flicked to the cousins before settling back on Ethan. "We don't talk about Cassidy like that."

Ethan's brows lifted, feigned innocence dripping from his expression. "Like what? We were just admiring her...charm." His grin widened, his tone deliberately provocative.

Duke clenched his fists at his sides, the room around them seeming to grow quieter. He took another step closer, towering over Ethan. "Watch your tone."

Ethan's smirk faltered, but he masked it quickly, leaning forward with an arrogant shrug. "Relax, Duke. We're just talking. No harm done."

"You're right," Duke said, his voice dangerously calm. "No harm done. Yet."

The unspoken warning hung heavy in the air, and for a moment, Ethan's grin slipped entirely. Duke stared him down, his dark eyes unflinching, until Ethan looked away, muttering something under his breath.

Satisfied, Duke straightened, casting one last glance at his cousins before turning and walking away.

"Hey," she said, her voice light and warm. "You finally decided to join the party?"

Duke let out a faint huff of a laugh, his tension easing as he looked down at her. "Something like that."

She tilted her head, her green eyes searching his. "You okay?"

"Yeah," he said, his voice quieter now. "Just keeping an eye on things."

Cassidy's lips curved into a knowing smile, her fingers brushing his arm briefly. "Well, if you're done being a wallflower, I could use a drink refill."

Duke nodded, his chest loosening at her easy presence. "Lead the way."

As they moved toward the bar together, the warmth of her laughter made the room feel less suffocating. For a moment, Duke allowed himself to believe that this was what the holidays could be—something real, something worth holding onto.

And as Ethan's sharp grin faded into the background, Duke knew one thing for certain. Cassidy wasn't just someone he wanted to protect—she was someone worth fighting for.

* * * *

The snow fell in soft flurries, the cold air biting at Duke's skin as he stood outside on the darkened patio. The Armstrong retreat was quiet now, the glow from the windows casting long, warm shadows across the pristine snow. Most of the family had retired for the night, but Duke's blood was still running too hot to rest.

The door creaked open behind him, and Duke didn't have to turn to know who it was. The sound of boots crunching on the snow told him everything.

"Thought I'd find you out here," Ethan drawled, his tone smug as he stepped out onto the patio. He had a drink in his hand, the amber liquid sloshing as he walked. "Taking a break from playing hero?"

Duke clenched his jaw, his hands curling into fists at his sides. "What do you want?"

Ethan leaned casually against the railing, his grin sharp. "Just thought we should clear the air. About Cassidy."

Duke's temper simmered just beneath the surface. "Leave her alone."

"Leave her alone?" Ethan repeated, feigning innocence. "Why? She's cute, fun. And she seems...available." His grin widened, the implication cutting like a blade. "Unless, of course, she's not. Is she,

Duke? Because from where I'm standing, she looks very single."

Duke took a step forward, his dark eyes flashing. "She's not yours to mess with."

"Oh?" Ethan tilted his head, his smirk widening. "And why's that? Is she yours? Because I don't see a ring on her finger. Don't see her hanging off your arm, either. If anything, she seems to be avoiding you."

"Fuck off, Ethan," Duke growled, his voice low and dangerous. "You don't know what you're talking about."

Ethan's smile faded slightly, his eyes narrowing. "But I think I do. You're jealous." He laughed, the sound harsh in the cold air. "That's what this is about, isn't it? I think she likes me."

Duke's fists clenched tighter, the words hitting a nerve. "Stay away from her."

"Why?" Ethan pressed, stepping closer. "Are you in love? Is that it? Big, bad Duke Armstrong has finally found a girl he wants to keep? That's rich."

Duke's jaw clenched, his teeth grinding as his patience snapped. "She's mine," he said, his voice low and fierce. "And you don't get to touch her. Not now, not ever."

Ethan chuckled darkly, shaking his head. "We'll see about that. Like I said, she looks single to me."

That was it. Without another word, Duke's fist shot out, connecting with Ethan's jaw with a sickening crack. Ethan stumbled back, his drink spilling into the snow as he clutched his face.

"You son of a—" Ethan started, but Duke didn't let him finish. He grabbed Ethan by the collar, shoving him against the railing.

"I said, stay the fuck away from her," Duke growled, his voice deadly quiet.

"Duke."

The sharp voice cut through the tension like a knife. Both men froze, turning to see the president standing in the open doorway, his expression dark and unreadable.

"Inside," the president said firmly, his tone leaving no room for argument. "Now."

Duke stood in the president's office, his shoulders squared and his fists still aching from the punch. His uncle sat behind the massive desk, his hands folded neatly in front of him as he regarded Duke with a look that was both disappointed and assessing.

"You've had a hell of a night," the president said finally, his voice calm but edged with steel.

Duke said nothing, his jaw tight as he met his uncle's gaze.

"What were you thinking?" the president continued. "Punching your cousin? It's Christmas Eve, for God's sake. There are reporters here. You can't be civilized for two days?"

"Someone needed to put Ethan in his place," Duke replied, his tone clipped. "He was out of line."

The president raised an eyebrow. "And you thought violence was the solution?"

"It got the message across," Duke said, his voice hard.

His uncle leaned back in his chair, letting out a long sigh. "Son, you're walking a fine line here. And I have doubts — about your ability to keep your temper, to make good decisions. Head of security — does he punch his cousin?"

Duke remained silent.

The president continued, "I don't think so."

Duke's fists clenched at his sides, but he forced himself to take a breath. "I'm not going to stand by and let him treat her like she's some game."

The president's eyes narrowed slightly. "Here comes the truth."

Duke didn't respond, his silence speaking volumes.

His uncle leaned forward, his expression softening slightly. "I need to know something, Duke. Is this about her? About Cassidy?"

Duke hesitated for a moment, then nodded. "Yeah. It is."

The president studied him, his gaze heavy. "And what do you plan to do about that?"

Duke straightened, his voice steady. "Whatever it takes to protect her. To prove I'm not the man you all think I am."

The room fell silent, his words hanging heavily between them. The president nodded slowly, his expression unreadable. "Then I suggest you start proving it. And fast. Because she's my writer, writing my biography, and you are leaving in two days."

Chapter Seventeen

The lodge was wrapped in the deep stillness that came only when everyone was fast asleep, waiting for Santa. The kind of quiet where the world seemed to hold its breath, waiting for dawn to break. Cassidy sat in a small room off the kitchen, the scent of cedar and peppermint mingling in the air. A cylindrical wood-burning stove crackled in the corner, its flames casting flickering amber light across the shelves of jars lining the walls, their glinting glass making the shadows dance.

She had curled up on the edge of a cushioned bench, a thick wool throw draped around her shoulders. Her hands clutched a mug of peppermint tea, the warmth seeping through her fingers, grounding her in the strange, heavy quiet.

She wasn't sure how long she'd been there, but time felt slippery, dissolving as her thoughts spiraled. Every look, every charged word from Duke lingered in her mind, tangling with everything unsaid. And everything inevitable.

The faint creak of a floorboard snapped her from her thoughts. She turned sharply, her breath catching.

Duke stood in the doorway, his broad frame shadowed against the faint golden glow spilling in from the kitchen. His dark hair was mussed, his T-shirt clinging to his chest and shoulders. His socks muted his steps on the wooden floor as he shifted, watching her with a look that felt both cautious and unshakable.

"You're still awake," he said, his voice low, roughened by the late hour.

"So are you," she replied, her tone sharper than she'd intended. She glanced away, embarrassed by how raw she felt under his gaze.

He stepped into the room, his movements quiet, deliberate. Without a word, he sank down beside her on the bench, his long legs stretching toward the fire. The heat seemed to draw him closer, his shoulders relaxing as the glow flickered over his face.

"Waiting for Santa?" he asked, his voice dry but softer now, almost teasing.

Cassidy gave a faint laugh, more breath than sound. "Maybe. Wanted to see what he's bringing me."

"Well," Duke said, leaning back against the bench, his gaze catching the firelight. "Have you been good?"

She hesitated, the words slipping out before she could stop them. "I hope so. Maybe not."

His head turned toward her, his dark eyes locking on hers. Something shifted in his expression, the teasing edge fading. His gaze softened, the weight of it pressing against her, and she swore she felt the air grow warmer between them.

Neither of them spoke for a long moment, the fire filling the silence with its steady crackle. Cassidy tightened her grip on the mug, suddenly hyperaware of the closeness between them.

"Why are you really here?" she asked finally, her voice quieter, gentler. "Are you tracking me?"

Duke's hands rested loosely on his knees, and he exhaled. "Couldn't sleep," he admitted, his voice low. "And then I found you. So, maybe yes."

Her heart stumbled, the honesty in his words hitting her in a way she didn't expect. She lowered her gaze, watching the firelight flicker across the floorboards.

Before she could respond, Duke shifted. His hand reached out, his fingers brushing hers. The touch was deliberate but unhurried, his calloused thumb grazing her knuckles. He picked up her hand, lifting it to his lips.

The kiss was soft, fleeting, but the warmth of it lingered, spreading up her arm and settling somewhere deep in her chest. He didn't let go. Instead, he held her hand in his, resting it gently on his thigh.

Cassidy felt herself inch closer, drawn by a pull she couldn't quite name. Her shoulder brushed against his, the warmth of his body seeping through the layers of the wool throw and the thin fabric of his T-shirt.

Duke turned slightly, their faces now just inches apart. The shadows danced across his features, the sharp lines of his jaw and cheekbones softened by the firelight. His gaze searched hers, something raw and unspoken flickering in his dark eyes.

"So, Miss Evans," he said, his voice low and rough. "What do you want for Christmas?"

"You're ridiculous," she said, but her tone was warm, and her gaze softened as she took him in — the way the firelight kissed his sharp jawline, the faint shadow of stubble, the rare and genuine care in his expression.

His free hand brushed against her side, playful but firm. "Be careful, or you'll end up on the naughty list."

"Seriously," he said, his voice dropping, the teasing edge fading. "What do you want, Cass?"

The change in his tone sent a shiver through her, and her smile faltered slightly. She looked away, her fingers curling into the fabric of his shirt. "I don't know," she said quietly.

"Yes, you do," he pressed. "Tell me."

She hesitated, her gaze fixed on the flames. "I want to feel like I belong," she said.

Duke stilled for a moment, his grip on her tightening slightly. "You do belong," he said, his voice firm but gentle. "Don't let anyone here — or anywhere — make you think otherwise."

Cassidy's chest burned at his words, the sincerity in his voice pulling at something deep inside her.

"And," he added, "you belong with me."

Cassidy blinked back the sudden sting of tears, her heart swelling at the quiet conviction in his words. She leaned into him, resting her head against his shoulder as his hand resumed its steady rhythm on her back.

"And what about you?" she asked softly, her breath warm against his neck. "What do you want for Christmas?"

Duke let out a low hum, his chin brushing against her hair. "Nothing I can ask Santa for," he said, his voice tinged with something heavier, something unsaid.

"Try me," she said, tilting her head to look up at him.

The President's Bodyguard

His gaze met hers, dark and unflinching. For a moment, the world seemed to still, the fire crackling in the background. "You," he said simply, his voice barely above a whisper. "I want you."

Cassidy's breath hitched, her heart pounding in her chest. She couldn't look away, couldn't breathe, as his words settled between them.

"You already have me," she said, her voice trembling with honesty.

Duke's hand slid up, cradling her face as he leaned in, his forehead resting against hers. "Then don't let me screw this up," he said, his voice raw.

She leaned into his touch, her breath catching as her heart raced. The quiet between them stretched, heavy with something neither of them dared to name. And yet, in that moment, it didn't feel like they needed words.

Because here, wrapped in the glow of the firelight, the world asleep around them, there was nothing else but this. Nothing but them.

"Cassidy," he said, her name a quiet confession. "There's so much I need to say to you."

She didn't push him to say more—he'd started and stopped so many times before that she knew it had to come in his own time.

Finally, he exhaled long and slow, turning to face her. His dark eyes were shadowed with guilt, his jaw tight. "You deserve to know the truth," he said, his voice low and rough. "And I've been thinking about this for a while."

Cassidy sat up straighter, her pulse quickening. "Okay," she said softly, her voice steady. "I'm listening."

Duke ran a hand through his hair, his frustration evident as he let out a long breath. "You want to know why I'm being banished?"

She chewed her lip, anticipating what it would turn out to be.

He continued. "It started last year. I met her at a charity event in DC. She was...beautiful. Sophisticated. The kind of woman who turned every head when she walked into a room."

Cassidy nodded, keeping her expression neutral.

"She was Italian," he continued. "At first, it was just small talk. Harmless. I knew she was a diplomat. We started seeing each other. But the more I saw her, the more I started noticing things. Bruises on her wrists. The way she'd flinch when someone spoke too loudly or moved too quickly."

Cassidy's grip on her mug tightened, her heart sinking.

"She then told me she was married. And her husband was...hurting her." Duke's voice wavered slightly, and he glanced away, his jaw clenching. "She didn't go into details at first, but I could see it. The fear. The shame. She was trapped, Cassidy. And I—I thought I could help her."

"You did help her," Cassidy said gently, her voice trembling.

Duke let out a bitter laugh, shaking his head. "Not enough. She'd come to me when things got bad. I'd keep her safe for a few days, make sure she had everything she needed. But she always went back. Said she had to. Said it was her duty, her responsibility, to stay."

He paused, the silence stretching painfully between them. Cassidy's heart broke for the woman, but also for

Duke, who clearly carried his decisions like a millstone around his neck.

"One night," he said, his voice quieter now, "she came to me...and it was different. She was terrified, crying. She said she couldn't go back this time. That he'd kill her."

Cassidy's breath hitched, her chest tightening.

"I kept her with me that night," Duke said, his eyes dark with guilt. "I told myself I was protecting her. That I was doing the right thing. But we crossed a line, Cassidy. She told me she loved me. She wanted to run off together. I didn't know what to do."

The words hung in the air like a thunderclap, and Cassidy's stomach twisted. But she didn't speak, waiting for him to continue.

"I cared for her," Duke said, his voice rough. "Maybe too much. But it was wrong. She was married. And as much as I wanted to help her, I didn't know what else to do. She kept going back, no matter what I said or did."

"What happened?" Cassidy asked quietly, her voice barely above a whisper.

"Her husband found out. Turns out, he's not just some businessman or minor official, Cassidy. He's one of the highest-ranking members of the Italian government. He's the type of man with his own Wikipedia page. A man with connections, power, and a vindictive streak a mile wide."

Her eyes widened, her heart sinking further. "I'm guessing he didn't take it well?"

"He demanded blood," Duke said bitterly. "Made a political mess of it. Claimed I'd seduced his wife, dragged her into an affair, disrespected his family and his country. It didn't matter that she'd come to me because she was scared for her life. All anyone saw was the playboy nephew of the president, screwing around with a married woman."

Cassidy stared at him, her chest aching as she processed his words.

"And that's the problem. No one knew what really happened. I wasn't going to sink her by telling the real story. The president — my uncle — was dragged into it. Gagged the press. The Italians wanted me fired, prosecuted, publicly shamed. It was a shit show." Duke paused, his gaze dropping to the floor. "This went on for a while. And, the only thing that saved me was eventually my uncle's promise to get rid of me. To remove me from the political spotlight completely. The Italians finally calmed down. That's why I'm being sent to Iraq. It's exile. A way to make me disappear quietly. And I think someone is hoping I'll just die there."

Her mug trembled in her hands as she set it down, her heart breaking for him. "You were trying to do the right thing," she said, her voice trembling. "You didn't deserve this."

Duke's head snapped up, his dark eyes locking onto hers. "Didn't I? I crossed a line. I let my feelings get in the way of my judgment, and now I'm paying for it. And I'm bringing everyone else down with me, including you."

"You're not," Cassidy said fiercely. "You're not a bad man. Please stop saying that."

He shook his head, his jaw tight. "You don't understand, Cassidy."

"I see you," she said, her voice soft but firm. "The real you. The man who protects people. The man who does what's right, even when it costs him everything."

Duke's gaze softened, the vulnerability in his eyes cutting through her. "Cass…"

She reached up, her hand brushing his cheek. "You don't have to do this alone. You don't have to keep punishing yourself for trying to save someone."

Duke closed his eyes, leaning into her touch, the warmth of her hand on his cheek grounding him in a way he didn't know he needed.

Cassidy quickly found herself perched on Duke's lap, straddling him as if it was the most natural thing in the world. His arms wrapped securely around her waist, holding her steady, while one of his hands slid down her thigh. His strength grounded her, his warmth spreading through her like the fire crackling beside them.

Her lips parted slightly, her breath quickening under his gaze. The tension between them coiled impossibly tighter, a magnetic pull drawing them closer.

And then he kissed her.

It wasn't tentative or careful — it was everything he'd been holding back. His mouth slid against hers, fierce and consuming, a raw clash of frustration, longing, and something deeper that neither of them dared name.

His embrace was firm, desperate, his grip almost bruising as he held her like she was the only solid thing in a world that had slipped out of control. Her body molded against his, soft and strong at once, and he exhaled a shuddering breath against her hair.

Cassidy gasped against him, the sound swallowed by his kiss as his hands slid up her back, pulling her impossibly closer. The wool throw she'd wrapped around herself slipped to the floor, forgotten, as her fingers tangled in his dark hair. The strands were soft and thick under her touch, and she tugged lightly, earning a low, guttural sound from him that made her knees weak.

The firelight danced across their faces as the kiss deepened, the warmth of the room nothing compared to the heat igniting between them. Duke angled his head, his lips moving against hers with a hunger that left her breathless. She responded in kind, her body pressing into his, her heart pounding so loudly she was sure he could feel it.

His hands slid lower, settling on her waist, his thumbs brushing over the curve of her hips. The touch was reverent, almost hesitant, as if he couldn't believe she was real. But then he pulled her closer again, their bodies aligning perfectly, and all hesitation vanished.

Cassidy's fingers trailed from his hair to his jaw, her palms pressing against the stubble that rasped under her touch. She could feel his chest rising and falling against hers, each breath uneven, ragged, as if he'd been holding it all in for far too long.

When he finally pulled back, his lips hovered over hers, his forehead pressing gently against hers. Their breaths mingled in the small space between them, the air thick with unspoken words and undeniable connection.

"I—" he started, his voice hoarse, but the words faltered as his hand came up to cradle her face. His thumb brushed her cheek, the simple touch sending another shiver down her spine.

Cassidy reached up, her fingers brushing over his hand as her eyes searched his. "Duke…" she said, her voice trembling with a mix of wonder and fear.

But instead of answering, he kissed her again, slower this time, softer. It wasn't a clash anymore—it was a promise, a surrender to something neither of them could stop. It was warm and tender, the kind of kiss that made the world disappear.

"You're the only thing I've ever wanted that doesn't feel like a mistake," he said, each word cutting straight to her core.

Tears stung her eyes, but she didn't blink them away. Instead, she cupped his face with trembling hands, forcing him to meet her gaze.

"Then don't leave me," she said, her voice barely audible. "Stay."

For a moment, his dark eyes searched hers, and she could see the war raging within him. She thought he might argue, might give her the same clipped excuses he'd been using for days. But then his lips brushed hers again, softer this time, like a question he was too afraid to ask.

The kiss was tender, a touch that carried everything he couldn't put into words. And yet, when he pulled back, something in his expression shifted. His hands curled into fists at his sides as he stepped away, his jaw tightening.

"I can't," he said, his voice breaking.

"Why?" Cassidy stood abruptly, her tears threatening to spill as desperation laced her tone.

Duke froze, his broad shoulders rigid. For a moment, she thought he might just walk away, his silence leaving her with nothing but questions and heartbreak. But then he turned back, his eyes burning with an emotion so raw it left her breathless.

"Because he killed her."

Cassidy's breath hitched. "What?"

"He killed her," Duke repeated, his voice rising, trembling with pain and rage. "Because of me. Because

I fucked her. Because she loved me. And it was my fault."

The room spun. The words didn't seem real, didn't fit into anything she could understand. But the agony in his eyes was undeniable.

"Was he charged?"

"No, not enough evidence. Looked like an accident. But I know exactly what happened. He did it. And I failed her," he continued, his voice cracking. "I failed to protect her. I thought I could keep her safe—I thought I could save her. But I didn't. And now she's dead because I wasn't enough to stop him."

Cassidy's knees nearly gave out, but she steadied herself, her hands clutching the back of the chair. "Duke..." she said, her voice breaking.

He shook his head violently, his hand raking through his hair as he turned away. His shoulders shook, and she realized with a jolt that he was fighting back tears. "She trusted me," he said, his tone bitter. "And I let her down. I let her die, Cassidy. And that's on me."

Cassidy stepped forward, her instincts screaming to comfort him, to hold him, but he flinched as if her presence hurt more than the memories.

"Do you understand now?" he demanded, his voice sharp and raw. "Do you see why I can't stay? Why I can't let myself be with you? I ruin everything I touch, Cassidy. I can't—" His voice broke, and he turned away, his hand swiping at his eyes.

She reached for him, her fingers brushing his arm, but he pulled away. "Duke, that wasn't your fault—"

"It doesn't matter what you think," he cut her off, his voice hollow. "I know the truth. And I won't let it happen again. Not to you. I deserve Iraq—and if I'm lucky, someone will put me out of my fucking misery while I'm there."

And with that, he was gone.

The door clicked behind him, but the echo of his words stayed with her, reverberating in her chest until it hurt to breathe. Cassidy sank into the nearest chair, her tears finally spilling over.

For the first time, she felt a pain inside of her that she had never known before — deep, aching, and unbearable. And yet, beneath it, there was something else.

Chapter Eighteen

Duke woke with a groan, the cold weight of reality settling over him even before he opened his eyes. The faint light filtering through the heavy curtains told him it was morning, but he didn't need a clock to know what day it was. Christmas.

Perfect. Just what he needed.

He rubbed a hand over his face, the rough stubble scratching against his palm. His head wasn't pounding — he hadn't drunk nearly enough for that last night — but the emotional hangover was worse. Cassidy's voice still echoed in his mind, soft and steady as she'd tried to convince him he wasn't the villain he'd painted himself to be. He wanted to believe her. God, he *wanted* to. But the knot of guilt in his chest refused to loosen.

Lying flat on the bed, he stared at the rustic wooden ceiling, the faint sound of wind brushing snow against the windows. Normally, waking up in the Armstrong family lodge brought a small sense of nostalgia —

memories of childhood Christmas mornings, sledding down the hills, pretending for a brief moment that they were just a normal family.

But not today. Today, it felt suffocating.

His phone buzzed on the nightstand, dragging him from his thoughts. He grabbed it, his thumb swiping across the screen before his eyes had even focused. The notification made his stomach churn: *Flight Itinerary: Washington D.C. to Erbil – Check-in Now Available.*

Duke sat up, the warm cocoon of blankets falling away. He scrolled through the email with mechanical precision, his jaw tightening as he read the details.

Departure: December 26th, 6:45 PM
Connecting Flight: Doha, Qatar (Layover: 8 Hours)
Arrival: Erbil International Airport – December 28th, 3:15 PM

It was all there, cold and impersonal, like a countdown to his own execution.

The government hadn't spared any expense, of course. He'd be on a cushy flight out of Dulles, seated in first class, but after the first connection, it was military transport—packed into a steel tube with uniformed soldiers heading to the same volatile region.

One last Christmas in the cozy lodge, he thought bitterly. *How festive.*

Duke tossed the phone onto the nightstand and swung his legs over the edge of the bed. The wood floor was cool against his feet, the air sharp and cold, even inside. His gaze flicked toward the door, knowing the family would already be awake, bustling about the lodge in holiday cheer. He could practically hear the chatter, the clinking of glasses, the laughter forced by tradition.

The last thing he wanted to do was join them.

He dropped his head into his hands, his elbows braced on his knees as the ache in his chest swelled. He couldn't face Cassidy either, not after last night. He'd said too much, cracked himself open in ways he hadn't meant to. And she'd looked at him like he was someone worth saving, someone who deserved more than he was willing to believe.

What a joke.

He stood abruptly, grabbing a sweatshirt from the chair by the window and pulling it over his head. He needed air, space—anything to avoid the suffocating weight of Christmas cheer and Cassidy's green eyes looking at him like he mattered.

As he slipped out of the room and into the quiet hallway, the smell of pine and cinnamon filled the air, a sharp reminder of the holiday he wanted no part of. He passed the family's Christmas tree in the main hall, its lights twinkling mockingly at him as if to say, *Cheer up, Duke! It's Christmas!*

"Go to hell," he said under his breath, pulling open the front door and stepping into the crisp, biting cold.

He walked aimlessly, his breath visible in the icy air. The lodge sat nestled in the heart of the mountains, the landscape a picturesque postcard of serenity. But to Duke, it felt like a cage, the countdown to his deployment ticking louder with every step.

He stuffed his hands into his pockets, his thoughts circling like vultures. He couldn't stay. He couldn't leave. And he sure as hell couldn't keep pretending he was okay.

Some Christmas.

The cold air cut through Duke's sweatshirt, but he didn't care. He welcomed the sting, letting it bite at his skin as he trudged through the snow. His boots left heavy tracks in the pristine white, following him toward nowhere in particular.

He'd walked these woods a hundred times before as a kid, escaping the chaos of Armstrong family gatherings. But today, the quiet offered no relief, only the echo of his own thoughts — Cassidy's voice, the flash of her eyes, the weight of his failures.

The crunch of snow behind him broke his train of thought.

"Rough morning?" Reed's voice was calm, even, but Duke could hear the edge of curiosity in it.

Duke sighed, shoving his hands deeper into his pockets. "Don't you have a Christmas to celebrate?"

"I do." Reed caught up, falling into step beside him. "But I saw you sneak out like a teenager trying to dodge chores. Figured I'd see what's eating you."

Duke shot him a sidelong glance but said nothing. Reed wasn't the kind of man to fill silences unnecessarily, and they walked in relative quiet for a few moments.

"You're usually better at hiding it," Reed finally said, his tone almost conversational.

"Hiding what?" Duke asked, his voice flat.

"That you're pissed off. Or maybe just pissed at yourself. Hard to tell."

Duke let out a bitter laugh, his breath visible in the cold. "You always did have me pegged, didn't you?"

Reed shrugged, his hands tucked into his coat pockets. "Maybe not as much as I thought."

Duke's brow furrowed, but he didn't respond. Instead, he kept walking.

"I've been watching you this week," Reed continued, his tone steady but probing. "And I have to admit, I'm starting to wonder if I've been wrong about you."

That stopped Duke in his tracks. He turned to Reed, his eyes narrowing. "What's that supposed to mean?"

Reed met his gaze without flinching, his expression thoughtful. "It means I've been so used to seeing you as the president's playboy nephew that I didn't bother looking any closer. But the way you've handled yourself this week — especially with Cassidy — " He paused, his words deliberate. "You're not the man I thought you were."

Duke's chest burned, a mix of emotions swirling — frustration, guilt, and something dangerously close to hope. "You're saying this now? After everything?"

Reed nodded slowly. "Maybe I should've said it sooner. You're not just some screw-up, Duke. And I think Cassidy sees that, too."

Duke turned away, his hands clenching into fists inside his pockets. "She sees what she wants to see," he said.

Reed stepped closer, his voice firm. "No, she sees the man you're trying to be. And for what it's worth, so do I."

Duke let out a sharp breath, Reed's words pressing down on him. He wanted to believe it, wanted to let the approval sink in, but all he could feel was the cold, heavy reality of what was waiting for him in twenty-four hours.

"It doesn't matter," Duke said finally, his voice tight. "I'm leaving. I've got a one-way ticket to Erbil, and there's nothing I can do to change that."

Reed studied him for a moment, his eyes sharp but not unkind. "Maybe not. But that doesn't mean you're the same man who got himself sent there. You've got time to figure out what kind of man you want to be when you come back."

Duke barked a bitter laugh, shaking his head. "Five years in the middle of a warzone. You really think there's a version of me that makes it back?"

Reed's gaze didn't waver. "I think if anyone can, it's you. And I think Cassidy would agree."

Duke stiffened at the mention of her name, his throat tightening. "She deserves better," he said, more to himself than to Reed.

"Maybe," Reed said, his tone softening slightly. "But I think she's already decided what she wants. And if it's you, you'd better find a way to be worth it."

He didn't respond, couldn't. Instead, he turned back toward the lodge, his steps heavy and deliberate.

Reed didn't follow, staying behind as Duke walked away. But as he reached the edge of the woods, Duke glanced back. Reed stood there, hands still in his pockets, his expression unreadable.

For the first time, there was no judgment in Reed's gaze—only something that looked like quiet approval.

Duke turned away, his jaw tight as he marched back toward the lodge. He didn't want Reed's approval, didn't deserve it. And he certainly didn't know what to do with it.

All he knew was that the clock was ticking, and for the first time, he wasn't sure if he was running toward something or away from it.

* * * *

The Armstrong dining room shimmered with curated holiday polish—fine china, crystal, garlands, and enough candlelight to make the whole night feel like a staged photo op. The table was long, the conversations rehearsed, and Duke's tolerance was wearing thin.

Duke sat near the end, half-turned from the table, nursing a glass of wine and a headache. Across the room, Cassidy sat beside Caroline, upright and composed in that way that said she was trying not to flinch.

She shouldn't have had to try this hard.

"Cassidy," Paul Armstrong said smoothly from the head of the table. Duke's intimidating father. "You're the journalist, yes? Writing the piece on my brother?"

Cassidy looked up, her smile poised. "Yes. A profile piece. I'm focusing on the administration's human impact—how the president's policies play out on the ground."

Paul raised an eyebrow. "So, feature writing."

"She's been embedded with us for months," Reed interjected from farther down the table, his tone even. "The draft is thorough. Thoughtful. She's done her homework."

Paul hummed, swirling his wine. "I'm sure it's very heartfelt."

"There's plenty of substance," Reed said.

"Well...substance of a different kind. Being so story-driven," Paul said.

Cassidy's smile didn't move, but Duke could see the tension in her jaw.

"I'd argue the opposite," she said, voice calm. "Sometimes narrative cuts deeper than numbers. When people feel something, they remember it."

Across from her, Ethan leaned in, all teeth and laziness. "So basically, puff journalism. Human tales, light on the facts?"

Duke felt it then—the shift in Cassidy's expression. Not obvious. Just a flicker of disappointment behind her eyes. Her fingers clenched slightly around her fork.

"I wouldn't call it light," she replied. "It's a different kind of weight."

Ethan shrugged. "Sure. But I guess it's easier than digging into real policy."

That was it.

"That's enough," Duke said, his voice slicing through the room.

Silence fell. Every head turned.

Duke didn't raise his voice. He didn't need to.

"She's not here to entertain you," he said, looking directly at Ethan. "And her work isn't easy. It takes more guts to sit down with someone who's at the top and ask the right questions than it does to throw out shitty commentary at a dinner table."

Paul leaned back slightly, a flicker of disapproval in his eyes.

"Duke—" he began.

Reed cut in instead. "Cassidy's piece is the real thing. It's not fluff. From what I've seen…she's held a mirror up to this administration in ways no one else could from the inside."

The table was still quiet.

Duke pushed his glass aside. "So maybe show some respect."

A beat passed. Then Caroline, smooth as always, stepped in. "Well said," she offered with a diplomatic smile. "It's clear Cassidy's work matters. I, for one, look forward to reading it."

Cassidy glanced at Duke—surprised, grateful, a little stunned.

He didn't look back. He didn't have to.

Because she got it now.

She wasn't alone at this table.

Not while he was sitting at it.

The Armstrong family drifted into the expansive living room after dinner, their laughter and chatter filling the space like a low, comfortable hum. The room was a perfect portrait of Christmas elegance. A massive stone fireplace dominated one wall, its flames crackling and glowing, casting a warm, golden light that flickered over the grand pine tree trimmed with ornaments that sparkled like tiny stars.

Cassidy perched on the edge of a plush armchair near the piano. The lingering taste of the robust cabernet warmed her throat as much as the fire's glow warmed her skin. Despite the earlier tension at dinner, she felt more settled now, her shoulders relaxing as the festive atmosphere carried on around her.

Her eyes flicked across the room to where Duke leaned by the fireplace. His dark hair caught the firelight, and his sharp profile looked almost sculpted, a contrast to the soft glow of the room. He wasn't looking at her, but his presence felt steady and grounding, like an anchor in a sea of polished elegance and unspoken judgment.

She replayed the moment from dinner, her heart skipping at the memory.

The way he'd stood up for her—his voice cutting through the quiet dismissal, his words deliberate and unflinching. The Armstrong family, with all their carefully masked superiority, had been silenced. He'd seen her, really seen her, and defended her like it was the most natural thing in the world.

And in that moment, for the first time all night, she'd felt like she belonged.

"You okay?" Caroline's soft voice pulled her from her thoughts. The president's wife eased into the armchair beside Cassidy, her movements graceful as ever.

Cassidy nodded, offering a small smile. "Yes. Thank you."

"You handled yourself beautifully tonight," Caroline said warmly, her tone low enough not to carry beyond their corner. Her gaze swept the room briefly before returning to Cassidy. "But Duke...well, I think he surprised all of us."

Cassidy's cheeks flushed, and she ducked her head, trying to hide the heat spreading through her chest. "He's...full of surprises," she said, taking a sip of her wine.

Caroline's lips curved into a knowing smile as she raised her glass, her eyes twinkling in the firelight. "Indeed he is."

"Across the room, someone called out her name, and Cassidy glanced up to see Ethan, his glass raised in an overly cheerful toast. "Cassidy! You're an artist, right? Play us something!" His grin was too wide, the kind that made her wary of the intention behind it. "The piano's been neglected all evening."

A ripple of agreement moved through the room, and Cassidy felt her chest tighten as more eyes turned toward her.

"Oh, I'm not sure," she started, her voice faltering. "It's been a while since—"

"Oh, please," Caroline interjected, her voice warm and inviting. "We'd love to hear something."

A murmur of agreement rippled through the room, the kind that left no room for refusal. Cassidy felt her stomach tighten as their collective gaze settled on her.

Her cheeks flushed, her pulse quickened, and her first instinct was to shake her head, to laugh it off.

But then she saw Caroline's encouraging smile. And when she glanced toward the fire, she saw Duke, standing tall and silent, his dark eyes fixed on her.

Something in that look steadied her, gave her the courage to stand. Her knees felt a little shaky as she turned to the grand piano, its polished surface gleaming under the soft glow of the room's golden lights. The flickering firelight danced along the edges of the space, making everything feel both intimate and vast, like she was walking into a dream.

The faint hum of conversation faded, replaced by the quiet anticipation of an audience. Cassidy slid onto the piano bench, running her fingertips lightly over the keys. They were cool and smooth, their weight familiar under her touch despite how long it had been since she'd last played for anyone. Her reflection in the lacquered wood looked as uncertain as she felt.

"What'll it be?" Ethan called out, his lazy smirk cutting through the silence like a blade.

Cassidy ignored him. She closed her eyes, taking a deep, steadying breath. The sound of the fire crackling, the clink of glasses, the soft murmur of the wind outside—it all faded as she let herself sink into the moment.

Then, she began to play.

The opening notes of *The Nutcracker Suite* floated into the room, delicate and deliberate. The familiar melody wrapped itself around her like an old friend, her fingers moving lightly, almost timidly at first. The soft, cascading notes seemed to shimmer in the air, settling gently over the gathered family.

The room grew still. Conversations stopped. The clinking of glasses ceased. The only sound was the piano, its voice filling every corner of the space with haunting, crystalline beauty.

Cassidy let herself lean into the melody, her fingers gaining confidence as they moved over the keys. The music began to swell, taking on a richness that mirrored the emotions swirling in her chest. The weight of the evening, of trying to belong, of wanting to be seen — it all poured into the music. Each note carried a piece of her, a reflection of the parts of herself she rarely showed anyone.

The silence of the room deepened. She opened her eyes briefly and saw the family transfixed. Caroline sat with her hand pressed to her chest, tears glimmering in her eyes. Paul's usual air of detached authority was softened, his brow furrowed in thought as he listened. Even Ethan, his smirk long gone, looked genuinely stunned.

But it was Duke who caught her attention.

He stood by the fireplace, his face shadowed and golden in the flickering light. His glass hung loosely in one hand, forgotten. His eyes were locked on her, and the intensity of his gaze stole her breath. He wasn't just watching her play. He was watching her — seeing her in a way that made her chest ache.

She faltered for the briefest of moments, her fingers slipping, but the music carried her forward, rising and falling like a tide. She looked away from him, focusing on the keys as her hands moved faster now, the melody swelling into something bolder, more triumphant. It was as if the music itself had taken hold of her, pulling her forward, pulling her out of the smallness she'd felt all night and into something vast and limitless.

Her heart raced as she let the final chords ring out, their resonance hanging in the air like a spell that refused to break. When silence finally fell, it wasn't the heavy, uncomfortable kind she feared. It was the kind that hummed with awe, with something meaningful.

Then, applause erupted.

Caroline was the first to stand, clapping her hands together, tears sliding down her cheeks. "That was...breathtaking," she said, her voice thick with emotion. Others joined in, their applause genuine, their murmurs of appreciation filling the room.

Cassidy sat frozen, her hands still resting lightly on the keys. Her breath came in shallow gasps, her chest tight with the enormity of what she'd just done. She hadn't played like that in years. She hadn't felt like that in years.

"She's remarkable," Caroline said, her voice carrying easily over the noise. "Absolutely remarkable."

Even Ethan, for once, seemed at a loss for words. "You've been holding out on us," he managed, his tone devoid of its usual bite.

Cassidy turned her head, her gaze searching for Duke. He hadn't moved, still standing by the fire, but his expression was different now. The sharp lines of his face had softened, and his dark eyes glimmered with something she couldn't quite name. His lips curved into a faint, reverent smile, and he lifted his glass in a silent toast.

Her heart squeezed painfully, her cheeks burning as she looked away. But the warmth in her chest didn't fade. For the first time, she didn't feel like an outsider. She didn't feel like the girl trying too hard to prove she belonged.

She felt like the hero of her own story. And the way Duke looked at her, like she was the most extraordinary thing in the room, only confirmed it.

When she stood and turned to join the others, her hands were still trembling. But for once, it wasn't from fear.

It was from something closer to joy.

Chapter Nineteen

The lodge was quiet now, the echoes of laughter and music from the Christmas celebration fading into the stillness of the snow-covered mountains. Cassidy stood alone on the wide wooden deck, wrapped in a wool blanket that didn't seem to offer enough warmth against the cold. Her cheeks stung from the bite of the air, though she barely noticed. Her eyes were fixed on the snowbanks stretching into the dark woods, bathed in the pale glow of the moon.

The buzz from the wine still lingered, warmth creeping over her skin, but it was the memory of the evening's praise that made her feel a little unsteady. The piano. The applause. The way the room had gone still as her fingers moved over the keys, a hush falling over the guests. The emotion, raw and sincere, had been almost overwhelming. And Duke. Duke's unwavering gaze had followed every note, every chord. It was unsettling, and it had stirred something in her — a feeling she didn't know how to place.

A flicker of movement pulled her from her thoughts. A winter rabbit, small and swift, darted across the snow, its soft body leaving a trail of tracks behind. Cassidy couldn't help but smile faintly, watching it pause for a brief moment, ears twitching before it vanished into the snowdrifts, as if it had never been there at all.

She let out a soft breath, visible in the frigid air, when the creak of the door behind her made her heart skip, even before she saw him.

Duke.

He stepped onto the deck, his silhouette framed by the warm glow spilling from the lodge. He wasn't wearing a coat, just a thick sweater that clung to his broad frame, and his dark hair was tousled, like he'd run his fingers through it more than once in frustration.

"My favorite follower," Cassidy teased, her voice barely above a whisper, betraying the mix of emotions she couldn't quite hide. "Never fails."

He gave her a tired smile, his hands shoved deep into his pockets as he walked toward her. "You're not exactly hard to find."

Cassidy turned away, letting her eyes wander over the snow again. She pulled the blanket tighter around her shoulders, her breath shallow. "I had too much wine," she said, unsure if she meant the alcohol or the emotions still swirling inside her.

He stopped beside her, his presence warm even in the chill of the night. The familiar scent of him — woodsmoke, pine, and that trace of something uniquely him — cut through the crisp air, and Cassidy couldn't help but inhale.

They stood there in silence for a moment, the only sound the faint rustle of snowflakes drifting down, settling on the ground. Cassidy's eyes followed the spot where the rabbit had disappeared, her chest tightening with a quiet, inevitable dread.

Then Duke spoke, his voice low but clear, the kind of tone that always made her feel like he was looking right through her.

"You were incredible tonight," he said, his words so unexpected they made her stomach flip. "You brought everyone to tears. You don't even realize how rare that is, do you?"

Cassidy turned her head slowly, surprised by the intensity in his voice. His eyes were fixed on her with a steadiness that made her breath catch in her throat. She couldn't tell if he meant it—if he was just trying to soften the blow of everything that had been left unsaid between them—or if he truly believed it. But the sincerity was there, undeniable.

"I didn't expect…" She trailed off, the words lost for a moment. "I didn't expect it to matter that much."

Duke shook his head, a small smile tugging at his lips. "It matters. You matter. You don't need to play down your talent, Cassidy. Not here, not with me. What you did tonight…it wasn't just about the music. It was the heart you put into it. You made people feel something. That's something."

The weight of his words settled around her, and she swallowed hard, unsure of how to respond. The tension in her chest, the ache she'd been carrying all evening, seemed to melt a little in the warmth of his gaze. But there was still that distance. That barrier.

"Thanks," she said quietly, her voice soft against the stillness. "I… I needed to hear that."

Duke stood in front of her, his gaze distant, unreadable. The cold air between them seemed to press down, thick with everything unsaid. He nodded slowly, his expression hardening as if bracing himself for the inevitable.

"I don't know if I'll see you in the morning," Duke said, his voice steady but tight. "Before I leave."

"So soon?" she breathed, the words heavy, unwilling to come out.

"It came fast," he said, eyes falling to the ground for a moment. "I've got to pack the truck, head back to DC, grab a few things. Then straight to the airport."

Her heart sank, a wave of cold dread washing over her. "And that's it?" she asked, her voice trembling, finality settling in like an anchor in her chest.

Duke's gaze flicked up to hers, his eyes dark and soft, filled with the ache she'd been trying to ignore. "That's it."

Silence descended between them, thick, suffocating. Cassidy's throat burned as she tried to swallow the lump that had formed there. The cold bite of the night seemed to invade her, but it was nothing compared to the chill creeping into her bones at the thought of him leaving.

Finally, she said, barely able to make the words come out. "Why does this feel like goodbye, for real?"

"Because," he said, his voice low, rough around the edges. But he didn't say anything more, and Cassidy's heart twisted painfully in her chest.

Her breath hitched, and she turned to face him fully, feeling the blanket slip from her shoulders as she stepped forward, urgency burning in her. "So, can I write you?" she asked, the words tasting foreign on her tongue, sharp, as if she didn't belong in this moment.

"Yes," he said, his voice barely a whisper. He reached out then, brushing her arm lightly, his touch lingering for a second before it fell away. "I can't leave without telling you...how much you mean to me," he added, his voice cracking as raw emotion gripped him. He blinked, his eyes turning glassy, and Cassidy's chest tightened, her own breath ragged.

Tears blurred her vision, but she fought them back, her heart shattering with each passing second.

"I've been to Iraq four times. And countless other deployments," Duke continued, his jaw tightening as he spoke through the pain. "But this...this is the hardest thing I've ever done." His voice trailed off, raw and torn.

Cassidy exhaled sharply, the ache in her chest unbearable. "I wish you would stay," she said, the words feeling like a plea, but nothing more.

He shook his head, eyes dark and filled with anguish. "I know."

Her pulse raced, desperation clawing at her chest. "Is there nothing we can do?" she demanded, her voice breaking. "What if we —"

"Don't say it." Duke's voice cut through the air, a painful quietness filling the space between them. "I've already been asked this question before. It doesn't end well."

Tears spilled over, hot against her cold cheeks. She wiped them away quickly, but her voice faltered. "You don't get to decide that for me."

"I already have." His voice softened, barely a whisper now, but his words was enough to silence her. "I'd rather break my own heart than risk breaking yours."

Her heart cracked open at his admission. Cassidy looked away, her gaze lost in the distance, focusing on the spot where the rabbit had disappeared into the snow, its fleeting presence echoing the fragility of everything between them. Everything she wanted, everything they could have had — gone too soon.

Duke reached out again, his rough fingers gently brushing her cheek. The warmth of his touch sent a shock through her, even in the cold. "I'm sorry," he said.

Cassidy closed her eyes, leaning into his hand, even as the cracks in her heart deepened. "Me too," she said.

He stepped closer, and in that moment, Cassidy held her breath. His lips brushed her forehead in a kiss that felt like both a promise and a final farewell, everything he couldn't say wrapped up in that one, delicate touch.

When he pulled back, his hand lingered on her skin for just a moment longer, as if unsure whether to leave or stay. But then, slowly, he dropped his hand, stepping back, the distance between them widening.

"Goodbye, Cass," he said, heavy with everything they hadn't said, everything they couldn't. "Be good."

Cassidy stood frozen, unable to speak, the words stuck in her throat, her heart racing with the weight of what was happening. As he turned and walked away, she remained rooted to the spot, watching him disappear into the golden glow of the lodge, his shadow swallowed by the darkness.

And in that moment, Cassidy knew — this was really goodbye.

* * * *

The silence in Cassidy's room was thick, oppressive, broken only by the quiet crackle of the fire in the hearth. She stood in front of the mirror, brushing through her long, curly blonde hair with a wide-toothed comb. Her red silk robe clung to her skin, the fabric soft against her body, but it couldn't ease the tightening in her chest. She wasn't sure what she was feeling anymore — grief, longing, uncertainty. Maybe all of it.

The goodbye. The way his words had hung in the air, heavy and final.

She stared at her reflection, her eyes dull and distant, the soft glow of the candlelight casting a pale hue across her face. Her fingers gripped the brush tighter. Was this really goodbye? Was it really over, just like that? No more words, no more chances to say what they both were clearly feeling but never admitted.

A surge of panic gripped her. He was leaving. She might never see him again. Never feel the heat of his touch, hear the raw edge in his voice. Never know if they could have been something more. Something real. Could she really let that go? Could she let him go?

She dropped the brush onto the vanity and stood, the soft silk of her robe slipping down her shoulders as she moved to the door. Every step felt like an electric jolt, each one vibrating with uncertainty. But the thought of doing nothing, of letting him walk out without her fighting for him, cut deeper than the pain of her heart breaking. She wouldn't regret it. She couldn't.

Her bare feet made no sound as she crossed the floor, her body moving on instinct, her mind consumed with a singular thought. *One more night.* That's all she wanted. One night with him — uncomplicated, raw, no more goodbyes. Just one night to feel something, anything, that wasn't the unbearable emptiness filling her chest.

The house was quiet, the halls bathed in a pale, ghostly moonlight, and she knew exactly where to go.

His room. She had seen him disappear into it earlier, his broad shoulders hunched, his jaw set tight, as though he were trying to outrun whatever this was between them. But there was no escaping it. Not now.

When she reached his door, Cassidy hesitated, her fingers brushing the cool wood of the handle, her heart racing in her chest. She could hear the soft thrum of her pulse in her ears, the familiar mix of fear and resolve pooling in her stomach. But she couldn't stop now.

She just wanted the night.

She gripped the handle, the metal cold beneath her fingers, and took a deep breath, steeling herself. Then, without another thought, she twisted the knob and pushed the door open.

The room was warm, the glow of the fireplace casting long shadows across the walls. Duke stood in front of the hearth, his back to her, a glass of scotch in his hand. His broad shoulders were relaxed but heavy, his head bowed as though lost in thought.

The door clicked as she closed it behind her.

He turned at the sound, his eyes widening when he saw her standing there. "Cass," he said, his voice low and rough. "What are you doing here?"

Her throat tightened, but she held his gaze. "I couldn't let you leave," she said quietly, her voice trembling slightly.

He prayed to the ceiling. "You are not here in this room with me. Wearing that thing." His jaw tightened, his dark eyes blazing as he set the glass down on the mantel. "Cass," he said, his voice a low growl. "You can't—"

Cassidy swallowed hard, her pulse pounding in her ears.

He took a step toward her, his expression torn between disbelief and something darker, something heavier. "You shouldn't be here," he said, his voice sharper now. "If anyone finds out—"

"I don't care. I love you."

Her hands trembled as she reached for the tie of her robe. He froze as she pulled the knot loose, the silk sliding off her shoulders and pooling at her feet.

She stood before him, completely bare, her body trembling but her gaze steady.

"One night," she said, her voice shaking. "Please." She trembled in front of him, waiting.

Duke's breath hitched, his eyes raking over her body before snapping back to her face. In two long strides, he closed the distance between them, his hands cupping her face as his lips crashed down on hers.

"You," he said hoarsely, his voice breaking. "You have no idea—"

The kiss was fierce, consuming, filled with all the things he couldn't say. His hands roamed down her back, pulling her closer, his body trembling against hers.

Cassidy clung to him, her fingers digging into his shoulders as the heat of the fire mirrored the heat between them. Her skin burned under his touch, her breath coming in ragged gasps as he kissed her like she was the only thing holding him together.

He let out a harsh breath, his dark eyes blazing with a mix of desire and torment. "You're impossible," he said, his voice low and rough. "You're everything I want, and I can't have you."

"You can," she said, her voice cracking slightly. "Right now, you can."

When he pulled back, his forehead rested against hers and his breath was hot against her lips. "You're my dream," he said, his voice rough with emotion. "And I never want to wake up."

Cassidy's heart ached at the rawness in his voice. "Show me," she said.

Duke's hands tightened on her waist, his chest heaving as he fought an internal battle she couldn't begin to understand.

His lips found hers again, softer this time but no less desperate. His hands moved over her body, reverent and aching, as if memorizing every inch. She felt his goodbye in every touch, every kiss, and it broke her heart even as it made her whole.

Chapter Twenty

Cassidy barely noticed the glow from the fireplace casting flickering shadows along the walls. She couldn't have cared less about the snow piling up in the windows.

Her senses were consumed by the man holding her.

And that meant the world outside felt far away, muffled by the warmth of Duke's touch and the sound of their lips meeting.

To Cassidy, there was no tomorrow.

Duke laid her back on his bed, his gaze intense. She sank into the thick, worn blanket that stretched across it. She was weightless, untethered, completely caught in him.

Her breath came faster as he stood by the bed, the tension between them thick. He moved on top of her as her head fell against a pile of pillows, the scent of cedarwood and something distinctly Duke surrounding her.

She tugged at the hem of his shirt, her fingers trembling but insistent. "Off," she said, her voice barely audible.

Duke gave her a half grin, the corner of his mouth lifting in that infuriatingly confident way that made her heart race. He didn't hesitate. In one swift motion, he pulled the shirt over his head, tossing it carelessly to the floor.

God.

Cassidy's breath caught in her throat. Her eyes roamed over his chest, her lips parting as she took him in. His body was hard and lean, every muscle etched in sharp relief, the firelight casting golden highlights across his skin. But what made her heart throb were the tattoos.

Her hand reached out instinctively, her fingertips brushing the ink that wound its way up his ribs, over his chest, and down his arms. The designs were intricate, the lines bold yet precise—symbols, words, and patterns that told a story she hadn't expected. She traced one with her finger, a soft gasp escaping her lips as she followed the curve of a feather that extended from his side up to his ribs.

"You didn't tell me," she said, her voice trembling.

Duke's dark eyes met hers, and for a moment, the tension between them softened. "Didn't think it mattered," he said gruffly, his voice low and rough.

"It matters," she said, her hand trailing up to rest on his chest, where a compass was inked just below his collarbone. Her fingers brushed over the northward arrow, her eyes searching his as her voice softened. "It all matters."

He didn't respond, not with words. Instead, he leaned down, his hands bracing on either side of her as his lips found hers. The kiss was hot, insistent, stealing the air from her lungs. Cassidy moaned softly, her hands sliding up his chest and over his shoulders, her fingers tangling in his hair as she pulled him closer.

Her legs shifted, the blanket beneath her crumpling as Duke's weight settled over her. His skin was warm under her palms, the hard lines of his body fitting against hers as though they'd been made for this moment. She broke the kiss just long enough to catch her breath, her lips brushing against his ear as she said, "You're...incredible."

Duke's hand moved to her hip, his grip firm but careful as his other hand trailed up her side, leaving a trail of heat in its wake. "You're one to talk," he said, his voice thick with desire.

Cassidy's fingers slid back down his chest, tracing the line of another tattoo—a phrase in a script she didn't recognize running along his side. She paused, her fingers trembling as she looked up at him. "What does this one mean?"

His gaze darkened, and for a moment, he hesitated. "It's...a reminder," he said finally, his voice quiet. "That no matter how far I've gone, I can always find my way back."

The weight of his words hung between them, raw and unspoken, but Cassidy didn't press him. Instead, she leaned up, her lips brushing against the tattoo as her fingers pressed against his ribs. "You already have," she said.

Duke groaned softly, his head dipping to rest against her shoulder for a moment before he lifted it again, his lips capturing hers in another searing kiss as he held himself on top of her.

She found her way to him.

Now, there they were, in the dim light of his room, everything else in the house slipping away as his tongue played with hers, savoring every moment of their kiss.

And then, as if he couldn't wait any longer, he pulled back. His dark eyes locked onto hers, and she could feel what remained unsaid between them, the pull, the longing that had been simmering beneath the surface for too long.

He cupped her face gently, brushing his thumb across her wet lip with a tenderness that made her heart ache. His touch was so familiar, so right, but also so new, like every second with him held the promise of something she hadn't even dared to imagine.

"Cassidy," his voice was rough, like he was trying to make sense of everything that had been building between them. "I need…" He didn't finish the sentence. Didn't need to.

Because in that moment, he leaned in and kissed her again, biting at her lip. He kissed down her jaw, her throat, to her chest. Her breath caught as his mouth found each breast, warm and insistent, worshipping each hardened tip in turn.

His hands brushed up her thigh, tentative at first, like a question.

"Open for me," he said.

She relaxed her thighs and pressed up to him, feeling the pull between them, irresistible, undeniable. His hand ran farther up her thigh as she spread, and he found her soaked opening.

It was everything.

Her head tipped back as his mouth moved down her breasts, his stubble scraping deliciously against her skin. Each kiss was unhurried, deliberate, making her feel like time itself had stopped.

Her fingers tangled in his hair, pulling him closer as her breath hitched, her body arching instinctively toward him. He responded with a low, rough sound that sent a thrill coursing through her.

He moved farther down her body, drawing circles with his tongue around her belly button until he found her clit and licked.

The way he licked her was slow, firm, and all-encompassing, like he was trying to consume her in the best way possible, like he wanted to leave a mark and ruin her for any other man. His hand slid to her ass, pulling her closer to him, angling her pussy to his face, and she responded instinctively, wrapping her legs around his body as he worked harder. Every inch of her body seemed to hum with need, with the unspoken promise of what this meant.

And where this was going.

His lips found her clit again, the kiss deep and consuming, his weight pressing her into the bed in a way that made her feel entirely claimed. He licked her faster as she throbbed in his hands. His fingers pulsed into her hot core, needing and aching from the tension of the past few days — the long days watching him, the conversations that never seemed to end, the emotional whirlwind that had taken over her.

So here she was, her eyes half-closed, trying to get everything out of her mind, focusing instead on the sensation of Duke's lips on her pussy.

One night.

The bed shifted as Duke moved below her, and she heard the rustling of his arm as he adjusted his cock in his pants.

"Lie back," he said, his voice low and steady, a soft promise in the stillness of the room. "Let me take care of you for once."

Cassidy nodded like a good girl, sinking further into the bed, the plush surface enveloping her. Her breath was slow, steady, and she let her body ease, trusting him in a way she hadn't been able to with anyone else.

Duke's mouth was warm as he lapped at her wet slit again, running up to her clit, his fingers pumping intently into the tight opening. She exhaled, the sensation spreading heat through her whole body, melting the tension away with each deliberate stroke. He was firm but demanding, steady, as if he knew exactly where she needed him.

"I need to watch you fall apart," Duke said, his voice barely above a whisper. "For me. This last time."

"I'm almost there," Cassidy moaned, letting the words drift off as she surrendered to the rhythm of his tongue working her. "Duke…" she said, her voice trembling with emotion she couldn't quite contain.

"I've got you," he said softly, his breath warm against her clit. "Just let go."

And she did. For once, Cassidy let herself stop thinking, stop worrying, and simply feel. She arched into his touch, her fingers caught in his thick hair as his tongue trailed up and down her slit, lingering just long enough on the sweetest spot to drive her over the edge.

And then she was climaxing.

She closed her eyes, her head tipping back as he moved lower, his lips pressing tender kisses along her mound. Each kiss felt like a promise, a reassurance that this was real, that she wasn't imagining the emotion in his touch.

Cassidy swallowed hard, her heart pounding in her chest. She felt raw, exposed in a way that wasn't just physical. He wasn't just touching her body, he was touching every part of her, the pieces she kept hidden, the parts she didn't even know existed.

Cassidy let herself go completely, surrendering to him, to the moment, crying out his name again and again as she hit the peak of her pleasure.

But when she opened her eyes, his dark eyes were fixed on her, an intensity in the way his gaze lingered on her.

Cassidy's breath caught, her heart swelling with a mix of vulnerability and something deeper, something she hadn't let herself feel in a long time. "I've never —" She broke off, her voice faltering.

"I know," Duke said quietly, his lips curving into a faint, reassuring smile. "And that's okay. You don't have to say it."

Duke's hands skimmed back up her body, firm yet reverent, like she was something sacred to him. His touch sent shivers racing along her skin, his fingers tracing paths that left her gasping.

She reached for him as he moved on top of her again, her hands feeling the hard planes of his chest, his warmth searing against her palms. Her fingers brushed again over the tattoos that wound across his ribs and arms, their meaning as enigmatic as the man himself.

Her breath hitched as his hands found hers, pinning them gently above her head. He put pressure on her wrists, holding her in place. He leaned down, his forehead brushing hers as he said, "You're all I see, Cassidy. Do you know that?"

Her chest tightened, tears pricking at the corners of her eyes as she nodded, unable to speak. No one had ever looked at her like this, touched her like this — with equal parts passion and care, as though she was the only thing that mattered.

"You're so damn perfect," he said, his voice thick with emotion. "And you don't even know it."

His thumb brushed her lip, his touch so gentle it made her heart ache. The scent of the woodsmoke from the fire mingled with the soft, almost heady sweetness of her orgasm on his fingers.

She opened her eyes, her gaze locking with his. The firelight reflected in his dark eyes, making them shimmer like molten gold. "I need you inside me," she admitted, her voice barely above a whisper. "Now."

In one quick motion he tore off his pants and returned over her fully bare. He was still as tall and commanding as ever, his broad frame silhouetted in the firelight, his expression intense. Holding her hands above her head, he kissed her — slowly, deeply, as though he wanted to memorize every detail of her. His broad shoulders were tense, his back curved, the muscles in his arms flexing as he held her hands to the bedframe.

His generously hard cock bounced in between her thighs as she opened to him. Duke didn't hesitate. He sunk his cock inside of her, slowly meeting the ache deep within.

Each thrust of his hips made the entire bed rock beneath them. She could feel the weight of him leaning into her, his muscles rippling with each movement. His focus was entirely on her, his body pressing into hers with a force that made her forget why it could only be one night.

He slid hands, strong and calloused, over her skin with purpose, leaving a trail of heat in their wake. She gasped as his fingers gripped the curve of her hip, his touch possessive as he held her and fucked her harder, though he were memorizing every inch of her.

He pumped his cock faster inside her, worshipping her. Her breath came fast and shallow, her heart pounding as she fought to keep it together.

Because she was about to lose her mind.

Her chest tightened, tears pricking at her eyes as she gazed up at him. "I feel like I'm dreaming," she moaned, her voice breaking. "Like this isn't real."

His dark eyes softened as he cupped her face, his thumb brushing over her cheek. "It's real, babe," he said, his voice low but steady. "It's as real as it gets."

Duke was a force of nature. His dark hair was damp with sweat, his chest rising and falling with each deep breath. A slick sheen covered his body, highlighting every hard muscle, every ridge and line. His arms flexed with every motion, veins standing out against his forearms as he gripped the bed frame above her, pushing himself harder into her, finding the top of her cave and everywhere in between.

She moaned louder, digging her nails in his back. She felt the heat of his gaze on her even as she opened her eyes to find him watching her with that same intensity. His dark eyes sparkled with a mix of challenge and amusement, like he knew what was going to happen to her.

She was going to cream again — right on his cock.

His mouth parted, just the slightest bit, as though he wanted to say something, but his gaze dropped to her lips again. She could see the dark hunger there, the tension building in the way his jaw clenched.

He was nearing the edge, too.

He was thrusting faster and deeper into her, grasping her wrists with one hand and her hip with the other. Her eyes rolled back. Tears prickled. She was falling — and she couldn't catch herself.

He turned her body slightly, his cock head sliding deliciously along the most sensitive ridge in her pussy. And then she saw stars.

"Oh, babe," she cried. "Baby."

"Take it."

"I love you so much," she said as he groaned, biting her shoulder in agony and something else.

A rush of pleasure coursed up and down her body. She twisted underneath him, barely cognizant of the fact that he was spilling his seed, the hot, sticky liquid shooting into her pussy.

He collapsed beside her, breathless, drawing her waist toward him and embracing her.

She could feel the tightness in her chest, the way her body responded to his touch instinctively.

The thought of letting him leave, of walking away from this, was unthinkable. She wanted more. Wanted him more. She wanted to feel every part of him, just as she felt the heat of his eyes on her.

"It's never felt like that before," he said, running his hands through his damp hair. "Unbelievable."

She snuggled into him, pressing her lips to his once more.

"You feel too good in my arms," he said, his voice deep and raw, as though he were struggling to hold onto consciousness. His lips trailed from her ear down her neck, brushing against her skin.

"You belong here," he added. "With me."

Cassidy felt a rush of heat spread through her chest, her stomach tightening in response.

"I don't want to let you go," Cassidy said, her voice catching on the words as they escaped her.

His lips brushed against her forehead in a soft, lingering kiss, and she felt the reverberation of his heartbeat against her own chest. "Then don't," he said, his voice like a balm, like a promise that settled deep inside her, comforting the ache that had been there for so long.

"After all this, it could be that easy?"

"Everything's changed now."

Cassidy closed her eyes for a beat, savoring the sensation of his embrace. The scent of him wrapped around her—smoky wood from the fire, the faintest hint of pine, and something deeper, something undeniably Duke that made her head spin. He smelled like home, like safety, like something that had always been just out of reach but was finally right here, in this moment.

"Don't ever forget how beautiful you are," he said, his voice low and rough. His lips found the sensitive curve of her neck, his stubble grazing her skin in a way that made her toes curl. "Inside and out."

His arms tightened around her as though he, too, was trying to hold onto this moment. He kissed the side of her neck as he slowly fell asleep, holding her like he was marking her, staking his claim on her soul.

For the first time in what felt like forever, Cassidy felt truly home.

The fire in Duke's room had burned low, its faint embers casting a warm glow across the walls. The snow outside had slowed to a gentle fall, soft flakes catching on the windowsill and melting against the glass. Cassidy lay nestled against Duke's chest, his arm draped heavily around her waist, his breathing slow and deep in sleep. His warmth enveloped her, his presence grounding her in a way she hadn't felt in years.

She tilted her head slightly, her eyes tracing the sharp lines of his face in the dim light. Even in sleep, his expression was intense, his brow furrowed like he was carrying the weight of the world. Her heart ached knowing what the morning would bring — knowing this might be the last time she'd ever be this close to him.

Carefully, she shifted, her movements slow and deliberate so as not to wake him. His arm tightened briefly around her, and she froze, her heart pounding in her chest. But then he sighed softly, his grip relaxing as he sank deeper into sleep.

Cassidy leaned in, her lips brushing against his temple, lingering there for a moment as her throat tightened. "Goodbye," she said, the word barely audible, her voice cracking under its weight. "Don't ever forget that I love you."

She slipped out of bed, shivering as the cool air kissed her bare skin. Pulling on her red silk robe, she tied it around her waist and glanced back at him one last time. He looked peaceful, the firelight flickering across his face. She wanted to stay, to crawl back into his arms and pretend the morning wouldn't come.

But it would. And she couldn't bear to be here when it did.

Back in her room, Cassidy paced, her thoughts a tangled mess of regret and longing. The clock on the bedside table glowed faintly, each passing minute pulling her closer to the moment Duke would leave. She sat on the edge of the bed, her hands clenched in her lap, trying to convince herself to stay — to face the day, to say goodbye properly.

But the idea of watching him go, of standing there as he walked away, was unbearable.

The decision came suddenly, a sharp clarity cutting through her haze of emotion. She couldn't stay. She couldn't watch him leave. She had to go first.

Her movements were automatic as she grabbed her bag and began packing, her hands trembling as she folded clothes and stuffed them into her suitcase. Her breath caught in her throat as she caught sight of the dress she'd worn to the holiday dinner, the memories of his defense at the table and his gaze during her piano playing rushing back. She shoved it into the bag with shaking hands and zipped it closed.

Pulling on her coat and boots, she slung her bag over her shoulder and stepped into the hallway. The house was eerily silent, the kind of quiet that only came in the early hours of the morning. Her steps were soft as she descended the staircase, her heart pounding with every creak of the old wood.

Outside, the cold hit her like a slap, the heavy snow biting at her cheeks as she made her way to the car. The snow was turning to ice again, blanketing the retreat in a thick, threatening layer. She hesitated for a moment, her gaze drifting toward the house, the windows glowing faintly with the remnants of the night.

What if he wakes up? What if he comes looking for me?

The thought made her chest tighten, but she shook it off. This was the only way she could survive today — by leaving before she had to say goodbye.

Sliding into the driver's seat, she started her car, the engine sputtering before roaring to life. The headlights illuminated the swirling snow ahead, a near-impenetrable curtain.

But she couldn't stay. Not now.

As the car pulled away, the retreat faded into the distance behind her, its warm glow disappearing into the storm. Cassidy's hands tightened on the wheel, her vision blurring as tears spilled over, hot and unrelenting. She didn't know where she was going, only that she had to keep moving.

The snow fell heavier, the road ahead uncertain.

Chapter Twenty-One

Boxing day. It was time to leave.

Duke woke to the pale gray light of early morning, the dim glow creeping through the curtains as ice pellets hammered against the windowpane. The soft, persistent tap of the storm outside was the first thing he registered. He stretched, pulling the covers up tighter against the cold that crept into the room.

For a moment, there was a strange warmth in the air—a memory of Cassidy's body pressed against his, her said goodbye still lingering in the edges of his dream. It felt like a rare comfort, but it was gone the moment his hand reached across the bed. Cold. Empty sheets.

His chest tightened instantly. The fleeting peace evaporated, replaced by a sharp pang of something he couldn't name. "Cass?" he called hoarsely, his voice rough from sleep, but there was a quiet panic rising in his throat. His eyes scanned the darkened room, half-expecting her to be there, but the place was still—too still.

She was gone.

He swung his legs over the side of the bed, the chill of the hardwood floor jolting him fully awake. Throwing on a sweater and a pair of jeans, Duke hurried out of the room, his pulse quickening with every step. The house was quiet now, but there was a hum in the air—voices from below, the soft clink of dishes, the rhythm of a life going on without him.

The storm raged outside, its force slamming snow against the walls, the windowpanes rattling with the weight of it. He paused at the top of the staircase, staring out of the window at the swirl of white in the air, the world outside veiled in a thick sheet of snow. It felt like the whole world was shut off, as if the storm had trapped them all inside, alone.

With a knot in his stomach, Duke rushed down the hallway and into the living room. Empty. He moved swiftly through the house, his footsteps echoing on the hardwood floors, his ears straining for any sound of her. The place felt foreign without her presence—like the storm had taken her too.

The Armstrong family sat around the long oak table, the smell of coffee and pastries filling the air, the kind of farewell breakfast they'd planned for him—a proud send-off for the golden nephew, the family's protector.

But Duke couldn't care less about any of it.

He stormed into the room, his eyes locked on Reed, who stood by the president and First Lady, casually stirring his coffee. Duke's jaw tightened. His chest burned with anger.

"Where the hell is she?" His voice cut through the room, raw and violent.

The chatter stopped. Heads turned, eyes wide. Everyone went still, as if they could feel the storm inside him.

Reed glanced up, too calm, too casual. "Who?" he asked, feigning ignorance.

"Cassidy," Duke growled, fists clenching. "Where. The. Hell. Is. She?"

Reed's nonchalance didn't crack. "She left early this morning," he said, setting his coffee down like it was any normal conversation. "Would you like some coffee, Duke? There's plenty."

"I don't want any goddamn coffee," Duke roared, his voice ripping through the silence. "I want to know where Cassidy is."

The force of his shout made the room flinch. The First Lady's hand flew to her chest. Caroline looked from Duke to Reed, her face tight with confusion. Even the president straightened in his chair, a flicker of discomfort crossing his face.

Reed's eyes flickered briefly, but his tone remained maddeningly calm. "She left a message. She decided to leave. Her choice."

"In this storm?" Duke snapped, his voice dripping with disbelief. "In that tiny car, with no cell reception, and a visibility that's barely ten feet? You didn't stop her?"

"She's an adult, Duke—and left before any of us knew," Reed said.

"She doesn't know these roads!" Duke bellowed, his fists trembling with the effort not to strike something.

Reed raised a hand dismissively, as if Duke were overreacting. "She will be fine. She's a good driver."

"A good driver?" Duke spat, furious. "I've seen how bald her tires are. There is no chance in hell she's staying on the roads."

The president stood, his tone placating. "The storm should clear up by midday—when it's time for your flight out."

Duke snapped, spinning on his uncle. "I'm not leaving until I know she's safe. Do any of you realize how stupid this was? To just drive away in the dark, in the storm, with shitty tires—when she doesn't even know the fucking roads."

Reed's calm finally faltered, his brows furrowing in annoyance. "She would call if there was an issue," he said, quieter now.

"There's no fucking cell signal on half of these roads. What the fuck is wrong with you? Do you not give a shit?"

Reed stared at him with his mouth parted, as if he was finally realizing it.

"Someone needs to fucking find her." Duke snapped, spinning on his heel. He didn't need to hear any more. He wasn't staying here while Cassidy was out there. "If anything happened to her..." He stopped himself, words too heavy, too final. The thought was too much. "I swear to fucking God, Reed—it will be your goddamn head."

Without another word, he stormed out of the room. The sound of his boots slamming against the hardwood floor echoed through the silence, his anger and panic hanging in the air.

He reached the coat rack, yanking his jacket off the hook and forcing his arms into the sleeves. The storm outside howled, the wind biting into his face as he shoved his keys into his pocket.

His mind raced. Worst-case scenarios flashed by, each one darker than the last. He didn't care about the snow. Didn't care about the breakfast. Didn't care about any of it.

All he cared about was Cassidy.

The door slammed open. The wind smacked him in the face, but he didn't flinch. He didn't hesitate. He was already in his truck, engine roaring to life, his hands gripping the wheel so tightly his knuckles went white.

"Hang on, Cass," he said under his breath. "I'm coming for you."

The Armstrong cousins poured out of the lodge as Duke's truck lurched forward, headlights cutting through the storm. The snow whipped around him in a blur of white, the road disappearing under the heavy flakes. But he didn't care.

He wasn't stopping until he found her.

Duke's hands gripped the wheel so tight his fingers ached. The storm outside was unforgiving, the snow falling in thick, violent sheets, reducing the world to a blur of white and gray. He knew this route. This was the usual way back to D.C. — through the winding mountain roads that cut deep into the heart of the Appalachians. It was supposed to be familiar, comforting even, but tonight it felt like a cruel maze. The clock ticked down. He had hours until his flight, but nothing about the airport mattered anymore. Cassidy was missing, and nothing, nothing, would keep him from finding her.

Her name ran through his head like a mantra, the one thing he couldn't shake. "Cassidy, Cassidy, Cassidy." Her number had gone straight to voicemail too many times. Not that it mattered — she wouldn't have been able to hear him over the storm. Hell, she probably couldn't even see the road in front of her, with the visibility barely reaching ten feet.

His jaw clenched. *Damn it. Where the hell are you, Cass?*

The tires of his truck skidded on the slick asphalt, the snow piled high on either side of the road, and every mile felt like it added weight to his chest. What had she been thinking?

Then he saw it—a wall of brake lights in the distance, hazard lights flashing red and orange against the white. Duke's heart thudded hard as he slammed the brakes. The truck skidded to a halt behind the crowd of vehicles lining the narrow shoulder.

He jumped out.

People were standing in the road. Staring.

"What's going on?" Duke barked, but he didn't wait for the answer.

A bystander pointed toward the cliffside. "Car went over. Rescue team's not here yet. They think someone's still inside."

Duke moved before the words registered. He pushed past them, boots crunching over snow and loose gravel, until he saw it—Cassidy's car. A mangled blue sedan, wedged into the side of the mountain twenty feet down, the front half hanging into open air.

And Cassidy was inside.

The car creaked beneath her.

Someone grabbed his arm. "Sir—you need to wait. The rescue team is on the way—"

He shook them off. "There's no time."

He was already climbing down.

Cassidy's fingers gripped the steering wheel, knuckles bloodless, body locked in place. Ten minutes ago, she'd skidded on black ice, her car crashing through a snowbank before tumbling twenty feet down the mountainside. Now it sat precariously, the driver's side hanging over the cliff, creaking with every breath of wind.

Blood dripped from her temple, hot against the icy air seeping through the cracked window. Her arm throbbed with a sharp, pulsing pain—possibly broken—but worse was the knowledge that she couldn't move. The slightest shift might send the car over the edge. The passenger side was angled just enough to offer a chance at escape, but the act of reaching for it could kill her.

Outside, snow still fell in slow, swirling sheets, and in the distance, through the haze, she could make out vague figures—onlookers. Watching. Waiting. No one moved.

Until he did.

Duke.

She saw him break from the line of spectators like a man on fire, his frame unmistakable, his expression sheer focus. He was already halfway down the slope before she could draw breath.

"Cassidy!" he shouted, his voice cutting through the wind. "Don't move. I'm coming to you."

Her throat tightened. She wanted to scream, to cry, to beg him not to—but she didn't. She just watched as he climbed down, ice and rock scraping at his boots, each step dangerous. He reached the car, bracing himself on the passenger side, breath heaving.

"Trust me," he said, voice low and steady now. "I'm going to open this door and get you out. I've got you."

The door creaked under his grip. She flinched, but he was careful—mindful of the car's balance, of her injuries. His hands reached in, one supporting her broken arm gently, the other anchoring around her waist.

"I'm not letting you fall," he said, meeting her eyes.

She nodded.

Then, with a sharp pull and a desperate prayer, Duke lifted her free.

Her body collapsed against him as he backed away from the car. He cradled her close, his steps careful, his weight shifting for balance. The moment they cleared the slope, he passed her up into the waiting arms of an onlooker.

"Got her!" someone yelled.

And that's when the car fell.

The metal screamed as it slid, tumbled, and vanished into the abyss.

The ground beneath Duke shifted. His foot slipped on the ice. He hit hard, skidding down several feet before slamming into a rock outcropping. Pain burst across his ribs.

"Duke!" Cassidy screamed from above.

He couldn't see her face—just the blur of movement, the sound of her voice—but it was enough. Enough to reach for the rocks. Enough to try.

He clawed at the icy ledge, his arms shaking, the injury in his side screaming louder with every inch. Blood bloomed on his jacket. Every breath was a war.

Voices echoed above.

"Duke, come on!"

"Get him up!"

"Don't quit now!"

He heard the president. His father. The cousins. But it was Cassidy's voice that cut through the fog.

"Duke, please," she cried. "I love you. Don't let go. Not now."

And somehow, that made him move. Not for himself. For her.

With a guttural roar, he found leverage, his boots scraping for purchase. One hand, then the other. Blood in the snow. Wind in his ears. And then—he was up.

Cassidy was there, dropping to her knees beside him, her hands cradling his face, trembling.

"I love you," he said hoarsely, voice broken and raw. "I'm sorry. I love you."

Then he collapsed.

His father caught him before he hit the ground, easing him back.

"Call an ambulance!" someone yelled.

Cassidy knelt beside him, clutching his hand like it was the only real thing left in the world. His chest rose and fell beneath her palm, weak but steady.

His father crouched beside her, a hand on her shoulder. "He's going to be okay."

She nodded, the tears spilling now. She leaned down, pressing her forehead to Duke's.

"I love you," she whispered. "You came for me."

Chapter Twenty-Two

Cassidy sat on the hospital bed, her body wrapped in blankets, her skin pale from the trauma of the day. The steady beep of machines and the sterile smell of antiseptic filled the room. A doctor was finishing up with her, checking her vitals one last time, but Cassidy couldn't focus on anything except the need to be by Duke's side. Her heart was pounding, her legs restless, even as the fatigue weighed her down. She kept glancing toward the door, her eyes searching for any sign that someone was coming to tell her what was happening with him.

Caroline, who had stayed by her side, stood by the window, her posture tense. She was watching Cassidy closely, her concern evident. Cassidy hadn't said much, but she knew Caroline was reading her — knew what Cassidy needed, what she was going through.

"Are you feeling all right?" the doctor asked, his voice kind but professional.

Cassidy nodded absently, too distracted to really answer. "When can I go see Duke?" she asked, her voice sharp with urgency. She couldn't stay still any longer. Every minute felt like an hour, like she was being ripped away from him, like she couldn't breathe without knowing he was okay.

The doctor glanced at Caroline, his brow furrowing. "You should rest for a little while longer, Cassidy. You're lucky, but your body needs time to recover. Duke's still in critical condition. I need you to stay put for now."

"I don't care about me," Cassidy replied immediately, her voice a little too raw, a little too desperate. "I need to be with him. He saved my life, and now he's—" Her voice cracked as the memory of Duke hanging onto the cliff edge, bloodied and barely hanging on, surged through her. She swallowed hard, fighting the tears that threatened to break free.

Caroline moved to her side, placing a gentle hand on Cassidy's shoulder. "Cass, you have to take care of yourself first. We can't help Duke if you're not well enough to help him."

But Cassidy wasn't hearing it. She shook her head, pushing the blankets off her legs. "I have to see him," she insisted, her eyes wide and pleading. "I have to be there. I need him to know that I'm okay, that…that it's not his fault. Please. I'm the one who's okay. I can't sit here while he's—"

She broke off, a sob escaping her before she could hold it in. The dam inside her cracked, and suddenly, she was crying, hot, desperate tears streaming down her face. She felt it all—the fear, the relief, the love for Duke and the terror that she might lose him.

Caroline's eyes softened as she wrapped her arms around Cassidy, pulling her into a hug. "I know," she said, her voice thick with emotion. "I know you do. But

Duke's strong. He made it through, Cass. He's going to be all right."

At that moment, the door opened quietly, and Cassidy's breath hitched. It was the president. He stepped into the room with calm authority, but the worry on his face was unmistakable.

Caroline straightened, gently letting go of Cassidy, who immediately wiped her eyes, her heart racing at the sight of him.

"Sweetheart, how's Duke?" Caroline asked, her voice steady, but Cassidy could hear the anxiety behind it.

President Armstrong paused for a moment, his gaze steady, scanning both Cassidy and Caroline with a sharp eye. His face softened when it landed on Cassidy. "He's stable for now. But still unconscious. Wyatt's with him," he said, his voice low. "He saved your life, Cassidy. If it weren't for him, you wouldn't be here."

Cassidy wiped her tears, trying to pull herself together. Her voice was raw. "He...he's still out?"

The president nodded. "Yes — the ice knocked his head and got an artery in his shoulder. He lost a lot of blood. But we're hopeful. The doctors say he's strong. He'll come around."

Cassidy's breath caught, and a soft sob escaped her lips. *He'll come around.* She hadn't realized just how much she needed to hear those words. But even now, she wasn't sure she could wait. Every minute without knowing if Duke would open his eyes was torture.

She looked up at the president, her voice breaking through the silence, raw with emotion. "He was dying, Mr. President. He almost didn't make it. He pulled me out of that car. He — he was hurt, but he kept fighting. He didn't give up. He was hanging on by a thread, and he saved me. He saved me, and now he — " She paused, not knowing how to finish. Her words were lost in the overwhelming flood of gratitude and terror that filled her chest.

The president's gaze softened, a rare vulnerability in his eyes. He nodded slowly. "He's a solid man, Cassidy," he said, his voice deep and full of weight. "A man of integrity. That's who Duke is."

Cassidy nodded, her heart swelling with an overwhelming mix of emotions—love, fear, admiration. The president gave her a knowing look before turning toward Caroline, everything shifting between them.

"Take care of her, Caroline," he said, his voice heavy with concern. "Duke will pull through. He's a fighter."

Cassidy swallowed hard, her throat tight. She wasn't sure if she was the fighter or if Duke was, but one thing was clear—everything had changed.

The man she had once been uncertain about, the man she had struggled to understand, was now the one who had saved her. And now, as she looked at the president, she knew. Duke Armstrong was everything he had seemed to be from the start. A protector. A fighter. A man worth loving.

* * * *

Duke's head throbbed as he slowly regained consciousness. His eyes fluttered open, the sterile light of the hospital room cutting through the fog of his mind. The air smelled faintly of antiseptic, and the dull hum of machines was the only sound, a constant, mechanical reminder that he was somewhere unfamiliar. Somewhere he didn't want to be.

His body felt strange, foreign, like he didn't quite belong in it. The dull ache in his limbs, the tightness in his chest, the kind of exhaustion that clung to his bones — it all felt wrong. He shifted and looked down at himself. Hospital gown. And then... *Wyatt's joggers?* He let out a dry, irritated laugh. "What the hell am I wearing?"

Wyatt, sitting in a chair near the window, stirred at the sound. He glanced over at Duke with a half-smile, but it didn't quite reach his eyes. "Those are mine, man. You're welcome. Didn't want you freezing your ass off when they moved you here," Wyatt said, his voice calm but with an underlying tension that Duke immediately picked up on.

Duke frowned, rubbing his face. His skin felt like it had been stretched too tight. "Wait — hold on. What the hell happened?" His heart started to race, the confusion swirling through him like a storm. "Why am I in the hospital?"

Wyatt's eyes darted briefly to the door before he sighed, standing up and leaning against the wall. "There was an accident," he said quietly, avoiding Duke's eyes. "A bad one."

Duke's chest tightened at the lack of detail. The more Wyatt said, the more Duke realized something was off. He couldn't remember anything. His mind was a blank, like a fog had swallowed up the last month. He couldn't even place how long it had been. *A day? A week?*

"What the hell do you mean an accident?" Duke's voice was rising, agitation taking hold of him. He felt trapped, like something was wrong but he couldn't put his finger on it.

Wyatt's jaw clenched. "I'll get the doctor," he said, turning on his heel and walking toward the door, clearly not wanting to explain further.

But Duke's mind was already racing, panic creeping into his chest. "No. No, wait. I'm fine. I don't need the doctor. Just tell me what the hell is going on."

But Wyatt was already gone, and the door clicked shut behind him, leaving Duke alone in the sterile quiet of the room.

Alone.

Duke sat up, feeling lightheaded as he swung his legs over the side of the bed. He looked down at the IV in his arm, at the cords that snaked across the floor. His heart was hammering in his chest, his head spinning. Something wasn't right. He didn't know what happened—didn't remember the last month, hell, didn't even know how long he'd been in this damn bed—but something about this felt off, like he was missing the most important part of the picture.

He watched nurses in the distance moving around in the halls. It was dark. Sometime in the evening.

He stood, swaying slightly, the room tilting around him, his head swimming with disorientation. His legs felt like jelly as he moved toward the door, the beeping of machines following him like a relentless countdown. He reached out for the doorframe, steadying himself, then yanked the IV from his arm. The small sting of the needle didn't register—nothing mattered except getting out of the room, getting some answers.

He wasn't going to wait. He had to find out where he was, what was going on, what the hell had happened to him. And why he felt this gnawing in the pit of his stomach.

His bare feet slapped against the linoleum floor as he walked down the hospital corridor. The fluorescent lights above flickered, and everything felt eerily quiet. There were a few other patients in the rooms he passed, nurses scurrying by, but it felt like they were in another world. None of it was his. None of it made sense.

He was looking for something, someone, though he didn't know what. He couldn't focus — everything was fuzzy, like he was stumbling through a dream. His mind was locked in a haze, unable to latch onto anything concrete.

He passed a nurse's station but didn't stop, just kept walking. He didn't even know where he was going, only that he had to keep moving. Had to keep searching. There had to be an answer.

Her.

Blonde curls and green eyes. A woman. He knew her. He remembered her. But who was she? What had happened to her? The panic grew, his heart racing even faster as he walked faster, the walls around him closing in.

Everything was hazy. Everything was wrong.

He rounded a corner, nearly colliding with a nurse, but he barely noticed. His breath was shallow, chest tight, a pressure building in his head, but all he could think about was her — blondie — and what had happened to her. He had to find her.

He stumbled into another hallway and froze.

There, at the far end of the hall, he saw the silhouette of a familiar figure, standing in the doorway of a room. A figure he recognized but couldn't quite place at first. His chest constricted. The figure turned and —

It was her.

She was standing there, looking at him with wide, tear-filled eyes, her face pale but alive.

Her presence shattered the fog in his mind, the fragments of memory falling into place as he took a shaky step toward her. He could feel his heartbeat in his ears, his legs barely holding him up.

"You…" His voice was hoarse, barely a whisper, but the look on her face—the relief, the confusion, the fear—made everything else fade away.

She didn't say anything at first, just stepped forward.

He took another step, reaching for her, desperate to understand. To make it all make sense.

Duke's legs felt like they were made of lead as he stumbled down the sterile hospital hallway. The fluorescent lights above flickered, casting an almost otherworldly glow across the scene, but none of it mattered to him. The only thing that mattered was her.

His head throbbed painfully with every step, a searing ache behind his eyes, but he didn't care. He didn't stop. Every step he took felt like it drained him, but he couldn't—wouldn't—turn back. He had to reach her. His body burned with exhaustion, but his chest burned with something stronger, something he couldn't ignore.

The hospital had turned into a quiet, watching theater, the muffled voices of doctors, nurses, and patients blending into one distant hum. And then there was a silence that fell, thick and palpable, as Duke's unsteady footsteps echoed down the hall. The president was there, the First Lady, Wyatt, the Armstrong cousins, all of them, watching him. But he didn't care about any of them. All that mattered was the woman ahead of him.

She was ahead. He could see her now, standing there, waiting for him. Her hair was golden, her face streaked with tears, her hands trembling as she clutched at something—nothing. It didn't matter. It was her.

He couldn't think of anything else, not even the pain tearing through him. The hallway seemed to stretch on forever, but every breath, every shaky step, brought him closer to her.

Finally, he was standing in front of her.

And her bright green eyes.

He knew those eyes, filled with an ocean of emotion — relief, sorrow, and something else he couldn't quite name. Something familiar.

She reached out, and before he could think, his arms were around her, pulling her into him, his chest aching with the intensity of the moment. His head was spinning, but he couldn't let go.

"I love you," he said, the words tumbling out of his mouth without warning, raw and unfiltered, as if they had always been there, waiting to be said. "I don't know who you are, but I love you."

Her eyes welled up again, and she kissed him — soft, desperate, like she was trying to make him remember, make him understand everything they had been through, everything they were.

When she pulled back, tears still streaming down her face, she said, "You saved me."

His breath hitched. "From the accident?" he asked, confusion still fogging his thoughts.

"No," she shook her head, her voice thick with emotion. "From everything."

And just like that, it all came rushing back.

The White House lawn. The bet. The protest. The red paint. Reed's holiday party. The green velvet dress. Christmas Eve. Her playing the Nutcracker. Her tears. Their kisses. Her visit at midnight. How she'd walked into his life and shattered everything he thought he knew.

Her.

Cassidy Evans.

Duke kissed her again, fiercely, as if to make up for the time he'd lost, as if to erase the doubt that had clouded his mind. And in that kiss, in the heat of the moment, everything clicked into place. Every touch, every look — they made sense now. Every part of him understood.

She was the one he had wanted all along. The one he'd kept running from. The one who'd saved him, without even realizing it.

Finally, he pulled away, his chest heaving and his face wet. He turned to the president who was standing nearby, still in stunned silence. His voice, firm and clear, broke through the quiet. "I'm not going to Iraq."

The president blinked, his lips twitching into the hint of a smile. "We will discuss it," he said, the moment lifting for just a second, a shared understanding passing between them.

Duke turned back to Cassidy, who was looking at him with a mix of awe and relief, and smiled. There was no more uncertainty. No more hesitation. He knew what he had to do. And he was done running. Done pretending.

Because in that moment, in the hospital hallway, surrounded by a crowd of people who had watched his every step, Duke knew one thing for sure — he was going to fight for this. For her.

And he wasn't going to let anything — anyone — stand in his way.

Chapter Twenty-Three

Cassidy stood in the corner of the grand hall, her back pressed against the cool wood-paneled wall as the clock began its final countdown. The Armstrong family and their guests filled the room, champagne glasses raised high, their faces illuminated by the soft glow of chandeliers and the flicker of firelight. The air buzzed with anticipation, the kind that always accompanied the last seconds of a year.

She glanced down at her phone, the screen glowing with the time — eleven-fifty-nine p.m. The article — her article — had just gone live. The notification from the network's website had popped up moments earlier, and she'd felt her heart skip a beat at the sight of it. The culmination of weeks of work, countless edits, and every ounce of determination she'd had in her.

It was done. Out there for the world to see.

"Ten! Nine! Eight!" The crowd's voices swelled with excitement, glasses clinking, laughter spilling over as they joined in the countdown.

Cassidy's heart raced, but it wasn't for the New Year. It wasn't for the countdown or the confetti or the champagne. Her thoughts swirled with anticipation for what would come next—for what people would say about her piece. Whether they'd see what she had poured into it—the humanity, the complexity, the truth behind one of the most powerful men in the world.

She glanced down at her phone, the screen lighting up with notifications faster than she could process them. The article was live, and the flood of kudos had already begun. But the buzz of the crowd, the glittering room, and even her achievement faded into the background when she felt a warm, steady hand slide into hers.

She turned, her breath catching when she saw Duke standing beside her. His dark eyes were intense, the flickering light of the chandeliers reflecting in them as they held hers. His presence was grounding, and yet, her pulse quickened under his steady gaze.

"Three! Two! One! Happy New Year!"

The room erupted into cheers, confetti raining down from above as glasses clinked and couples embraced. Cassidy barely noticed. All she could focus on was Duke—his hand tightening around hers, his gaze never wavering.

"Happy New Year, Cass," he said, his voice low, his tone rough with something unspoken.

Her lips parted, her heart thudding in her chest. "Happy New Year, Duke."

He didn't say anything else. He didn't need to. The way he looked at her said it all—an intensity that made her knees weak, a tenderness that stole her breath. Slowly, he lifted their joined hands, his thumb brushing across her knuckles in a gesture so gentle it made her chest ache.

And then, without warning, he pulled her closer, his free hand settling on her waist as he leaned in.

Cassidy barely had time to register the movement before his lips were on hers, claiming her in a kiss that was as passionate as it was inevitable. The noise of the room faded away, the world narrowing to just the two of them. His hand cupped her face, his fingers threading into her hair as he deepened the kiss, and she melted into him, winding her arms around his neck.

The kiss was electric, consuming, a promise wrapped in fire. Her heart pounded against her ribs, her body igniting under his touch as the confetti fell around them like snow. She could feel the eyes of the room on them, but she didn't care. This moment — this kiss — was theirs.

When they finally pulled apart, their breaths mingling in the space between them, Cassidy opened her eyes to find Duke staring at her, his expression open and raw in a way she'd never seen before.

The president's face — the person of the year — was everywhere, her words quoted across headlines and social media.

She barely had time to process it before the president himself stepped into view, flanked by Caroline and a small cluster of family members. His presence, as always, commanded attention. But tonight, when his gaze landed on Cassidy, there was something warm and genuine in his expression.

"Well done, Cassidy," he said, his voice steady and carrying easily over the noise. The room hushed, people turning to look as he extended his hand to her.

Cassidy hesitated for a split second before taking it, his firm grip and approving nod sending a wave of relief through her.

"You captured the heart of the story," he continued, his tone sincere. "And more importantly, you captured the heart of the people. Thank you."

Her cheeks flushed, and she managed a quiet, "Thank you, Mr. President."

The applause that followed was overwhelming, the sound wrapping around her like a warm blanket. For the first time, she felt like she belonged — not just here, but in this world of polished, poised professionals who had doubted her every step of the way.

She'd earned her place.

Later, as the celebrations spilled out onto the snowy lawn, Cassidy found herself standing beneath the wide, star-speckled sky. Fireworks burst overhead, painting the night in brilliant colors, their echoes rolling across the retreat like distant thunder. The cold nipped at her cheeks, but she barely felt it, her thoughts too tangled in the events of the night.

"Cassidy."

The sound of his voice sent a shiver down her spine. She turned, and there he was — Duke, standing a few feet away, his broad frame silhouetted by the soft glow of the retreat's lights.

She'd barely seen him since midnight, the swirl of celebration keeping them apart. But now, as he stepped closer, the intensity in his dark eyes made the rest of the world fall away.

"You fought to stay," she said softly, the words slipping out before she could stop them.

He nodded, his gaze steady. "I did."

"Why?"

Duke exhaled, his breath visible in the cold night air. "Because of you," he said simply. "You made me believe I could be better. And I want to be better — with you."

Cassidy's chest tightened, her heart pounding as his words settled over her.

"You're everything I didn't know I needed," he continued, his voice low but sure. "You don't just see the good in people — you make them want to live up to it. You make me want to live up to it."

Tears pricked at her eyes, but she blinked them back, a small, wobbly smile tugging at her lips.

"I don't want to run anymore," he said, stepping closer, his hand reaching out to cup her cheek. "Not from you. Not from us."

She didn't trust herself to speak, so she nodded, leaning into his touch.

And then he kissed her.

It wasn't like their previous kisses — those had been filled with passion, urgency, and fire. This one was different. It was slow, tender, and unguarded, a promise in the form of a kiss.

When they pulled apart, their foreheads rested together, her breath mingling with his in the cold night air.

"I love you," he said, his voice trembling slightly.

Cassidy smiled, her tears finally spilling over. "I love you, too."

As the fireworks began to fade, the crowd drifting back toward the retreat, Duke took her hand in his. His grip was warm, steady, grounding, and she felt a sense of peace settle over her that she hadn't felt in years.

They walked together through the snow, the retreat fading into the distance as they followed a quiet path toward the woods. The night was still, the only sound the crunch of their boots and the faint rustle of the trees in the breeze.

Neither of them spoke for a while, content to let the silence fill the space between them. But as they reached a clearing, Cassidy stopped, turning to face him.

"Do you think we can do this?" she asked, her voice soft but steady.

Duke met her gaze, his dark eyes filled with a quiet determination. "I know we can," he said. "Because we're doing it together."

She smiled, her chest swelling with a mix of hope and certainty.

Whatever came next, they would face it. Together.

Sign up for our newsletter and find out about all our romance book releases, eBook sales and promotions, sneak peeks and FREE romance books!

Want to see more from this author?
Here's a taster for you to enjoy!

Secret Service:
A Patriot's Promise
Zoe Normandie

Excerpt

Palm Beach, Florida

Pixie's three-inch patent heels clicked sharply through the halls of President Armstrong's Palm Beach estate. Four years of serving the First Lady in this fortress of security.

The low murmur of voices and the hum of authority filled the air. With the President entering campaign-mode, the Secret Service was running on high alert, updating risk assessments.

She rounded the corner — and there he was. Wyatt Steele. At the center of a group of agents, giving orders with effortless command.

Broad-shouldered, impossibly self-assured, his gray suit tailored to perfection. He radiated quiet intensity, making everyone snap to attention.

Pixie pressed herself against the wall, unnoticed for now. She'd known he was here — but seeing him again still sent a jolt through her.

Wyatt Steele was dangerous. Not in the obvious way, but in a way that could unravel everything. A rogue who didn't play by the rules. Every time she tried to rein him in, he either ignored her, argued her down, or made her feel like she was the one out of line.

And it drove her mad that it worked.

The agents around him nodded, muttering acknowledgments before scattering, leaving Wyatt standing alone, his back to her. His stance was relaxed, his hands in his pockets, but there was an undeniable alertness to him, like he was ready to spring into action at any moment.

Pixie straightened her posture, schooling her expression into its usual mask of scorn, and stepped forward.

"Steele," she called out, her tone clipped and professional.

Wyatt turned slowly, and for a moment, his gaze locked with hers. His blue eyes, as piercing as ever, scanned her face, lingering just long enough to send a ripple of heat down her spine. Then his mouth curved into a faint, maddening smirk.

"Sinclair," he drawled, his voice low and deliberate. "To what do I owe the pleasure?"

Pixie's jaw tightened. "I assume you've been briefed on the First Lady's expectations for her detail this week."

Wyatt tilted his head, a mock-thoughtful expression crossing his face. "Oh, you mean the list of rules you sent over? Yeah, I saw them."

"And?"

"And I'll take them under advisement," he said with a casual shrug, the corner of his mouth twitching like he was trying not to laugh.

Pixie's hands tightened around the folder she was holding. "This isn't a suggestion, Steele. Those expectations are non-negotiable."

His smirk widened, and he stepped closer, closing the space just enough to make her pulse quicken. "Non-negotiable?" he repeated. "That's cute, Sinclair. But you know I don't work for you, right?"

Pixie's nostrils flared, her calm slipping. "No, you work for the First Lady. And as her Chief of Staff, I represent her interests, which means —"

"You get to boss me around?" he interrupted, his tone laced with sarcasm. "Is that it?"

Her lips pressed into a thin line. "I expect you to respect the chain of command."

Wyatt leaned in slightly. "And I expect you to stop wasting your breath trying to control things you can't."

For a moment, the air between them crackled with tension, sharp and heavy. Pixie's heartbeat thundered in her ears, but she refused to back down, lifting her chin in defiance.

"You're a liability, Steele," she said, low and cutting.

Wyatt's smirk softened into something harder, his gaze unwavering. "And you're still trying to figure out why that bothers you so much."

Before she could respond, he turned and walked away, leaving Pixie standing there, her fists clenched at her sides, her carefully maintained composure shattered.

She hated him.

And most of all, she hated that, for all her disdain, he still got into her head in a way no one else ever had.

* * * *

Wyatt Steele stood at the edge of the great room, his sharp eyes cutting through the crowd. His team was in perfect formation, guarding every angle of the First Lady's appearance. Caroline Armstrong was the picture of grace, her smile magnetic, her poise effortless, charming donors and supporters.

But Wyatt's focus wasn't on her tonight.

It was on Pixie Sinclair.

Wyatt's gaze lingered on Pixie longer than he intended, his trained eyes taking in every detail with the precision of a man who noticed everything — whether he wanted to or not. Her highlighted, bleach-blonde hair was pulled into its usual tight bun, not a strand out of place, a sharp contrast to the dark, enigmatic eyes that could cut through him with a single glance. That skin of hers, always tanned to a golden olive tone, made her seem like she lived in perpetual sunlight, though her personality was anything but warm.

Wyatt had dealt with every personality imaginable during his career in the Secret Service — politicians who thought themselves untouchable, celebrities who couldn't stop testing the boundaries of their protection, even the occasional agent with a chip on their shoulder. But Pixie Sinclair? She was a different beast altogether.

The First Lady's Chief of Staff was supposed to be diplomatic, someone who could effortlessly navigate the tightrope of politics and public scrutiny. Pixie, however, wielded her words like weapons, cutting sharp and clean. There was no tact in her commands, no deference in the way she addressed people.

Wyatt's jaw tightened as he watched Pixie approach Caroline, her black heels clicking like gunfire against the marble floor. She leaned in close to the First Lady, whispering something into her ear. Caroline laughed, her eyes lighting up, but Wyatt didn't miss the faint exasperation that grew across Pixie's expression. Concern? Empathy? No. That wasn't a word he'd use with Pixie Sinclair.

The First Lady needed a Chief of Staff who understood her, someone who reflected her grace and priorities back into the world. Pixie was more like a bulldozer, smashing through subtlety with a confidence Wyatt might have admired if it weren't so grating.

And then there was the matter of respect.

Pixie had none for him.

Wyatt clenched his fists at his sides, careful to keep his expression neutral. He could recall half a dozen instances in the last two weeks where Pixie had overstepped. She barked orders at him like she ran the Secret Service. She didn't just question his decisions — she outright undermined them.

Like last week.

Wyatt's jaw ticked at the memory. They'd been preparing for Caroline's visit to a new children's hospital. He'd outlined the security detail in painstaking detail, accounting for every possible risk. But Pixie had breezed into the room, glared at his plans, and called them 'overkill'. She'd insisted the First Lady didn't need to be treated like a 'fragile doll', and when he'd tried to calmly explain why each precaution was necessary, she'd cut him off with a sharp, "You work for me, Steele. Not the other way around."

I don't work for you, he'd wanted to snap. But he hadn't. Because Wyatt Steele didn't lose his cool, not even when someone like Pixie Sinclair made it damn near impossible not to.

He sighed, his gaze flicking back to Caroline. She deserved better. She deserved someone who could be assertive without being a tyrant, someone who could advocate for her without stepping on everyone else in the process. Someone who didn't make him grit his teeth every time they walked into a room.

As if summoned by his thoughts, Pixie appeared at his side.

"You're standing too close to the First Lady," she said, barely sparing him a glance.

"I'm exactly where I need to be," Wyatt replied, his tone calm but firm.

She crossed her arms, her icy blue eyes narrowing at him. "Well, your 'need' is obstructing her photo ops. Shift back."

Wyatt held her gaze, refusing to move. "Her safety comes first. The cameras can work around it."

Pixie huffed, her irritation radiating off her in waves. "You're impossible," she muttered, spinning on her heel and stalking away.

Wyatt watched her retreat, biting back the urge to say something he'd regret. She was svelte and fit, the kind of woman who moved with the fluid grace of someone who cared about every inch of herself. And tall — taller than most women, especially in those ridiculous heels she wore like weapons.

He took a slow, deep breath, forcing himself to refocus. He should have been thinking about Caroline Armstrong, the First Lady he was sworn to protect. About the entrances, the exits, and the agents stationed at each. About the shifting crowd dynamics and the potential threats lurking in plain sight.

But instead, his attention was stuck in one place.

Pixie moved like she owned every room she entered, chin high, shoulders squared, her sleek pencil skirt swaying with an infuriating kind of rhythm. Even in retreat, she was impossible to ignore.

And that was the damn problem.

Wyatt gritted his teeth, his jaw clenching as he forced his eyes to track the room again, scanning for potential threats. *Focus, Steele. Do your job.* But his gaze betrayed him, flickering back to her.

It wasn't just her disdain for him — though there was plenty of that. It was the way she carried herself, with all the subtlety of a lightning strike. The way she seemed to thrive in conflict, like sparring with him was less about the job and more about sheer enjoyment. She wasn't deferential, not even a little, and maybe that's what gnawed at him. He was used to people treating him with respect, acknowledging the weight of his position. Pixie Sinclair didn't just ignore that weight — she stomped all over it with her designer heels.

And yet, despite everything, she *fascinated* him.

Wyatt hated that word. Fascinated. It made him sound like some starry-eyed rookie instead of the hardened professional he prided himself on being. But how else could he describe the way his attention snagged on her whenever she entered the room? It wasn't her looks — though she was beautiful, objectively speaking. Blonde hair always swept into a no-nonsense bun, sharp cheekbones that looked like they could cut glass, and those ice-blue eyes that could freeze him in place with a single glance. No, it wasn't that.

It was the fire underneath it all. The passion in the way she argued with him, the way her lips pressed into a tight line when he pushed back, like she wanted the fight but hated to admit it. She was so tightly wound, so fierce, that Wyatt couldn't help but wonder what it would take to crack that icy exterior. To see what was beneath all that armor she wore so well.

He dragged a hand through his short, dark hair, exhaling slowly. This wasn't the time or place to dissect his feelings — or whatever the hell this was. He had a job to do, and getting tangled up in his fascination with Pixie Sinclair wasn't part of it.

But damn it, she was under his skin.

As if she could feel his gaze, Pixie turned, her cold gaze cutting across the room to meet his. For a moment, neither of them moved, the distance between them crackling with unspoken tension. Then she lifted one perfectly sculpted eyebrow, a challenge clear in her expression, before spinning on her heel and disappearing into the crowd.

Wyatt sighed, shaking his head.

"Get a grip, Steele," he muttered under his breath.

But deep down, he wasn't sure he wanted to.

About the Author

A little snapshot on who is Zoe Normandie…

After 10 years working with the police and attending a military university, I weave stories filled with danger, heart, and the grit of those who serve. An army brat, I grew up on military bases across the country, giving me front-row seat to the world of duty and sacrifice. With a veteran husband, my passion for writing military-themed romance, suspense, and mystery is rooted in real-world experience, supporting him through every mission.

Zoe loves to hear from readers. You can find her contact information, website details and author profile page at https://www.firstforromance.com

ENTWINED PUBLISHING